349982

ACCIDENTS
WILL
HAPPEN

ACCIDENTS
WILL
HAPPEN

Julian Rathbone

This first hardcover edition published in Great Britain 2000 by
SEVERN HOUSE PUBLISHERS LTD of
9–15 High Street, Sutton, Surrey SM1 1DF.
This first hardcover edition published in the USA 2001 by
SEVERN HOUSE PUBLISHERS INC of
595 Madison Avenue, New York, N.Y. 10022.

British Library Cataloguing in Publication Data

Rathbone, Julian, 1935-
    Accidents will happen
    1.   Suspense fiction
    I.   Title
    823.9'14 [F]

    ISBN 0-7278-5619-7

Printed and bound in Great Britain by
MPG Books Ltd, Bodmin, Cornwall.

This book is for Pieke Biermann and Thomas Wörtche. They helped me develop the basic idea, suggested characters, and finally checked the text for any stupid errors about German institutions, or even just day to day life. And it's also to celebrate six years of friendship and collaboration: here's to the next six!

AUTHOR'S NOTE

Accidents Will Happen is fiction and takes place in a fictional city called Burg in a fictional German autonomous region or *Land* with the same name. Germany is a federation of autonomous regions called *Land (Länder)*. I thought of keeping the word, as it appears in the Collins dictionary, but unfortunately it has no adjectival form that is acceptable in English. Therefore I have used Region and Regional, usually capitalised to give them an official, political status. Germany, however, is not fiction and it has its geography. Any reader who has a nodding acquaintance with the geography of Germany will realise that fictional Burg occupies the same bit of the map as real Bremen.

I have not been to Bremen. I have deliberately avoided reading anything about Bremen. Nevertheless, I have constructed my fictional Burg out of recollections of other north German and Dutch cities which I have visited—as a result Burg will almost inevitably have some things in common with Bremen: just as, say, a fictional town situated where Derby is, but constructed out of the author's recollections of Nottingham and Mansfield, would doubtless share some characteristics with the real Derby. Nevertheless, my Burg, and all who live and die in it or pass through it, is and are fiction.

JR

PART I

CHAPTER 1

'Autobahn five for thirty kilometres.'

'We're already on it.'

'Yes.'

Eloise, twenty-five, bilingual, Brit Dad a regimental sergeant-major, German mother, folded up the booklet of maps, reached forward to put it in the glove compartment, looked round the seat pillar. The Boss was lying back against the butter-coloured hide, camel coat thrown open over his silky grey suit. He looked tired, the purple circles that surrounded his closed eyes bruise-deep in colour.

'And so we say farewell . . .'

'To fucking Frankfurt.'

She faced forward again but then reached up to adjust the courtesy mirror on the back of her sun-shield so she could see his face.

'We didn't do so bad. Did we?' To get the visual angle right she crossed her ankles and swung her knees outwards: woolly black tights beneath a grey tweed fanny pelmet.

'Not good enough.' A squeaky voice, you'd guess a small fat man if you couldn't see him. She couldn't, which was a blessing, and she didn't have to guess, she knew. 'Frankfurt too big for us.' He squeaked on, a small furry denizen of the financial jungle, coypu perhaps, something with a bit of rat in it. 'I always said so. No way firms as big as Siemen and Hoechst are going to admit to problems they can't handle.'

'If you fucking say that once more Herbert will pull on to the shoulder and kick your arse for you all the way back to fucking Frankfurt.' The Boss said it all without moving his lips or opening his eyes.

Eloise glanced sideways at their driver. A thick lip in a thick face lifted: a snarl with enough amusement in it to suggest kicking squeaky Sam Pratchard almost any- where was a task he'd willingly undertake. His eyes flicked up to a passing gantry.

'Bad Homburg.' A laugh like wet concrete slipping off a shovel. 'Why didn't they call it Bad Hat and be done with it.'

'"Bad" means "bath". It means it's a spa town.'

'I know that. You don't have to tell me that. Last Year in Marienbad. Mary's bath, see? I don't suppose you remember that. Before yor time.' Delicately he used the nail of his right pinkie to lever a scrap of Westphalian air-cured ham from between a gold crown and the heavily filled molar next to it. 'And a Homburg is a hat. Anthony Eden was famous for wearing them. But I reckon he was before yor time too an'all.'

Shit, she'd done it again. For about the twentieth time in twenty days she'd assumed ignorance in one of her three companions and been caught out. Manners do not necessarily make the man, she thought, as Herbert's huge paw dropped to within six inches of her thigh so his thumbnail could flick the shred of stale meat out of his pinkie nail and on to the floor. Then he half lifted his left buttock, massaged the point of pain where an arthritic hip joint played up if he stayed in the same position too long.

'How long before we get there, El?'

She looked up. The Boss's eyes were open now. He stretched and yawned, elbows up, fists by his ears. He put his right index finger in his right ear and shook it.

'Three fifty kilometres. Three hours. A bit more.'

'OK, Sam. Time to crunch the numbers.'

Eloise looked out of the window, tried to smother the wave of fatigue and boredom that flooded over her as the Boss and small fat Sam behind her flicked up catches on the red leather brief-cases, opened out the laptop and the calculator.

'Sunday,' Herbert growled. 'Not much traffic, we might do it sooner.'

'Only if you speed,' El said. 'And often they do major road works on a Sunday.' She sank back in her seat, brought her eyes almost to the level of the long bonnet in front of her, used the three-pointed silver star in its circle as if it were a gunsight. She tried to manoeuvre her head so the centre fixed on the Garfield suckered to the back window of the Opel in front, but you couldn't do that on these newer models, the bonnet sloped down too much. It was a game she used to play in her Dad's old Merc when he took her to school.

Behind her Harry Sheen, old mucker of her Dad's from BAOR days, more of an uncle really, continued to growl irritably at Fat Sam who whimpered and whined in reply; Herb sat back in the big bucket seat, gloved hands just resting on the wheel, occasionally caressing it, hooded eyes fixed ahead. And El was bored, bored and disappointed. It had seemed such a glam thing to do, tour Germany in a fat Merc, stay at posh hotels, drumming up the business which would get Sheen Associates out of the shit the recession had dumped them in ... But it wasn't working out, and she knew it, and meanwhile there had been far too much cruising at a steady 110 kph down endlessly identical autobahns, and hanging around doing nothing in hotel rooms which were as similar to each other as the autobahns.

*

Sunday. Renata Fechter stretched her long lithe body between pink silk sheets, sniffed the coffee smell that filtered across the corridor from the kitchen. There were such good things to be said for having an Italian lover. It was, for instance, a matter of pride for Aldo, duty even, that he should help her to reach heights of physical pleasure she had not, in the thirty years since she reached puberty, previously discovered. And that was not all. He also had a Gaggia coffee machine that worked as well as the ones in Italian cafés do. She felt a little rush of what she supposed must be happiness. Anyway, deep satisfaction: is there a difference?

She turned on her side, plumped up the pillows, rolled on to her back, hoisted herself up on them, gave the question some thought.

Satisfaction she had felt often before. Even really deep satisfaction, especially when she achieved something she had set out to do. Her last promotion for instance, even though it had meant transfer to a department that her friends said must mean professional suicide. Satisfaction also came when she contemplated her fitness and good looks, her restrained but stylish dress sense. Not that she was particularly vain: they were simply signs that she had set herself goals and achieved them. Forty-three and it was still no problem cracking ninety minutes on a half marathon; she still entered amateur downhill skiing competitions to reach speeds in excess of a hundred and twenty kilometres an hour.

Still? A diet, rigorously maintained except on Saturday evenings and Sunday mornings, of fresh uncooked vegetables and fruit with fat free white meat and fish, no more than four spaced out units of alcohol a day, and as much wholemeal multi-grain sugar- and salt-free bread or pasta as she wanted. With all this and daily exercise for at least an hour and a half either in a gym or a swimming pool, or jogging, she expected that 'still' to last another ten years. As a highly paid professional with no one to support but herself she could afford to get it right and was determined to do so.

Satisfaction, yes. But this, this *happiness*? She explored the peace in her body, listened to the tangle of slight but hard noises from the kitchen, savoured again the aroma of the coffee. The difference was that the satisfaction she now felt was the product not of her own knowledge, intelligence, perseverance but of someone else's. And that, she decided, was the difference between happiness and satisfaction. She knew which she preferred and realised that it could be a problem if she allowed it to matter.

In a kitchen equipped and organised as thoroughly as one hopes a theatre dedicated to open-heart surgery might be Aldo Nerone tipped steam heated milk into the coffee he had already poured, scooped a perfectly white egg, the only one she would eat all week, from a small stainless steel saucepan and popped it into a white egg-cup. Since the hot white crusty bread and a small glass tub of *beurre en motte* were already in place, all he had to do now was scoop the ice cubes out of the freshly squeezed orange juice, and carry it all through.

He paused with his hand (a Seychelles tan) poised over the immaculate sink and let the ice burn his palm. He should, he reckoned, feel satisfied. But he would have to vary the routine. He sensed, no, he knew, she would feel disparaged if he ran this Saturday night Sunday morning routine too often without variation. She was so bloody intelligent. And sensitive. If he didn't come up with a variant she'd find an overload of work one Saturday soon and go to the cinema instead. Even the opera perhaps. Yes. That might be the answer. A trip somewhere, Berlin, even Munich, he could borrow a Lear jet or one of those new Messerschmidts . . . No. If it's to be opera it has to be La Scala.

He let the ice cubes clatter into the sink and rubbed his palm down the side of his wild cotton djellabah. He realised he was frightened. He knew he wanted to please her, he wanted to give her things, he wanted her to be happy. And that was not part of the scenario. That she should be happy . . . Yes. But he was beginning to realise he wanted her to be happy not because his financial future might depend on her being happy, but just simply because he wanted her to be happy, it was becoming an end in itself.

Sensing a chip in the usually flawless veneer of his self-confidence, he shrugged, picked up the tray, padded through the deep carpet of the passage, pushed open the bedroom door. She was sitting up, her honey-coloured torso and breasts with brown nipples exposed against the rose pink sheets and pillows. Her streaked but basically deep chestnut hair was pushed back from her temples, a tendril or two just reaching her shoulders, and she smiled. Again the lurch in his diaphragm.

'I think I've overdone the egg.'

Her smile broadened.

'Never mind. You'll have killed off the salmonella.'

He set down the tray, kissed her lips lightly.

'You are much the nicest police person I have ever met.'

'And you are much the nicest crook I have ever been to bed with.'

'Crook? I'm no crook.'

He adjusted the tray, made its shallow legs straddle her thighs. She smiled up at him, happy to be made a fuss of.

'You're a businessman,' she said, with joking finality, 'you're a crook.'

*

Sunday morning. A short terrace of grey stuccoed town-apartments, five storeys if you include the attics. Their narrow dormer windows were squeezed between steep slopes of glinting slates held in place by pewter tags that burned the eye in the morning sunlight, thousands of tiny dots of cosmic light. There were ten street-level entrances, whose winding stairs were marble to the first floor, wood after that. They were the oldest unrestored buildings in the city, older than most people realised since their foundations and their shells of ancient brick dated back to the fifteenth century when the city-fathers first prospered as minor members of the Hanseatic League. They had survived the firestorm of 1943 because they were near the railway station. It was the railway station and its marshalling yards that the Royal Air Force had been trying to hit.

Sunday morning and only one entry had a body in it. Ayla Muren found it. She was on her way to the railway station where she worked as a cleaner. She lived in the tiny attic with her husband and her husband's brother's family. Turks work Sundays. Which is fine for those who don't. Someone has to work Sundays. Difference is Turks also work Fridays when they'd rather not. Never mind. Sundays they work.

She had a name for him—Albert, two syllables she had no trouble pronouncing. He lived, he had been living on the fourth floor, beneath her attic, in a small suite of rooms he would not have been able to afford in a less deprived area. She had rather liked him in a distant sort of way, and especially since the demonstration a year ago when he and a thousand or so more had marched to the Rathaus and law-courts to protest against the minimal sentence handed out to three youths who had raped a Turkish lady not much younger than her. Many of them were students and aped the fashions of twenty years ago, but not Albert. In his early thirties he had been a quiet man, always respectably dressed, worked one would guess as a clerk or technical assistant. But her sister-in-law was sure he was a homosexual and told her young boys to keep clear of him.

And here he was, dead from what looked like multiple stab-wounds, lying in a small patch of blood and bathed in sunlight flooding through the big semicircular fanlight above the door. His head was on the doormat, his feet on the bottom step of the stairs. She bent over him, felt for his pulse, checked that he really was dead. She stepped round him, unhooked the wall-mounted payphone and dabbed out the emergency number. And then, because she was fifty years old, had witnessed violent death three times already and natural death more often than she cared to think about, and also because she knew how unreasonable her immediate superior at the railway station could be about unpunctuality, she let herself out, closed the door behind her.

There was another reason too for hurrying away. Albert had been mutilated. There were cigarette burns on the inner side of the wrist she'd lifted, and she suspected someone had forced a toothpick under the nail of his index finger which was caked with blood. She knew about such things. Most Turks become guest workers so that they can earn the hard currency that will buy not just food but cars and washing machines for their families back in Anatolia. But some leave their native land to escape the attentions of police who do nasty things to those who try to change a society even more lopsided and evil than most. Here, in Germany, it was not a scene she wished to be caught up in again.

CHAPTER 2

Monday morning. Kriminaloberkommissar Andreas Becker was finding his relatively new job, he had been in it for six months, even more wearisome than usual. Over five years he had built up what he had felt sure was a secure niche in the Vice Squad, with promotion to Kriminalhauptkommissar virtually certain, but then it had all unwound in his hands: almost literally. An Ossi pimp with three Ashanti girls in tow (he claimed they were ex-students from the Humboldt University in East Berlin) had bought the lease on a small boarding house already used by local talent. These the Ossi pimp had attempted to evict by threatening them with petrol-bombing, razoring and so on. The girls hung on in and the Ossi duly torched one of their rooms, severely burning one of them. The only evidence against him was her word and that of her friends. It was not enough for the Regional Public Prosecutor: it was for Becker.

Becker paid a call on the Ossi whose weak heart caused him to die while Becker was beating him. One of the Ashanti girls witnessed the event. Again, her word was not enough for the Public Prosecutor though it was for Becker's superiors. For some time they had been worried by his readiness to use unofficial methods to maintain some semblance of order in an area where cases very rarely came to court: he was reprimanded, lost three years' promotion, and was moved to the newly formed Dezernat Umweltkriminalität: the Regional Department for Environmental Crime.

DUK was the cheque the Green Party cashed following an election which left them with the balance of power in the Regional Assembly. Nobody but the Greens liked it. The Interior Ministry, with its close links to local industry, hated it; the public prosecution officers abhorred the expertise they were expected to take on board with every case that was brought; and above all the police themselves abominated it until the chiefs realised it served one very useful purpose: it was a sin-bin where they could dump officers who were misfits, incompetent, or difficult. Becker was classed as difficult.

He was in his late thirties, a big man, heavily built with huge powerful hands, a thick heavy moustache, rather dark in colouring—racially Bavarian, though he had been born in Burg. By no means stupid he nevertheless preferred to use direct if unorthodox action rather than painstaking sifting of evidence and its analysis. He had a temper. He was not, by his own standards, corrupt, but was not avidly interested in seeking out corruption in others: what he liked was order, and maintaining order was, in his book, what policing is about. Not law and order, just order. The Ossi pimp had been out of order.

Now he was deep in the paperwork that went with the first major case DUK had put together. A local firm, Vereinigte Biowerke, had developed a narrow spectrum antibiotic, which, used in conjunction with laser-based surgery, might cure certain intestinal cancers. The first batches of the drug had broken EU safety rules and had been dumped. Not disposed of, but dumped. In the River Weser. Investigation of the firm's books followed and showed that not all the batches had gone into the Weser. Others had disappeared. Some of them eventually turned up in a small warehouse in Rostock waiting shipment to Novgorod where, so manifests and so on indicated, a newly formed Russian firm of medical suppliers was waiting to take delivery. Yet still a small amount was not accounted for.

Enter Roger Vesper, a lab technician in the Regional Cancer Hospital. He had read of the case, and of the missing phials. He claimed they had been used on terminally ill cancer patients, without their permission, and in conjunction with surgery that had never been practised before. In short the case was that terminally ill patients, most of them geriatric, had been unwittingly used as guinea pigs for a treatment involving a drug that failed to meet EU safety standards. At this point this aspect of the case ceased to be of interest to DUK: it was a matter for the Serious Crimes Squad. However, it was still necessary that DUK should establish beyond doubt that every phial of the banned drug had been accounted for. And Vesper's account still left them thirty phials short.

Wearily KOK Becker, who still believed he ought to be KHK Becker, lifted the phone and dialled the number of the Regional Headquarters of the Green Party where Vesper now worked. Vesper was not in the building, had not come to work that morning. Becker tried his home number.

'Hallo. Could I please speak to Herr Roger Vesper?'

'Who is that? Who is calling?'

Wrong voice, not Vesper.

'Andreas Becker of the Regional Police. Herr Vesper knows me.'

'Is this some kind of sick joke?'

'Certainly not.'

'You are a policeman, one of the city policemen and you are asking me where Roger is?'

'Yes.'

'This is some sick joke, it has to be. You people really are psycho, you know that? Bastards, brutes, corrupt. Sadists who. . .'

Becker held on to his temper, but only just, sensed that the receiver at the other end was about to be smashed back into its cradle.

'Excuse me Herr ... I am sorry I do not know your name.'

That took the man or youth at the other end by surprise. The flow of abuse was cut off, there was a moment of stillness, then:

'You don't know my name?'

'No.'

'Yesterday you kept me at Police Headquarters for fifteen hours during which I was intensively interrogated, threatened, and physically assaulted, and you don't know my name?'

'That's right.'

'How is it you don't know who I am?'

'Because I do not work at Police Headquarters, because out of the five thousand policemen employed by the Region I should guess not more than thirty at the most are involved in whatever it is you were caught up in yesterday. I work for the Regional Department of Environmental Crime, whose offices are in the Interior Ministry Building out at Gründorf, and it is in that capacity I wish to talk to Herr Vesper. Now please tell me where he is.'

'Roger Vesper,' the voice at the other end spoke now as if to an idiot, 'is in the cells beneath Police Headquarters charged with a murder he did not do.' The voice broke on a sob and this time he did hang up, and none too gently.

In one movement Becker pushed his chair back on its castors and slammed his big hands on to his desk with a bang that made the two other people in the room with him look up and round with startled, even frightened, faces. He made as if to hurl the papers in front of him, even the VDT and keyboard, on to the floor with one big backhanded sweep and they held their breaths. But his palm again crashed flat on the surface.

He glared at them. A black, half black but that was black to him, woman fifteen years younger than him, and a grey alcoholic incompetent fifteen years older. His gaze swept across them, fixed on the big window and the tops of distant trees, tall poplars just beginning to green above a flat, dull hectare of useless grass. There weren't even any daffodils. It was all anathema to him. For all his working life he had worked out of the Police Headquarters next to the Rathaus, the Town Hall, and for the last five the streets, the cafés, the brothels, the casinos in the basements and on the upper floors of the restored baroque city centre had been his stomping ground. And now, now what?

A department that consisted of a black woman, whose father had been a sergeant in the US Marines, an alcoholic incompetent, both in the room with him now, and elsewhere a detective from narcotics who like most narcs had a habit he couldn't kick, and a Turk seconded, like their Chief, from Serious Crime. And the Chief? Another woman, and this one a real ball-breaker. And that was it. The back-up, secretaries, clerks and so forth, were all provided by the Regional Ministry for the Interior, which was why they were stuck out in the countryside, eight kilometres from the city centre, in a featureless modern block among grass and cows.

Becker hated it all, but especially he hated grass, cows and a chief who was a woman.

He looked around the large, airy, open-plan office, and then at the glazed door at the far end.

'Is the boss in?'

The black girl looked up, shifted the yellow ear-plug of her Walkman, looked a question. He repeated, loudly:

'Is the boss in?'

The black girl nodded, replaced the ear-plug, chewed on. Wearily, although it was still only half past nine in the morning, Becker got to his feet and headed for her office.

Monday morning. Renata Fechter hated Hans Roehl, Chief of the Serious Crime Squad (Delikte am Menschen und Organisierte Kriminalität—DAMOK), for while Becker was all for Order and she recognised only the Law Hans Roehl had little respect for either. She met him that Monday lunchtime beneath the high black rafters and mounted figureheads, all lovingly or at any rate accurately restored, of the mediaeval Schiffbauhaus or Shipbuilders' Hall. The occasion was a vast buffet lunch, part of the celebrations laid on to mark the twinning of Burg with Novgorod, hailed by the Mayors of both as particularly apt since Burg was almost the most southern and Novgorod the most northern city of the great mediae-val trading system known as the Hanseatic League.

Her eye ranged up and down the long laden tables seeking something she could eat without degrading her system. Eventually she found some cold salmon labelled as the product of a Baltic salmon farm, which was not reassuring considering the levels of pollution in that almost landlocked sea, but at least not too calorific, once she had scraped off the mayonnaise, even though it was mounted on a slab of black rye-bread. She took a mouthful, realised she did not really want it after all, but also sensed she would look naked if she were not holding a plate.

She looked around and marvelled at the way the hundred or so dignitaries and businessmen (and a few women) could so easily and apparently without self-awareness lose almost every shred of dignity in the process of shovelling rich food from a plate held in one hand by means of a fork held in the other, while talking loudly to two or three others all of whom were talking loudly to them. What made it all so depressing was the fact no one had the means, with both hands occupied, to redress the little spills and leaks that were bound to happen, staining cheeks, chins, and occasionally shirt-fronts, and in one instance the shiny Armani boot of the woman who ran the city's model agency.

But it was, she knew, an opportunity to catch Roehl on more or less neutral ground, and she looked out for him.

Even in a throng of tough, fat businessmen, he stood out. Taller than most, he had a big round head, bald apart from strands of grey hair combed across it like lines of latitude, huge black eyebrows above gold-rimmed spectacles that shielded hard agate eyes, a wide face with narrow hard lips, and, cased in a double-breasted suit and probably corseted, a body that looked like two giant hams squeezed together tapering to trotters hidden by gleaming black shoes. He was not a native of Burg but an import from Stuttgart and it was said that he had brought his own desk chair with him since he knew his backside would not slot into his predecessor's. She came up behind him, and flinching somewhat but steeling herself since she knew she would not get his attention otherwise, gave his elbow a tug.

'Herr Roehl. We are both busy people, so I won't waste your time later with what can be dealt with now.'

'Frau Fechter? Keep it short, I have a meeting in a quarter of an hour.' His voice rasped, a noise like crunching ice-floes.

'You have arrested Roger Vesper.'

'Yes.'

'Was that wise? Considering he is a prosecution witness in the case the State is bringing against the Regional Cancer Hospital.'

'Being a prosecution witness for the State does not normally give you immunity to commit murder.'

'Roger Vesper did not commit murder.'

'You have access to the forensic reports?'

'Vesper is one of the gentlest men I have ever met. He is a committed vegan and abhors all violence.'

'Vesper is a homosexual.'

'So?'

Roehl laughed, the sound an ice-floe makes when it sheds a small avalanche of year-old ice: 'Frau Fechter, you know as well as I do that relationships between perverts can lead to violence as bad or worse than more normal liaisons. Some of the nastiest disfigurements and maimings I have ever . . .'

'Herr Roehl, you are missing the point.'

'I was not aware you had one to make.' He ran his thumb round the inner rim of his plate, licked it, placed the plate and fork on the table at his other elbow, scooped a large tall glass of sub-zero vodka (courtesy of the burghers of Novgorod) from the tray of a passing waiter. 'If he did it, he'll confess. They always do. If he didn't he'll probably confess anyway . . .'

The enormity of this did not pass her by: but after twenty years as a police person it did not surprise. She drew breath.

'Vesper is also a witness in the case my department is bringing against Vereinigte Biowerke for falsifying their returns of . . .'

'Well Frau Fechter, I think you'll agree murder is a more serious business. You can have your pervert once the trial is over. Though who will believe a convicted murderer . . .?'

The huge fat man turned away, his attention caught by much the same means she had used, but this time by the owner of the City's Model Agency whose Armani toecap was still decorated with a blob of coleslaw. Her son had been caught in possession of enough cocaine to justify a dealer rap, and no doubt she was about to plead, or buy, his release on bail. Renata also turned away and into ... Death, who, as it were, belonged to Roehl and was attempting in the throng to follow him.

Death? Well, not exactly. But Roehl's companion could not have been more different from Roehl himself: he was tall, thin, with a high-domed head, bald and skull-like. He wore a floppy stylish black suit, silk and cashmere. Not a local, she was almost sure. He looked down at her (not many men were tall enough to look *down* on Renata) and she looked up into mirror shades, and her own reflected face. As he brushed past she took in a body long and loose-jointed, slender white fingers cradling a glass of clear vodka. She wondered who he might be and she shuddered. Then threw it off: the clothes, the emaciated look, the shades? Surely all they spelled out was one simple word: poseur.

She looked at her watch and saw with relief that it was time to go. The Environmental Section of the Federal Criminal Bureau had passed on to her a report from the Frankfurt DUK about an English firm who claimed to be able to export noxious and dangerous waste. They were giving a presentation to local business people that afternoon in a Burg hotel, and she thought she might drop by and see what it was all about.

CHAPTER 3

Renata Fechter paused on the top step of the Schiffbauhaus, pulled on smart leather gloves, and glanced over
the cobbled square with its gilded lamps whose big pear-
shaped globes were supported by mermaids with twined
tails. Enough of one had survived the firestorm to provide
moulds to make new ones. To her left was the Rathaus, a
neo-gothic structure modelled on Vienna's, with the
Lutheran cathedral behind it. Spring sunlight made the
colours of its patterned roof tiles glow. To her right the
Catholic cathedral, similar to Cologne's but smaller and
with only one spire; and the Regional Police Headquarters, nineteenth century flamboyant neo-baroque,
once the headquarters of a bank. Opposite, with a colour-
ful but orderly street market between, was the one
building that openly acknowledged its modernity, the
Hotel Intercontinental. For five hundred years its predecessor had been the Regional prison, and then for ten
years the headquarters of the Regional National Socialist
Party. Most people were glad to forget it had ever existed
and no one objected when the hotel chain bought the site.
Between these notable buildings gabled townhouses with
artfully stuccoed façades housed insurance companies,
commodity brokers, the best lawyers in town and on the
ground floors cafés and jewellers, and all, all of it apart
from the hotel, fake, carefully restored fake. Butcher
Harris had seen to that.

A slate grey 1958 Ferrari, soft-top Pininfarina-styled
250 GTS California, cruised round the far right hand

corner and on to the straight in front of the hotel. Momentarily it exposed its backside and private parts as it lurched on to the very steep ramp that would take it down to the underground parking below the hotel. The open car was unmistakable, the neat grey trilby of the driver not quite so distinctive, but clinching. Renata bit her lip. What's he doing there, she asked herself and looked at her watch. A quarter past two? Why does a rich middle-aged man call at an expensive modern hotel at the beginning of the afternoon? And since this was the hotel where the English presentation was to start at two-thirty, she thought, well, I might just find out.

She walked briskly across the black cobbles, threading the quickest route through fruit and vegetable stalls and stalls selling flowers, marvelling at the heaped strawberries from Spain already on sale, it did not seem right somehow, and then up the steps into the foyer. And there, she saw in front of her, moving across the carpeted spaces between ceramically potted exotics, Aldo—but not heading for the lifts as she half expected but towards the Conference Suite. She followed him into a gilded corridor and through double doors glazed with bevelled, carved glass. They were guarded by an easel like a child's toy and a uniformed flunkey with a clipboard. Aldo was held up, clearly did not have an invitation. Renata hung back, half hidden by a fern, and watched as Aldo produced ID.

She looked at the board. A large card, finger-marked in the corners, announced in flowing copperplate: *Sheen Associates—Invited Guests Only*. She waited until Aldo was through the doors before stepping up to the flunkey.

'I have no invitation But I think my name should be on the list. May I?' And she took it out of the flunkey's hands but before she looked at it, she peered through the glass at a large room laid out with twenty or so seats, most already filled, in front of a low dais. Aldo was just taking a seat near the front.

She scanned the list. Aldo Nerone's name was not on it. So, he had talked his way in or was expected as a late guest. But there were several names she recognised—indeed would have spotted the common factor even if she had not already known a little of what Sheen Associates were up to: all were involved in industries that either produced, or made a living out of processing, the Region's toxic waste. Relieved that Aldo was clearly there on business and not servicing a second lover somewhere upstairs, she handed back the clipboard and flashed her official ID out of her purse.

The flunkey hardly blinked, but flicked over the top sheet on his board and with a conjuror's aplomb handed it back to her with a ballpoint pen.

'Sign here,' he said.

She slipped in, took a seat at the back, as far from Aldo as she could get.

Upstairs Harry Sheen ran a comb through his corrugated silver hair, made a tiny and unnecessary adjustment to his tie. Finally he squeezed the bridge of his nose between the knuckle of his forefinger and the ball of his thumb, making the broken bone click: it was something he always did when he looked in a mirror, was a conscious assertion to himself that even now, at sixty-four, he was a hard man, a fighter. He turned back into the big room, the lounge of the four room suite he had rented for a week.

'Right then. Everyone ready?'

He looked them over, a sergeant checking his squad before the captain arrives on parade. First, Herbert. Everything about Herbert, whose massive shoulders were exaggerated by the cut of his dark but vibrantly blue pinstriped suit, said minder but minder with class, the impression Sheen wanted. On impulse he reached out towards the big man's left armpit but with six inches still to go found his wrist caught in an iron clamp. Herbert's reaction had been as instinctive and swift as a tiger's.

'Do you mind?'

'Sorry, boss.'

Sheen grinned, and his hand moved on to feel the shape of the lightly holstered Makarov pistol lying snug and well hidden behind the folds of Herbert's jacket.

'Just checking. I like to know it's there.'

He moved on. El. George Harman's daughter. He and George had been muckers on the Rhine at Mönchengladbach and later at Aldershot. Nice girl, though he wished she'd pluck her eyebrows, and her palms tended to sweat when she was nervous. Now in a neat beige linen suit, with a skirt that stopped just short of her knees and stockings the colour of dark chocolate, black seams, she gave off a warm scent that said money, money fast and maybe dodgy, but money.

'I'm not wearing them,' she'd said when he had proposed the stockings. 'Make me look like a tart.'

'Sure. A tart with class. The whole outfit has gotta have class. The scam won't work without it.'

'Chin up,' he said now.

'Yes, Harry.' She smiled wanly. She still got butterflies at the off even though they'd done this three times already, down the Rhine, Essen, Düsseldorf, Frankfurt. Now they were back north, on the last leg, just Hamburg to go after this one.

Nothing could be done to lend class to Sam Pratchard's appearance. Nearly bald, short, pear-shaped, piggy eyes, pendulous bottom lip, he'd always look like the fat man in a second rate comic duo. Sheen stood in front of him, shook his head, grinned but with pursed lips, brushed dandruff from his podgy shoulders.

'Checked it all through, have you? Got it all there?' He meant the compact soft leather bag that held the Amstrad laptop Alt 286 computer with the neat Canon bubble-jet printer, and the red leather document case with gold-plated locks and hinges which held Letters of Intent, Preliminary Contracts, and the rest. Sheen always bought Amstrad, for him Alan Sugar was something of a local hero.

'Yes Harry.'

'And up there too?' He tapped the fat man's forehead.

'All there, Harry.'

'Let's go then. How many positive replies did you say we'd had?

'Eighteen. Not bad, considering.'

'Gentlemen . . .' A slight frown passed over El's face. There had been no woman on the list, but there was a lady at the back, a lady with class, the real thing, a classiness that exposed the basic tackiness of Sheen's outfit. So who was she? 'If you're ready, we'll make a start.'

The fifteen or so men, several of whom had been at the reception in the Schiffbauhaus, shifted their bums in the upright armchairs, upholstered in squeaky leather, and for the most part shut up. As they did so El whispered to Herbert: 'Try to find out who the lady is at the back. She can't have got beyond the public rooms without signing in.' Sheen looked up from a chair slightly larger than the rest, set to the left of the screen.

'Where's Herbert going?'

'Find out who the lady is. She's not an invite.'

'Good thinking.'

She resisted the temptation to dry her hands on her skirt, rolled a pad of hankie-tissue between her palms instead, straightened, cleared her throat.

'Ladies and Gentlemen. Welcome to this presentation on behalf of Sheen Associates. My name is Eloise, you can call me El, El Harman. I am Mr Sheen's personal assistant . . .' Harry had said: make 'em think you suck me off when you say that, that way they'll know I've got balls. 'And also, as you can see, his personal interpreter. We are very conscious that most of you will speak English very adequately, however some of Mr Sheen's presentation will involve the use of technical, commercial and legal language. What we propose therefore is that he will give the presentation in English, pausing every now and then for me to summarise in German. Mr Sheen.'

Sheen did not stand up, and the care with which the chairs had been placed now became apparent—for everyone had a clear view of him.

'Thank you El. My name is Harry Sheen. I am a sterling millionaire six times over, and I have recently acquired from the government of Estonia a shipping line consisting of twelve freighters with a total tonnage in excess of . . .'

And on he went. As well as summarising every three minutes or so, Eloise manipulated a flop-over, revealing flow charts and pie charts at appropriate times, while Pratchard projected coloured slides of coasters, usually taken with the sun behind them but displaying the logo of the Sheen Star Line. And bit by bit they revealed just what Sheen Associates were up to. Not only had he acquired a shipping line, he had also obtained agreements to allow dumping of seriously noxious waste on land and in lakes belonging to those ex-USSR states which had access to Baltic ports. The actual sites were already so heavily polluted that a little bit more wouldn't do them any harm.

The first part took forty minutes, at the end of which Eloise announced a ten minute coffee break. This would be followed by a session devoted to the financial deals that were on offer, outlining how the lucky punters who got in first, especially those prepared to put down a deposit, would get guaranteed use of the fleet without any increase in costs for at least two years and, just as important, facilitating introductions to the agencies, and in some cases now the private individuals, who controlled or owned the land and lakes on which the dumps were sited.

'One of these,' said El, contriving to make a joke of it, even somehow a sexy joke, 'is, would you believe, a Count, a cousin of the Romanovs. He came back to claim what he believed to be a hunting lodge with adjacent forest and found a thousand hectares of sweetly steaming acid waste leaking out of a million drums. Bad news he thought, until he realised there was room for another million barrels. He lives in the hills behind Marbella now but is planning to move to the Virgin Isles.'

The formal meeting would close at a little after four o'clock after which Sam Pratchard, Mr Sheen's financial assistant, would be on hand with the necessary proformas for early applications to use the facilities on offer. El sat down and the classy lady at the back looked at her watch and left. A moment later Herbert limped back into the room, stuck his head between Sheen and El.

'Her name is Renata Fechter.'

'And?'

'The guy on the door let her in 'cos she's the bill. I says, why should the bill be 'ere? An' 'e says like she's not just the bill but in this town she's chief of the Eco-Cops.'

CHAPTER 4

Tuesday morning.

'There's an Englishman in town called Harry Sheen. He has a small entourage and he's staying at the Intercontinental. He says he's a businessman, a sterling millionaire but I reckon he's a crook and up to no good. I want a bio from research, and they can go to London if they want, but I suspect the Frankfurt DUK already have a file on him. Right?'

KHK Alfred Meier, the alcoholic incompetent, nominally equal in rank to Renata, made a note he hoped he would be able to decipher once the meeting had finished.

Renata paused, looked them over—the Eco-Squad. Six months almost to the day, and still she was very very conscious that they were not working as a team. Not surprising, really. Next under Meier came Becker whose idea of policing was smashing heads—a predilection that he had not yet been able to satisfy in DUK; he was also a sexist racist which was a problem for him since half the team were either female or ethnic or both. Then Firat Arslan, Turkish by birth, pushed, she presumed, out of Serious Crime because his colleagues wouldn't work with a Turk. It was an odd thing though. Renata herself had come from Serious Crime because she could no longer work with Roehl: it was a big section and she had hardly known Arslan at all, but what she had seen had led her to believe he was well-liked.

After Arslan came KOK Pieter Roth, Pieter because his mother was Dutch—indeed she had returned to Holland when he was five leaving him in the care of an alcoholic father who beat and later buggered him. A latent homosexual, he never married but lived alone. He was from narcotics and already a lot less twitchy than he had been—confidential reports from his rehab counsellor were encouraging.

And finally KOK Sharon King from Traffic. She was, in Renata's judgement, definitely a lightweight who possibly did not deserve the promotion she claimed she had been wrongly denied. At all events her habit of listening to her Walkman almost all the time was an irritant, as was her constant gum-chewing.

'Right. The Vereinigte Biowerke case. How important is it that we see Vesper and establish the facts about how many patients were treated with Diomycin and how often?'

Roth, the ex-narc, thin, grey, with a heavy jaw, looked up. 'Very important. Almost all the patients who underwent the treatment are now dead, and the two survivors suffer from advanced senility. The doctors and nurses involved have the right to remain silent, and of course any records there might have been have been destroyed. The point is, the point is, the point is, that our case is so much stronger if we can present a precise inventory, inventory of where every missing phial went. Serious Crime, dealing with the unlicensed use of untested drugs, are being most unhelpful—our only hope of presenting a neat package to the Public Prosecutor is Vesper.'

Renata turned to Becker.

'Andreas?'

'They've locked him up and thrown away the key, and they won't let any of us in to see him. It's unreasonable, uncooperative, but they're entitled.'

'Well. I shall have to find a way round that. All right, back to work.'

Chairs squeaked on the floor, dutifully they rose. Meier approached her.

'Frau Fechter, I have a minor family crisis on my hands. Do you think I could have the . . .'

'The rest of the morning off?' She eyed the almost elderly alcoholic. 'Certainly not. Harry Sheen, remember?'

He glanced at his pad, nodded, followed the others out. Those who had brought in chairs took them with them. Renata sat back in hers, pushed with her feet so the castors took her away from her desk, stretched her legs. With no formal appointments for the day she was wearing a dark blue track suit over a Lycra body stocking and Nike trainers. Her hair was held back by a simple elasticated cotton band. If the sun stayed out she'd spend her lunch break jogging the perimeter fences of the complex, if not she'd lane swim in the indoor pool a health-conscious ministry had provided. Now, she tried to think it all through.

She knew, though she could not prove it, that the Head of DAMOK, Serious Crime, Herr Roehl, was as morally corrupt as a gangrenous limb is physically corrupt. She had been denied promotion to be one of his three deputies because she would then have had access to areas where she could be an embarrassment to him, and that was why she was now where she was. She felt virtually certain that Vesper was not a murderer. So what was Roehl up to? Was the Vereinigte Biowerke case behind it all? But not even Roehl would arrange a murder just so he could frame someone else and bang him up. Unless this Albert Huber was connected with Vereinigte Biowerke, or the cancer hospital as well, and knew things that the drug firm and senior members of the medical establishment wanted to hide.

She searched her memory for what the Monday newspapers had said about the murder, about Huber. Very little really. Just that he had been stabbed to death in the entry to his apartment block, that he was a homosexual, that police enquiries were concentrating on the city's gay community and a man was already helping them with their enquiries. And that was it. There were anomalies. Roehl liked to present himself and his force as moral guardians of the community and usually would have let loose comments along the lines that this sort of crime was to be expected among such people, and so on.

She sighed. This was getting nowhere. Somehow she had to get to Vesper. Clearly Roehl was not going to let her or her officers get within shouting distance, but there were other ways. When the Vereinigte Biowerke case broke and Vesper came forward he had been represented by a lawyer paid for by the Green Party, Dr Anne-Marie Sonnenberg. Renata knew Sonnenberg, liked and respected her, had valued her help in getting together the case against the drug company. She sat up, pulled her chair back up to the desk, reached for the phone. Both busy professionals, they got through the courtesies with a minimum of fuss.

'You know Roger Vesper has been charged with murder. Would you act for him again?'

'I don't think I can. I've already been talking to the Greens about the possibility, but they don't feel justified in paying my fees this time: DAMOK are insisting that it's a domestic murder, and though Vesper is now employed by the Greens that does not in itself justify them footing the bill for a private matter, even one as serious as this.'

'So he'll be defended at the public expense by a lawyer appointed by the Justice Department?'

'Of course.'

'If I manage to get them to approach you, will you take it on?'

Silence for a moment. Then:

'Renata, what's behind this?'

'In the first instance Roehl won't let us see Vesper and we still have some details to clear up on the Vereinigte Biowerke case. But I think there's more to it. I'd just like to know what really happened, hear Vesper's side of it. Finally I'm sure he didn't do it and if anyone can get him off, you can.'

'If I am offered the job and I do take it on, then you know any consultations I have with him are privileged.' Anne-Marie's very clipped, precise voice seemed even sharper.

'Sure. So get his permission before you pass on anything you think might interest me. Vesper trusts me, I'm sure of it. And if I know a bit more about the background, which Roehl is keeping to himself, then I might be able to work out why he's being framed.'

'I'll think about it. But in the first instance you've got to get me appointed, right?'

Renata killed the call, dialled the Justice Department, asked for an extension, called in a past favour. She got a promise but it would be at least two days before it became effective — she would have to wait that long before Sonnenberg actually got to see Vesper.

She replaced the phone, looked at the pile of folders that sat in her in-tray, sighed, and wondered what Aldo was doing.

Aldo Nerone was out in the countryside down river, towards the estuary and the North Sea, driving his beautiful Ferrari at a not unduly fast speed round a two-kilometre concrete surfaced circuit, not too fast because the surface was cracking up. Beside him sat Wolfgang

Kurtz, about whom he knew very little: that he was Swiss, was fronting for other, even more shadowy figures who had hinted, through Kurtz, that if Nerone handled a particular problem that had come their way they might be prepared to invest money in Aldo's project.

Kurtz was tall and cadaverous with a handsome but emaciated face. His body was long and loose-jointed; his slender fingers clasped his knees as he lolled back in the low Connolly-upholstered passenger seat. His eyes watched the trees slip by beyond the tall fences with a cold intentness they never lost.

Presently Aldo spun the teak steering wheel and guided the sleek car into what had been the pits of a formula three race track. As they got out Kurtz slipped a glucose tablet under his tongue.

'Nice ride," he said and turned to look at the car. 'Tell me about it.'

To the untutored eye it could have been any of several models of sports cars from the late fifties and early sixties: sleek lines, close to the ground, wrap-round windscreen, wire hubs, and rather heavy chrome fenders with large over-riders—the yellow badge with its black prancing horse and the side vents just behind the front wheels declared its pedigree.

'1958 250 GT spider California, Pininfarina designed coach-work. The first civilised Ferrari: one you can talk to your passenger in.' Aldo stooped to lock his door, straightened. 'Though above two hundred K you need to raise your voice.'

'How much is it worth?'

'As much as anyone is prepared to pay. Although it was a production model there aren't that many around so the price can vary according to how quickly the seller needs the cash, how desperate the buyer is to have one.' He slipped the one simple key with its small Ferrari tab into his jacket pocket. Kurtz followed him up concrete stairs, then the steep terrace of a small stand to one of ten glassed-in hospitality units at the top.

Everything everywhere was shabby with disuse—paint peeled, damp patches formed, concrete edges crumbled— but one of the units had been smartened up, re-commissioned as a working office with desk, chairs, filing cabinets, fax, telephone and PC. There was also one big table, white laminate mounted on a white metal frame on which were spread architect's drawings and plans. On a side-table there was a large plate of gnocchi, flavoured with smoked salmon and mozzarella, with a choice of dips—garlic, tomato and anchovy. Mist formed on the bottle of Frascati Aldo took from the fridge.

Kurtz began to eat, popping into his mouth the flaky dumplings, in texture somewhere between pastry and soft bread, but bending intently over the drawings as he did so. Aldo opened the bottle, filled two glasses, took his to the window. Below him he could see Kurtz's black BMW with what looked like a minder rather than a driver standing beside it. Beyond that the concrete track wound through fields and then into woods. On the fur-thest skyline a row of container hoists, from this distance like tiny praying mantises, marked where the port was, and beyond them, no bigger than a golf ball on the horizon, a gleam of sunlight briefly illuminated the con-crete and steel containment vessel of a pressurised water reactor and glanced off the shallow dome.

'You have acquired the premises?'

'Yes. Leasehold, initially ten years, renewable.'

'But the acquisition has exhausted available capital.'

'That's right.'

'So.' Kurtz stabbed at the plan with a thin grey finger. 'I can see here you intend to convert these outbuildings into your principal showroom ... and these figurations signify underground petrol storage tanks, yes, so you will have pumps on the site, that makes sense. But a small motel, really? The clientèle you expect to attract do not stay in motels.'

'It will be no ordinary motel. Not more than ten units, with a luxury restaurant attached . . .'

'Ten units won't support a luxury restaurant.'

'No. But the way I see it is that people will drive out to eat here when they know what sort of person is using the motel.'

Kurtz gave it some thought, shrugged. 'Maybe. It's a nice idea. But nice ideas have a way of not working out. That's why market research was invented.'

'The sort of clients I have in mind don't fill in questionnaires.'

Kurtz began to riffle through the thin sheets.

'I like the drawings. Innovative, the way expo architecture should be, but not outrageous. Planning permission?'

'You don't recognise the designer's logo?'

'AD? No. Should I?'

'Andromed Drenkmann. She's the niece of Secretary Drenkmann of the Ministry of the Interior.'

'Ah. But even with him in the background there will be objections you know. Environmental damage, noise, fumes, that sort of thing.'

'None of those will be of the order, anywhere near, of what happened when it was a car-racing track.'

'Why did the track fail?'

'Who pays to watch formula three when they can watch formula one?'

Kurtz straightened, popped in the last of the gnocchi, stroked flakes of crust from his chin.

'Herr Nerone, my principals are interested. I imagine you have a prepared proposal. Send it to the Ramada

Hotel, suite fifteen. I'll want projections of turnover, profit margins, and so on, but basically what I shall be looking at is what the whole thing will be worth as collateral if you don't make money. It's a shame the lease is only for ten years.'

Aldo began to collect the papers together, rolling up the plans and slipping them into cardboard tubes.

'I need a decision fairly quickly.'

Thin eyebrows rose.

'You do?'

'A lot is tied up in this, and there's a lot to be done before we will actually see any return.'

With the papers under one arm he picked up a large bunch of keys with his free hand.

'Three weeks?'

'Two. I have a British merchant bank showing some interest . . .'

'Oh really?' Kurtz's incredulity was blunt. They went back out through the glass door and on to the top terrace of the stand. A draught of cold air off the distant North Sea gusted around them and a pool of weak sunlight drifted across the fields towards them. Nerone locked the door, turned, found Kurtz was eyeing him with a particularly nasty smile on his face.

'Herr Nerone, I know my principals will give very serious consideration to your project. However, before anything definite is settled, they would like to be assured that you will provide them with the facility they have asked for . . .'

Nerone smiled, small teeth for such an otherwise handsome if somewhat gone-over face.

'There's no problem there, no problem at all. Those English people you asked me to see, the Harry Sheen Company, whatever: they seem tailor-made for the operation. We can go ahead, no problem.'

'Good. Tomorrow then. Can you be here as early as nine in the morning?'

'Of course.'

Kurtz buttoned his gloves and set off down the steep terrace towards the cars. Suddenly he paused, looked back and up, over his shoulder.

'Oh yes. And there is one other thing. Naturally we have made enquiries about you. And naturally some of the material we received was not strictly germane to your financial credibility. And it has come to our notice that you are, um, acquainted with Kriminalhauptkommissar Renata Fechter . . .?'

Renata was standing and tidying her desk, prior to going home, when Alfred Meier knocked and put his head round the door. He was short but trim, with white close-cropped hair, clothes and shoes always immaculate: the chosen image of the controlled alcoholic. Only a tracery of tiny lines in the corners of his eyes and round his drooping mouth revealed the signs of premature aging. At the moment he was clean, but he was never able to keep it up for more than a few weeks. Then he would come in, looking just the same, just as neat, but his speech would stumble, he would suffer from short-term memory loss and by three o'clock in the afternoon his hands would begin to shake.

'Sheen,' he said. 'I've got a lot on him, and I didn't have to go to London for it. You were right: Frankfurt have already done the home-work. They have a small dossier on him which they've modem-ed to us. It's on the main-frame if you want to read it. Here's the access number.' As he slipped a small piece of paper on to her desk he sensed her impatience, that she had been just about to go. 'I'd have got to you earlier, but the lines were busy and the first version they sent was degraded, so we waited until things were less busy.'

'All right, Alfred. Many thanks. I won't keep you. It's your AA night isn't it?'

'Yes.'

'How long is it now?'

'Three weeks. I tell them six.'

'Naughty.'

'Well,' he shrugged, 'I had a little accident on the way home three weeks ago, but managed to pull myself up after the fourth. Since it's more difficult to stop once you've started I felt rather pleased with myself, thought I deserved a pat on the back rather than the sanctimonious shit they'd have given me.'

'I'm sure you're right. I'd better stay and have a look at this but you can go home. And no little accidents on the way, all right?'

As he went she mentally kicked herself for the patronising tone of that last remark. Should she call him back and apologise? No. Bosses, and she was his boss, do not apologise, and especially not if they are women bossing men. Yet ... Annoyed with herself she sat down, re-adjusted her keyboard and visual display, tapped in the numbers and letters he had written out for her in his old-fashioned script. The Frankfurt dossier scrolled down her screen.

Harold Sheen, UK nationality, dob 10/02/32. Address: Plunkett's Farm, Old Coddlings, Berkshire, England ... A farm? Was he a farmer? She read on and decided that he was not.

Sheen had been born in south-east London to a working-class family with gypsy roots. He joined the army at seventeen, made Sergeant, served in the British Army on the Rhine, then Northern Ireland where he had probably been seconded to the SAS. Honourable discharge at forty in 1972. He had then worked as a minder for a crooked casino owner and served a short sentence for Actual

Bodily Harm. Somehow, somewhere he got some capital together, possibly the proceeds of a major robbery he had played a small part in, and in the late seventies and early eighties had made several millions speculating in property, but had come unstuck when the property bubble burst in 1989. He was now trying to rebuild his fortunes in precisely the way he had laid out in the presentation at the Intercontinental: there seemed to be nothing illegal in what he was doing so far as German law was concerned and if it seemed likely he was breaking Russian and Baltic State regulations then that was hardly a matter for the German police. However, she smelled a rat, or two. If anyone had toxic waste on their hands which could not be explained, which should not have occurred, then the message was coming across. Sheen was your man.

Of the people with him Eloise Harman had a German mother and was bilingual; Herbert Doe was a chauffeur, ex-professional wrestler and had done time for being the driver in a major bullion robbery; Sam Pratchard was an accountant who had served a short prison sentence for fraud and was no longer a member of the British Institute of Chartered Accountants.

Decidedly a dodgy outfit, Renata thought, but no further action required right now. She took a printout which she left for the filing clerk, and was again preparing to leave when the telephone rang.

'Renata? It's Aldo.'

She felt instantly warm and happier.

'Listen, don't ask me how, but I've got two tickets for La Scala, Saturday week, Pavarotti in *Tosca*. What do you say?'

'Oh yes! But La Scala, how will we get there?'

'You can take your choice: plane, train or car.'

'Not car I think, not even yours. Train sounds interesting, but doesn't it take ages?'

'Twelve hours, but if it's train we should go the day before, from Hannover. Can you take the day off?'

'Yes. Why not. The Region owes me five days.'

'That's settled then. We can drive over to Hannover, be there at a quarter past nine. We can have a first class compartment to ourselves, there's a good restaurant, and we can take the same train back on Sunday. Happy?'

'Yes.' And breathless too.

CHAPTER 5

Dr Anne-Marie Sonnenberg was a round, short, compact woman, in her late fifties. Her iron-grey hair was always scraped back in a bun, she wore a black suit, thick stockings and sensible shoes.

She saw herself as a sort of lay secular nun, a Sister of Mercy working in the community but keeping the vows of chastity, obedience and, since she gave away most of what she earned, poverty. She was, however, an atheist and a communist/anarchist—of sorts. Intellectually she saw nothing in the last century or so to disprove the earlier texts of Marx and Engels and she hated what she called, with deep scorn, the Russian Aberration; emotionally though she ached for a world of Mutual Aid as described by Kropotkin.

On Thursday afternoon she climbed the stone steps between the bronze lions and entered the big marble hall of the Regional Police Headquarters. The duty officer recognised her and would have waved her through but for the fact he knew she would register a complaint to his superiors if he did not check her identity. The formalities completed she found her own way down to the remand cells in the basement where again her identity was checked and the enabling document from the Justice Department scrutinised. At last she was led along the immaculately clean modern corridor with doors like ordinary doors apart from the peep-holes. The warder even knocked before unlocking.

The cell would not have disgraced a not unpricey

Gasthaus: neat bed, washbasin, toilet and television set, two chairs and a built-in cupboard. The decor was cheerful if plain and there was even a picture on one of the walls: a photograph/poster of snowy mountains, pine forests and a lake. Better really than a window with bars.

Roger Vesper lay on the bed, eyes fixed on the ceiling, did not move as she came in, only registered her presence with a sideways flick of his head when he heard the locks clunk back into place.

'You're wasting your time, you know.'

This was not the man she had worked with on the Vereinigte Biowerke case. Vesper then had been jolly, intellectually stimulated by the problems in front of them. But then they had been the prosecution. She accepted deep depression in clients she defended, especially those accused of murder, but even so . . . She pulled a chair close to the bed, pushed back the clasps on her bag, which was an old-fashioned leather affair that concertina-ed out when opened and held far more and was far heavier than one would have thought possible. It had belonged to her father who had been a doctor. She extracted a folder.

'They've given me the usual digest of the case against you, not the details, I shall have to push for those later. Let's just now go over their version and you can tell me where it is wrong.'

'It's no use,' he repeated.

He was tall, in his early twenties, with long fair hair, pale eyebrows, a very big chunky nose. He still retained some of the charm and physical attraction of youth, but he would not be so prepossessing by the time he reached his thirties.

'We'll see. Let's go through the events of Saturday evening and night. You met Huber in the Hallöchen Bar at about nine o'clock. You were already in the company of two close friends. The Hallöchen is used by gays.'

'No.' He sighed. 'They've got that wrong right at the start. I actually spent Friday night and the whole of Saturday with Albert. But yes, we met up with Hans and Dominic at the Hallöchen.'

'That would be Hans Graf and Dominic Stieffen.'

'Yes.'

'Between nine and half ten you cruised through two or three more bars, during which period an argument began to develop between you and Huber.'

'Yes.'

'The matter of the argument related to whether or not Huber would come back to your apartment, where presumably you hoped he would consent to sexual intercourse. Apparently he did not seem attracted by the idea.'

'Wrong. That is not at all what the argument was about.'

'One of the men with you has attested that it was.'

'That'll be Hans. He was jealous.'

Sonnenberg checked back to the document. 'Yes. It was Hans Graf. Graf and Stieffen then left you and Huber. The contents of Huber's stomach indicate that he then had a meal which included fish prepared according to Thai cuisine. There are only two Thai restaur . . . Are you all right?'

'Sorry. I thought I was going to vomit. I think I would have done if I had been able to eat any breakfast.'

She sat back, looked at him. He had gone pale, his face glistened with sudden sweat, his respiration rate was up.

'I said: are you all right? Are you ready to go on?'

'I . . . was very fond of Albert.'

'Did you go with him to the Gold Temple Restaurant in Leopoldstrasse?'

'No.'

'Did you continue to quarrel with him?'

'NO!'

'A waiter there, a Thai, has identified you from a photograph and says you were there and that you were quarrelling violently when you left.'

'He has been bribed or threatened. Probably his papers are not in order and . . .'

'Maybe. It was now about one o'clock in the morning and the police admit that what follows is a reconstruction based on forensic evidence. You then took Huber along the canal towpath towards its junction with the river, and under the Leopoldbrücke you produced a knife and forced him to submit to sodomy and other sadistic practices. When he continued to resist you stabbed him repeatedly and left him for dead. In fact he managed to get back to the hallway of his apartment block where he collapsed and did indeed die. The most telling evidence against you is that preliminary tests indicate that the semen found in Huber's back passage could carry your DNA fingerprint. Now, if you do not want to spend the rest of your life in prison you had better tell me what really happened.'

'No.'

'Come on.' She was brisk, trying to give the impression that she was not ready to stand for nonsense. In fact, although she had witnessed and taken part in hundreds of similar scenes over the years, she was still touched, deeply touched by his despair.

'No.' He turned his face, literally, to the wall.

She softened her tone: 'Why not?'

Without turning his head he began to mumble and she had to pull in, bend close to hear him.

'Probably I'll confess. I'll say I killed Albert.' Manifestly he was choking back sobs.

'Why? Tell me, if you did not do it, why? Why confess to killing the man you loved?'

'They killed Albert. They can kill me.'

'You really believe that?'

'Yes. Look. You have to believe me. No one gay killed Albert. He was like a dormouse. Everyone was fond of him. He was timid and rather sweet. We loved him. We wouldn't hurt him, no one would.'

'But whoever killed him can't kill you. Not while you're here.'

At last he rolled back so his face was under hers. He spat the words out.

'Of course they can. Don't you see? The way I am being fitted up, this is a police job. If I don't go along with them then they'll take the other route.' He reached out a strong bony hand, caught her wrist, the words tumbled out: 'One thing I am not is suicidal. You know that. We've worked together before. I love life, I hate pain, I hate suffering, and that includes mine as well as anyone else's. To resist them now could be as bad as suicide ...' He stopped suddenly as the thought hit him and he raised his voice, almost to a shout.

'Doctor Sonnenberg, I am not suicidal, remember that. Please?'

'All right. But you could at least tell me your version of what happened.'

He sighed, turned away again.

'Perhaps another time,' she said. 'When you've thought about it a bit.'

It was after all still only four days since the murder, and only a little less since he had been taken into police custody. He would still be in shock, still deeply confused, and grieving. She got her things together.

'All right,' she said. 'I'll be back after the weekend.'

As she climbed the stairs, puffing slightly, it occurred to her to question that shout, that cry. Was he trying to convince himself that he was no suicide? Did he fear the temptation? She paused and shrugged. Yes, she had worked with him before, under entirely different circumstances, putting together the case against Vereinigte Biowerke. He was bright, intelligent, but sly and subtle too: above all she had been left with the impression of someone hypersensitive, especially to suffering, but someone who also had reserves of irony, who was amused not only by the absurd world he inhabited but by his own inner self too. A person who laughed at all pretension.

The Vesper she had just left was a broken shell of that person, yet somewhere in him the old Vesper still lived. So why had he shouted? At the top of the stairs she paused and felt a cold shiver run through her as an answer suggested itself: he believed his cell was bugged; he wanted the listeners to know that he had warned her that a presumed suicide on his part should be questioned. And if he believed the cell was bugged, then no wonder he had refused to tell her what had really happened that Saturday night five days ago. She turned, retraced her footsteps, called up the warder, got herself let back into Vesper's cell. Again the ritual of the locks, as he sat up on the bed, surprise written across his face.

'What do you want now?'

'Tell me. Have they beaten you? Tortured you?'

Again the despair as he rolled away from her.

'Can't you see? They don't need to.'

She reported back to Renata Fechter that she did not think Vesper was guilty of Huber's murder, that he had been framed, that some of the police, DAMOK, the Serious Crime Squad, were involved. She concluded:

'He is very, very frightened.'

Renata reacted, twisting a pen between her fingers as she leant back in her chair: 'I'm surprised. He seemed such a very complete sort of person. Integrated. Nothing about the Vereinigte Biowerke situation fazed him, nor the hostility of the bosses in the Regional Cancer Hospital. I'm surprised he scares easily.'

Sonnenberg reflected to herself, not for the first time, how wonderful it was that a position of authority, a little demesne of one's own, not only shelved reality, it obliterated one's recollection of what it was like. She spelt it out.

'Killing and beating are very nasty and extremely effective ways of getting people to do, and say, what you want them to do and say. This simple historical-physiological fact is generally shoved off into the attics of our minds together with any other lumber we prefer not to think of.' She took a breath, went on. 'But it is simply true that if you want almost anyone to do what you want them to do the simplest way to go about it is to threaten them with extreme pain and—or—death. Roger is not a coward. But his sensitivity sharpens what would be persuasive reasons for any of us to do as we are told.'

Silence filled the room for a moment or two, then Renata pulled in her chair, tapped her pen on the desktop.

'Sorry. OK. Where do you suggest we start?'

'With Albert Huber.'

'Who was he?'

'Precisely.'

'What was his job? It says . . .' she scrabbled through the paper, 'that he was a clerk. That's not enough. It doesn't even say who his employer was.'

Sonnenberg smiled grimly.

'I think you should find out, yes?'

'Yes.'

CHAPTER 6

'Turn left, the track coming up on the left.'

'Are you sure?'

'Yes.' El's voice registered irritation. Too often the others, and especially Herbert, questioned her interpretative abilities, whether of maps or German, and in this case both. Since she had made only one navigational mistake in the entire three and a half weeks she assumed he did so because she was female.

As the big Merc began to sway and pitch over deep ruts which splashed ochre mud and cowshit up the sides, she conceded he had other reasons for doubt, especially as they were on their way to pick up eight thousand three hundred and thirty-three pounds give or take what happened to the sterling rate over the next twenty-four hours or so. With double that eventually to come and apparently no cost to Harry Sheen Associates. She conceded to herself if not to the others that a mucky farm-track did seem an unlikely approach to that sort of money.

It had all started with a phone call the day before.

'Herr Sheen? I understand you export industrial waste to Russia?' A mystery voice speaking English though with a marked accent.

'Yes.'

'Ver' good.' The voice pronounced it 'goot'. 'I have a container, sealed, which I must ask you to take for me to Russia. But the circumstances are not quite usual so I am paying some big money for the work.'

'Yes?' Sheen was now very interested.

'Twenty thousand DM if you accept our terms and make an undertaking, another twenty when it is enshipped, final payment of third twenty when it is finally dumped.'

'Just the one container?'

'Ja, a cube container three by three by three metres. You must see to all the moving of it, but according to arrangements you shall be receiving tomorrow. Instructions to get where you should be will be deposited at your hotel desk for you at ten in the morning.' And the mystery voice rang off.

Sheen replaced the receiver and without telling any of them what had gone on simply asked Sam what sixty thousand DM was in pounds. Sam replied instantly— that was the sort of mind he had.

'Twenty-four grand, eight hundred and ninety six and some pennies, if the pound holds at two point four one. More if it drops. It won't go up. Not after that stupid budget.'

Herbert drove them in the hired Merc, and they left Sam behind, crunching numbers. The instructions, in German with a pencilled sketch map for the last part, had sent them north up the autobahn towards Burghaven, then, just as the dull suburbs of the port began to close round them and they could see the container hoists strung along the flat horizon beyond, they took an exit and El began to read out instructions. For ten minutes or so they threaded their way through streets of cheap post-war housing, then tatty allotments, and finally drab empty fields. They sensed they were approaching the river. Then came the turning into the muddy rutted lane, and the hedges, mechanically strimmed so bare shattered wood marked the end of every branch, closed in round them. Presently they came up behind a farm-cart, tractor pulled, laden with large tubers which occasionally rolled off, bounced, and hit the radiator grille.

'Back off, Herbert,' Sheen ordered.

But Herbert refused, instead blasted the horn.

'You silly fucker. What you do that for? He can't move over.'

El glanced across at the big ex-heavyweight professional wrestler and was startled to see that he seemed to be in the grip of an emotional maelstrom of which anger was the principal ingredient. He'd been in a bad mood ever since he had been told to drive towards Burghaven, and now it looked as though something was about to snap.

'What's the matter, Herb? Hip playing up is it?'

'Never you bloody mind.'

The cart pulled through an open gate into a field where big black-and-white cows stood around waiting for their feed: the lane opened out into a farmyard. All the buildings were modern: concrete and corrugated composite barns, mechanical dairy, cow-sheds and outbuildings, the farmhouse itself a sprawling bungalow.

'It says we should drive through the farmyard, through a gate into a wood, close the gate behind us, follow the track through the wood. It must be that gate over there.'

It was made from galvanised steel tubes. Herbert drove the car up to it and El realised he wasn't going to get out to open it. Cursing them all under her breath she opened her door and nearly slipped on the brown slurry that covered the cracked cement of the yard. The gate was heavy and she had to lift it an inch or two to get it to open.

The wood was mixed beech and oak, dank and still leafless, but the surface was now metalled, though crumbling at the edges and potholed. Presently it opened out and filtered on to a much wider concrete track that twisted and turned for a kilometre or so through more woods.

'What is it? Old airfield? From the war?'

'The doodle-bug launch sites were near here.'

Again the landscape opened and among fields they could see a small, dilapidated spectators' stand with outbuildings round it.

'Whatever it was first it got converted into a car-racing track later. What is it now?'

'A dump. Nice wheels though.'

Aldo's Ferrari. Fifty yards beyond it there was a container transporter but no pulling vehicle, and on the transporter a three-metre cube container. It was black, featureless: whatever lettering there was on it had been blanked out with black tape, which had also been plastered over the combination locks and keyholes.

Herbert turned to the others, gestured upwards.

''Ere 'e come then.'

Feet angled, knees slightly bent, a neat dapper figure in a good, lightly checked suit, grey trilby on his head, trotted down the terraced seating. He put El in mind of the classy gents you meet at the races (her dad often took her racing), though their hats tended to be brown. And though often they were quite dishy they were rarely as dishy as this guy, even though he was forty if he was a day. He was carrying a black heavy plastic brief-case.

'You found us then?' The English was good, though drawled—he lingered on the vowel sound in 'found', made an aria of it.

Herbert scowled up at him.

'We're 'ere, ain't we?'

He got out, walked round to the onside passenger door, opened it for Harry. When he felt there was the need to, he could do a good chauffeur. Harry got out.

'Meester Sheen?'

'That's me. My driver Herbert, my PA Eloise.'

No one shook hands. Sheen waited for what he had instantly identified as a wop spiv to introduce himself, but nothing came. Aldo simply gestured towards the cube.

'And that is the brute which has to go to Russia. When do you next have a ship calling in Burghaven, Mr Sheen?'

Harry looked at El, even though he knew the answer damn well: it was the first of their fleet due in. She fumbled a fat organiser from her shoulder bag, made a show of leafing through it.

'April Fool's day, Harry. Fortnight today. On-loading one thousand barrels of toxic from one of our Essen clients, seventeen tons of low-level waste from the Düsseldorf branch of Radwasthaus . . . well you don't need to know the whole manifest.'

Indeed not: she'd have had to make up the rest for that was all there was so far booked.

'There will be room for my little friend here?'

El made a show of it, pursed her lips.

'As deck cargo, yes.'

Aldo sniggered.

'Maybe there will be a storm and it will fall overboard.' No one else looked like laughing, so he didn't. 'Right. Here's what you must do. Monday, twenty-ninth of March, you will tell me the quay from which the cargo will be loaded and the name of the ship and so on, all the details. I shall see that there is enough documentation to satisfy the port authority and the master of your ship, but you are responsible for actually organising the move from here to the port. You will need to hire a trailer truck and a driver to pull it. Can you do that?'

Sheen looked at El. She nodded.

There was a pause, Aldo coughed, went on, tried to make an important question sound casual. 'In what sort of place, with what sort of waste will it share its final resting place?'

Sheen shrugged.

'Basically that's up to my Russian partners. And of course it depends on how you classify it. Is it chemical, noxious, how noxious, radioactive, recyclable and so on?'

'It is not recyclable. We wish it to be dumped and then left alone.'

Sheen was beginning to get the picture.

'We'll say highly toxic, not to be opened, but with a toxicity half-life of two hundred years. I'll get someone to do some research, find out what sort of substance fills the bill. Leave it to me.'

He had realised that the most important thing about the container, as far as his client was concerned, was that no one should know or discover what was in it, and that it should remain unopened for as many decades or centuries as it needed for the sixteenth of an inch welded steel plate that it was made from to fall apart. Probably decades rather than centuries, considering the corrosive atmosphere that would surround it.

'And,' he concluded, 'I can make sure that any documentation left at our end will disappear within a few months. All right?'

'Yes. That sounds satisfactory.'

'Arrangements have to be finalised. How do we stay in touch with each other?'

'I will telephone you at the Intercontinental, and we take it from there.'

'But we are moving to Hamburg on Sunday. We shall be there for two weeks before returning to England.'

'At the Hamburg Intercontinental?'

'That's right.'

'Fine. Now you will return the map and the instructions that brought you here.'

El went back to the car, found them, handed them over.

'I hope Herbert can find his way back without them,' she said. 'And the truck driver will need to know how to get here.'

'I'll make sure he knows how to get here. Finally, the first instalment.' Aldo lifted the black document case, thrust it towards El. 'You don't get to keep the case.'

She carried it back to the Merc, clicked back the lid, carefully counted out the two hundred used notes, each worth one hundred DM, stuffed them in her bag, handed back the empty case. A slow cold drizzle began to fall from the leaden sky. For a moment they all stood around, ill at ease and wondering what to do next, then Sheen turned on Aldo.

'How do you know we just don't take the money and run? Or take the money and go to the police?'

Aldo smiled, the friendliest of smiles.

'You came here for twenty K. You need twenty K? Then you need forty more.'

Aldo knew, all right.

Annoyed, Sheen turned to his associates.

'Bastard,' he said. Then, 'Come on, time to split.' He turned back to Aldo. 'Is there a more sensible way back to the motorway?'

'There is. But you go back the way you came, right?'

All three of them were a bit bemused as they drove back to the city. Conscious they had been outclassed, they spent a few minutes slagging off Mr Ice Cream, the name they all agreed on, following El's inspiration.

'Where's he coming from anyway?' El asked at last.

'Wherever, it's not the same place as the guy who rang us up. He was a kraut, this guy's a wop or a spic,' said Sheen.

'Wop,' said Herbert. 'An' I tell you another thing. He

were at the presentation. Uninvited at that. What's in that box then?'

'Don't even speculate, my friend. Don't even hazard a guess. Forget it. The main thing is: with this little windfall we've paid the expenses of this trip and enough over to buy a decent fish supper when we get home.'

'I tell you one thing, though,' said El. 'I don't know if you guys noticed it, but I did. When it began to rain, it gave off vapour. Not a lot, just a breath or two as the rain settled on it. That means whatever's inside is hot, warm anyway. So I hope it don't blow up before you get the rest of the loot.'

As they began to penetrate the city's suburbs, Herbert's mood lightened and he began to sing. Figaro's aria sung to Cherubino in Act I of *The Marriage of Figaro*, about the glorious life the young lad will have as a soldier. In fair Italian too.

To cut off the repeat El asked: 'What got into you back there Herb?'

'Well, I'll tell you. My old man, I never knew 'im, not like after I were a nipper. And you know why? 'Itler's lot 'ad a submarine base, what they called U-boats, at Burghaven and my Dad, see, was a tail-gunner in Wellingtons. Y'know what they were?'

'Bombers?'

'Right. Well, 'e were shot down in flames over Burghaven, which means cremated alive, and all the atoms and molecules that were 'im were scattered over the landscape. Back there, I was as near to him as I've ever been since he were called up. Like physically.' He drove on, peering past the windscreen wipers. ''E were a good bloke my Mum said. Any way up, she had a boyfriend or two after that, but never married any of 'm.'

CHAPTER 7

KOK Sharon King was, at twenty-four, the youngest operational member of the Eco-Squad. Her skin was the colour of coffee with a dash of milk, darker than cappuccino, and her face was more than pretty with high cheekbones and a neat chin and heavy lids. Because she was a touch overweight and her jeans were tight in her crotch and on her backside the male looks she got as she swung off the step of the yellow tram in front of the railway station amounted to psychic sexual harassment—and that pleased her. Some girls face out that sort of stare with smouldering anger, some pretend they haven't noticed, and some, like Sharon, make frank eye contact with a hint of a smile that says: Go on, say something, make my day. She checked the street number she was looking for from a slip of paper, binned it, crossed the busy street, took a left and presently a right into a quieter area.

Here the buildings were tall and old, covered with grey stucco, cracked and grubby. The few people about were mostly middle-aged women in shabby clothes with scarves over their heads, returning from the local DeSuMa laden with full shopping bags. The cars parked on the kerbs were five, ten years old with dents left unbeaten, rust untended. Five youths, dark, with heavy black hair above fake leather jackets, smoked on a street corner, idle on short time because of the depression. As she passed, one of them expressed a desire to stick it up her in the language of a country he had probably never seen, and the others laughed, but without spirit. It was automatic, a conditioned response, meaningless.

She took a left into a slightly wider street with tram-lines, and etiolated plane trees, pollarded back so they looked like arms with amputated hands thrust into the grey sky, walked past the DeSuMa with its absurd offers of five for the price of four on almost everything, and arrived outside a small Turkish agency: low-cost housing, insurance, travel back home by bus or bucket-shop plane. A large old woman, wrapped in at least two overcoats, sat on the window-ledge with an overfed sausage-dog between her feet.

Sharon pushed through the glazed door, a bell jangled harshly in her ear, and put her hands on the high laminate counter. In front of her the megalithic hemi-spheres crowned with gilded crescents of Aya Sofia were heaped into a cerulean sky: Fly Turkish Air-Lines. Beneath a little round man in shirt sleeves peered through half-moons at a computer screen. Tentatively he dabbed a keyboard: script scrolled, then froze. He swore sadly in Turkish and looked up at her.

'There's an apartment to let in Brüderstrasse,' she said. '13a. I'd like to see it.'

Ten minutes later he showed her through the narrow hallway, led her almost to the top of the long twisting staircase, and breathless now, unlocked the door, ges-tured that she should go in. He remained on the landing, occasionally showing his impatience by jangling a loaded keyring.

The apartment had one bedroom, two reception rooms, a bathroom and a kitchen. It was furnished rather well: an eclectic mixture of modern leather and chrome and old peasant closets and presses. The pictures were mostly art photography, exotic flowers posed to exaggerate their kinship with mammalian sexual organs of both genders;

studied male nudes, mostly black. Sharon did not recognise Mapplethorpe as the artist, but she felt she could get
to like them. There was a bookcase filled with paperbacks
and art books and a very fancy music centre. The kitchen
was particularly impressive: stainless steel everywhere,
non-stick pans, fridge-freezer, microwave, and so on. She
guessed: Albert Huber had worked as a technologically
trained clerk and lab assistant in high tech areas for ten
years or more; he had been single, he chose to live in a
low-rent area—if he spent little on clothes or holidays,
then he had had a very reasonable disposable income.

She found an escritoire beneath a window that looked
on to the street, glanced over her shoulder. None of the
drawers were locked though scratches seemed to indicate
that two had been forced. They were all empty. Homicide
standard procedure: anything personal, papers, clothes,
even toiletries had been cleared out in labelled plastic
bags. The rest left. She went back to the landing.

'What happened? He died or something?'

The little man shrugged, locked the door behind her.

'If you want the apartment I'll get it cleared,' he
said.

The last flight of stairs was faced with cracked old
marble and dropped into the gloomy drab hallway, lit by
a fan-shaped light over the door. Near the bottom Sharon
stopped, looked it over, let the agent go on ahead of her,
out into the street. It was a tall, narrow, empty place, the
place where Huber had died, or at any rate where his
body had been found. There was a payphone by the door,
and two rows of tin mailboxes, ten in all grey, with
narrow slits and lock-up doors. In the top row one was
full, envelopes protruding through the slit. It has to be
Huber's, she thought, and felt a little tingle of excitement.
She paused, listened to street sounds muted, and Turkish
pop music from somewhere nearer but behind closed

doors. Then she took the last four steps into the hall, reached for the envelopes.

'The fact they were there at all is odd,' Renata remarked, as she looked at the two envelopes and two handouts which added up to what Sharon had been able to extract from Huber's letterbox. 'Firat will tell you why.'

KOK Firat Arslan, tall, lean with black corrugated hair, pock-marked grey face and a very sharp suit, looked more like a man with a future in the Mafia, the second-hand car trade or the Christian Democrat Party than an Eco-Cop—but then Renata's image of high style and paid-for fitness hardly tallied either. He frowned, looked awkward for a moment as if he had been trapped into a situation he did not much like, then he shrugged.

'It's DAMOK standard procedure in a homicide case to collect the victim's mail and analyse it for as long as it continues to arrive.' His German was almost too perfect, not ghetto German but highly educated. His degree at Ankara University had been in German and English.

'So what's happened?'

Again he shrugged. 'I don't know. Maybe they changed the procedures. Perhaps the unit handling it has got a bit slovenly, lax. It happens. Tell the truth, in DAMOK it happens quite a lot. They've got Vesper and thrown away the key, why bother with procedures?'

Therein maybe lies the clue, Renata thought, as to why he is with us. If he let it be known to his immediate superiors in DAMOK that he was noting inefficiency and slothfulness, they'd quickly find an excuse to have him out.

She unfolded the handouts, using fingertips and the edges of the paper, handling them as little as possible. One was for a book-club, the other for car insurance on the cheap if you were a non-smoking non-drinker. She pushed them to one side, picked up the first of the sealed envelopes. It turned out to be a proposal for a private pension plan. The second bore the logo of the Green Party. She slit it open along the top with a paper knife, thereby interfering as little as possible with the parts that would have been handled, even licked, drew out the letter inside. Then she looked round the room, checking that her gang of misfits, incompetents and difficult police persons were all attending.

'It's a pro-forma letter from the Green Party answering an enquiry from a member of the public: the sort of thing which is made to look personal by getting the recipient's name printed in, but in fact is on a computer together with the personalised signature of someone at least fairly well-known. All the clerk has to do is keyboard in the name. Usually they spell it wrongly, but this time, since the words 'Albert Huber' present few problems even to the semi-literate, they have got it right.'

They all appreciated her sarcasm. None of them was a Green. None of them had chosen to be an Eco-Cop. There would not have been a DUK, a *Dezernat Umweltkriminalität* to be shunted off into if the Green Party had not won the eight seats that held the balance of power in the Regional Assembly.

'This is what it says: "Dear Albert Huber. Thank you for your enquiry. If you think you have a problem at work which has environmental significance, then you should contact your local district councillor, whatever party she or he belongs to. Then, if you feel you have not had a sympathetic hearing, contact the secretary of your local branch of the Green Party. In the meantime, since you clearly have an awareness of environmental problems, you may be interested in joining the Green Party. I enclose an application form." Signed, if I may so abuse the term, by the Regional Vice-president. And yes, someone did remember to put in the form. That's it.' She paused, thought. 'You know, I don't think this is entirely without significance. Yes, Pieter?'

KOK Pieter Roth, late of Narcotics, stroking his large jaw, had lifted a finger.

'If Huber worked in an environmentally sensitive area of the economy, and was having problems with it, and was a friend of Vesper, then he'd talk to Vesper about it. Maybe that's what they were quarrelling about on the night he died.'

'If indeed they quarrelled at all. Yes. Those are the sort of lines I was thinking along. Sharon. You set this all off. So you can go over to the Green HQ and see if they still have Huber's original letter.'

Arslan raised a hand.

'I'll go with her.'

Ignoring the sudden flash of anger Sharon King showed, Renata said: 'Yes. Why not? If you have nothing better to do. Take a car from the pool.'

Renata Fechter was prejudiced: Sharon was young and inexperienced was the way she verbalised the prejudice. Sharon was black and female were the barely conscious mutterings of a not entirely reconstituted politically correct police person. Forty years of indoctrination, even indoctrination that belittles yourself, do not get wiped overnight.

'I'll drive.' He held out his hand for the keys.

'No you won't.' Sharon scooped them up from the counter where they had applied for an Interior Ministry car. 'This is my show, and don't you forget it.'

They spoke English with some fluency and a self-conscious use of what they believed were up-to-date idioms: Sharon because her Dad had been an Afro-American soldier on the Rhine and, even though he had gone back to the States and re-married, she had spent at least one school holiday a year in San Diego; Arslan because ever since he was seven years old his father, a senior policeman in Ankara, had made sure he was proficient in English as well as German, hiring private teachers to supplement what he learnt at school.

She unlocked the driver's door of the small black Opel they had been allocated, got in, reached across and released the passenger door.

'I can't think why you want to come along anyway.'

'Because you have a gorgeous ass and I like to be near it.'

'Piss off.'

The previous user of the car had left a not quite empty pack of Marlboro and a disposable lighter on the dash. She rarely smoked, and thought he didn't, so she shook one out and lit it, coughed, and then with the cigarette clamped between her fingers set the car moving. Firat wound down his window. She stopped the car and this time spoke in German.

'If you don't like it get out.'

He closed the window again.

She drove in silence through the suburbs that separated the Interior Ministry building from the centre of town, but presently switched on the radio, retuned it, found a station playing German Heavy Metal: the Scorpions. She chucked the cigarette so she could snap her fingers to the music.

'Do you like this stuff?' he asked.

"Course I do. It's great. The greatest. I went to see them, to the Hameln concert. The one here sold out before I could get a ticket. They're really big in the States, you know? The Green HQ is behind the Lutheran cathedral, am I right?'

It was on the fourth floor of a modern office block,

textured concrete and tinted mirror glass. She strode in through the automatic doors, ahead of him, doing her best to ignore him but conscious that he was probably getting a hard-on from the sight of her backside. Then as they got into the lift, he grabbed her and held, his fingers searching into the groove between her buttocks. She turned on him and slapped him hard as the doors slid to behind him.

'Don't ever do . . .'

But he too was angry now, enraged in fact, and with both hands slammed her shoulders so her back crashed against the side of the lift.

'You fucking tart!' he shouted. 'You hit me. I'm your superior officer and you hit me.' And he raised his fist over his shoulder ready to backhand it into her face, but thought better of it, dropped it, straightened his jacket as the lift came to rest. 'Frigging nigger. I should have known better.'

Then he caught sight of his face in the small mirror, the finger-marks already coming up red across his pocked cheek. He pulled out a handkerchief, held it so it covered them.

Still panting with rage and outrage, her palm still stinging, Sharon showed her ID to one of the two women behind the enquiry desk and then the pro-forma letter addressed to Albert Huber.

'This is a murder investigation,' she said, 'and we need to have the letter Huber sent you, the one which this was an answer to.'

One of the women looked at it, checked the date.

'It's possible we still have it on file, though usually we clear that sort of thing out quite quickly. I'll see if I can find it though.' And she went through a door into offices behind.

'We get a lot of letters from nutters who just want to

stir things up for their bosses, that sort of thing. What's wrong with your friend?'

'Toothache,' Arslan replied before Sharon could answer. But she wasn't going to let him get away with that.

'He tried to feel me up in the lift so I hit him.'

'Well done.'

The first woman came back, handed a piece of cheap notepaper across the counter.

'Got it. You're lucky. Friday today, we'd have binned it just before closing time.'

It was a brief note, scarcely filled the page, neatly typed on a steam portable. Sharon read it aloud.

'"Sirs. My name is Albert Huber. I work as a clerk at the Radwasthaus terminal and processing plant in Burgdorf. Two days ago I came across a set of circumstances which has given me cause to worry that all may not be well and as it should be in the plant, circumstances which I think the Green Party would want to investigate. I should be pleased to disclose personally to you this cause for concern and look forward to arranging an appointment at your office, but preferably outside normal working hours." That's fine. I'll take it with me if you don't mind. You'll want a receipt.'

'Don't bother.'

'But I should give you a receipt. It's possible you may be called to witness that this is the actual letter I took from you. So a receipt, and also I think you should photocopy it and file the copy.'

As they crossed the entrance hall on the way out Arslan caught up with her, took her arm.

'If you ever do or say anything about what happened, I'll smash your face in, right?'

CHAPTER 8

Vesper was at least watching television when Sonnenberg called Monday morning, after the weekend, and
from one of the chairs at that. She had left after her first
visit with the impression that he never got off the bed.
She pulled up the second chair, swung her case on to the
bed. When he sat down again after turning the set off
they found that in the cramped space their knees were
almost touching.

'First,' she said, 'I should like to check that you are
getting all the privileges you should have as an untried
prisoner on remand. You should have use of the recreational facility for at least three hours a day, and open-air
exercise for at least half an hour. I know the latter is in a
tiny yard here, and if you think it's not enough I'll put in
a claim to have you moved to the new Willy Brandt
Centrum out in the country . . .'

'No. I don't use any of that much.'

'Why not? You'll rot if you don't. Mentally and physically.'

'The screws have told the other customers to watch
their arses if I get near them. And the criminal classes
traditionally pretend to be homophobes and beat us up
when they get the chance. Oh sure, they bugger each
other, but they're homophobes. What's that for?'

She had produced a small cassette tape-recorder, not
much bigger than a Walkman but with a built-in micro-
phone. She set it up using a flex and plug to a socket in
the wall rather than batteries, and as she did so reflected
that Vesper did indeed seem much better.

'I don't think I told you this when I saw you first but Renata Fechter, you know her, the Chief of the Dezernat Umweltkriminalität, is taking a keen interest in your case, and believed at first that possibly you were framed to prevent you from giving evidence in the Vereinigte Biowerke affair. But we now think there may be a lot more to it than that, and she is very keen that she should hear the conversation we are going to have. It is perfectly legal for me, as your defence counsel, to tape our interviews and play them to her, but only if you agree that I should. Yes?'

He thought for a moment, chewed a thumbnail already gnawed to the quick.

'There's no chance they . . .' he glanced up at the ceiling, 'will get hold of it?'

'None. Unless they are prepared to use force.'

'All right.'

She recorded preliminaries, date, place, who they were, and his authorisation that KHK Fechter could have access.

'Good. Now, Roger, we have discovered that your friend Albert worked as a clerk at the Radwasthaus plant at Burgdorf and that he had come on evidence that some sort of malpractice has been carried on there. That is precisely all we know, no detail, nothing else at all. Did Albert talk to you at all about any of this?'

She felt that if there had been room he would have got up and walked away from her. As it was, he pulled into himself, head sunk between his shoulders, his big bony pink nose dominating his suddenly pale face. And he shook his head, not in denial, but denying her.

'Come on, Roger. I don't have to tell you getting you out of here depends on you telling me all the truth, everything you know that might be relevant.'

He closed his eyes, a last refuge, shutting out this small tough woman, sensing her strength and fearing it.

'And if something is going wrong at Radwasthaus then lives could be at risk. Roger . . .'

He sighed tremulously, as if exhaling what could be his last breath.

'Are you quite sure what I'm saying won't get into the wrong hands?'

For a moment she felt a surge of impatience which she suppressed. After all this man's lover had been sexually abused and stabbed to death, possibly simply because he knew what Roger was about to tell her.

'I'm sure.' And she felt a twinge of guilt. How could she be utterly sure? But she went on: 'I'm sure. And I repeat, if we're to get you out of here, you have to tell me everything you know.'

'All right . . .' The slow sigh again, but at least his eyes left the ceiling and made contact with hers. With an effort that seemed physical as well as moral, he gathered himself together.

'As I'm sure you know, Radwasthaus collects low level waste from nuclear power stations,' he began slowly but picked up speed as his tale unfolded, 'and arranges for it to be safely dumped or processed. Shipments come in several times a week in containers that contain the radiating material. Each one is carefully logged, the dates, weight, contents and so on, and the level of radiation being given off. As a routine check each container is passed through a chamber or shed, I don't know, I've never been there, I'm just remembering what Albert told me. Anyway this shed has a . . . what are those things called that measure radiation?'

'Geiger counter?'

'Maybe. And it was part of Albert's job to record the readings that came up on the displays, in other words the levels of radiation. Well. The day before they killed him, the Friday afternoon, he was just about to check through

a cube container when there was a fire alarm in his sector
of the site. He stopped the process, or so he thought,
observed the fire drill, and then returned to set it going
again only to find that it had completed itself without
him there. He made a fuss, tried to call the container
back, but the foreman refused, said it was all routine
stuff, it would cause too much trouble. Well, this was a
clear breach of procedure, so when it came to his lunchtime he went into the marshalling area where containers
are kept before onward shipment, found the one in
question and stood near it. Now, anyone who works there
has a radiation monitor, a simple device, pinned to their
overall. As far as I could gather from Albert it was like a
plastic disc. If it went red you were in the presence of
potentially dangerous radiation. His went red.'

'So what did he do?'

'He told the site manager. Later the site manager told
him that the people at the originating reactor had made
a silly mistake, but that it was being put right. He
thanked him for his vigilance and responsible attitude.'

'So, after a mistake had been made, the danger was
discovered and the mistake rectified. Hardly a murdering
matter.'

'That's what I said. But Albert seemed to think there
was more to it than that. High level waste should never
come anywhere near the Burgdorf plant. It normally goes
somewhere else where it is monitored far more strictly,
and of course handled with far more care. And the
procedures are so tight it's impossible for high level
waste to get mixed with low level waste. By accident that
is. It's not so difficult to do it on purpose, because of
course no one expects anyone ever to try to do it on
purpose.'

'You seem to have a very complete understanding of all
this.'

'Not really. Tell the truth I'm not even entirely clear as to what radiation is, or radioactivity or if there's a difference. But Albert knew, he was well up in it all, and he explained it to me very carefully, and I questioned him, and so on. In fact we went over it again and again all through Friday night and Saturday, because I really wanted to understand it. There was another factor which bothered him.'

'Which was?'

'The checking system I've described to you is a two-way business whereby computerised machinery complements the human factor and vice-versa.'

'Explain.'

'I'm not sure if I've got this right, but I'll do my best. When the container goes into the scanning area, the operator taps in its serial numbers, the date and so on. But the actual reading is automatically printed on the form which is in the machine. It then comes out of the machine and the operator checks it against the visual reading he has taken from a display. The forms are serially numbered.'

'So there has to be a form on file that gives the high reading.'

'That's right.'

Sonnenberg let silence fill the room for a moment or two then dropped a stone in it.

'Why? Why did you bother about all this? Why didn't you just reassure him and tell him to forget it? Most people would have done. Why did you try so hard to understand it all?'

Suddenly he looked irritated, a bit more like the old Vesper she had dealt with in the past.

'Dr Sonnenberg, you know how I feel about Green matters, the environment and so on. I was trying to persuade him to go to the authorities, but that was asking him to risk his job, just his job I thought then,' bitter laugh, 'so I wanted to understand, be sure just how serious a matter it was.'

'So. Why was it a murdering matter?'

'If the high level waste was put into a low level waste container on purpose, then there had to be a reason. And the only reason Albert could come up with was that there had been an incident in one of the power stations, which had created more high level waste than usual, and that someone wanted to conceal the fact that the incident had taken place and so was getting rid of the high level waste through the low level waste facility.'

Silence for a minute, maybe more. Pipes hummed, then an air-changer came on automatically, a gentle whirring sound.

'Did Albert have any idea where this stuff had come from?'

'Oh yes. Didn't I say? From the Burghaven Reactor. It's actually on the other side of the estuary, but that's what it's called.'

'I know.'

Indeed, twenty years earlier, when it was proposed, she had been on the committees organising demos, marches and petitions against it. It was a Pressurised Water Reactor that now, in the early nineties, only had another five years or so to run. They had proved remarkably reliable, even though or perhaps even because one of the prototypes had been the American TMI2 which came within a whisker of the China Syndrome. Three Mile Island had proved an opportune if unpremeditated testing ground from which all sorts of safety procedures were developed.

Roger Vesper gave another deep sigh but this time it seemed of relief. He sat up, head up, nose in the air like a ship's prow and slapped his knees with his palms.

'I'm glad I've told you all that. I feel better for it. Albert wanted me to, I know.'

Sonnenberg felt a sudden surge of emotion which was not unusual for her. It was her normal response to any manifestation of courageous altruism and she came across examples more often than she thought she had any right to expect in a civilisation dominated by the values of Late Capitalism. Vesper went on:

'Anyway. By then, half ten or thereabouts on Saturday night, I'd had a lot to drink, and I didn't seem to be getting anywhere persuading him to go to the authorities. He kept making niggling objections, like arguing about which authorities we should go to and so on. Naturally I suggested the Eco-Cops but he just said they were a showcase, cosmetic, no one in the nuclear industry has any respect for them at all. So then I said the Greens, and he said he had written to them, but not saying anything specific. He was frightened all the time you see, and I kept telling him not to be. What a bloody fool I was . . .'

Again the sigh that was close to tears.

'As I said, I was a bit drunk and . . . I may as well admit it, when I've had more than I should I get impatient, bad-tempered. Albert hated that, really hated it. He was so . . . gentle. So I banged the table a bit, shouted at him and then went for a . . . went to the toilet. We were at the Ganymed disco by then. When I came back he and Hans had gone. Dominic asked me to go back to his pad and I did, partly thinking that Albert would be upset if he knew I had, and that would serve him right.'

'But that gives you an alibi!'

'No. I told you. I was in a bad way, both with the booze and about Albert. I only stayed there a few minutes, then I went back out and spent the rest of the night looking for Albert in all the usual places. I gave up about three o'clock, went back to my own place and crashed. I never saw Albert again. That's all.'

'Is that really all?'

'Yes. You can turn that thing off now.' She did and as she released the plug from the socket he smiled, albeit thinly. 'Thanks for listening. On your way out could you tell the screws that I will use my recreation privilege from now on? I believe they have table-tennis tables. I'm rather good at table tennis.'

She grimaced, braced herself.

'There's one more thing we have to clear up.'

'Yes?'

'The semen, your semen, in his back passage.'

'Oh come on . . .' Again the bitter laugh. 'No one does that any more, not even with a condom. Well, yes, if both partners are HIV positive I suppose they might not have anything more to lose, but neither of us are, were.'

'They have your semen, and impartial forensic scientists will attest it is yours.'

'But not from his back passage.' Suddenly his voice broke, and his eyes filled. 'Perhaps . . . a tiny smear or something, from the skin on his stomach . . . Oh I don't know.'

She leant forward, put an arm round his shoulder, made it a hug.

'I did love him, you know?' He choked back a sob.

'I know you did.'

She waited a moment or so until she felt sure he was under control again, then got her things together, held out her hand.

'Enjoy the table tennis,' she said, and left.

CHAPTER 9

'Fantastic!' Renata cried as Dr Sonnenberg clicked the tape into silence. 'Brilliant, couldn't be better.'

Almost it was a jump that brought her out of her chair. She circled her desk, put her arm round the lawyer's shoulder in a brief hug and stormed on to her big picture window which overlooked the lawns and trees that surrounded the Interior Ministry.

'It's an in, it's the nutcracker that will crack it open,' she went on.

'Because it's evidence unrelated to the actual murder charge?'

'Of course! Isn't it? Of course it is, precisely what it is. It's an eco-case, a case for DUK. DAMOK and the rest can't block our enquiries now.'

Sonnenberg shrugged. 'Maybe not. Maybe it is a base from which you can make nuisances of yourselves. I'll be interested to see how far you get. Meanwhile, Frau Fechter, you must remember where my interest lies in all this. I have a client. My professional concern is simply what is best for him.'

'So?' Renata turned, arms folded. 'Surely if I, my team and I, get proof that there was an undisclosed incident in the Burghaven reactor, and that Albert could have been murdered as part of the cover-up, then the case against Vesper collapses.'

'Maybe.' Sonnenberg's voice was level, dry. 'But you are going to be obstructed at every possible turn. Meanwhile there are two factors you should bear in mind. First, the danger to Vesper if the contents of that tape are known to the wrong people. Second, we don't know what Huber actually did after he split from Vesper. We don't know where he went or who he was with. The DAMOK investigation says he went to the Gold Temple Restaurant with Vesper. Maybe he did go there, but if he did it was not with Vesper. Now someone has to check all that out, find out what really happened.'

'Of course. Do you want me to put my people on to it?'

'It's either that or go private. And frankly though there are good private agents in the city there's no one I'd trust with this sort of thing.'

'All right. Of course if DAMOK get wind of what we're doing they'll try to pull the plug, but until they do we can try. I'll get someone on it, straightaway. Meanwhile I have to try to get inside both Radwasthaus and the Burghaven Reactor management.'

But Sonnenberg was right. Through four working days Renata leant on doors and found them immovably closed, or they flew open and she fell through into nothing or almost nothing.

Frustrating telephone calls to both concerns, which always had to be re-routed because people were out, or off sick, or snatching a last chance of spring powder in the Alps, took up most of the rest of Monday, but at least she got Becker, the ex-vice cop, and Roth the narc into Radwasthaus by two o'clock on Tuesday.

Becker and Roth hated each other, and, to be fair, all their other colleagues in DUK as well, which led them to synthesise a spuriously amicable flow of chat while Becker guided another Opel from the ministry pool towards Burgdorf: what chances the city had in the second leg of a midweek Euro-Cup tie of pulling back a two–nil deficit against Bayern-Munich; what bastards the Ossis, the East Germans, were, but they could at least speak the language and eat pork which was not true of the Turks or Moslems from Bosnia and Macedonia. Obviously the three things they did not talk about were narcotics, vice, and the job they were about to do.

The Radwasthaus plant was on the river and close to the junction with the canal and, like the station and its neighbouring streets, still had pre-war buildings in it. This area too had been a prime RAF target in 1943, and as a result several thousand hectares of ripening rye on the other side of the river had been burnt—which probably did more damage to the German economy than destruction of the river and canal-side warehouses would have done.

Brick warehouses with smashed windows but as big as cathedrals and less bigoted (anything can get into an unused warehouse) still loomed over patches of wasteland where, in March, willowherb and ladies' bedstraw began to renew themselves among rusting railway track. The problem was that because these ancient monuments to the first flowering of German industry in the fifties and sixties of the previous century still stood, while almost everything else in the city from stone-age settlements to baroque cathedrals had been torched and replaced with fakes, no one could decide what to do with them. Some said these are our genuine past and must be preserved. Others said, with equal accuracy, they are unbelievably ugly monuments to an ugly age, we should finish off what the British air force scarcely began and blow them up. What all could agree on was that it was an ideal area in which to site a plant that would accept, process and dispose of, or package and pass on, the low level radioactive waste from the three PWRs sited within eighty kilometres.

Designed, laid out and built in the mid-seventies, the

Radwasthaus plant had been a model of clean lines, clean efficiency, and user-friendly mendacity. After twenty years of over-use the mendacity remained.

There was a uniformed security guard on the gate, an ex-policeman who was also very big and sported a huge ginger moustache. Becker recognised him but said nothing as he handed the pass that had been sent round for them through the window together with their IDs. The guard kept them waiting for as long as he dared and visibly sneered when he handed them back.

'Eco-Cops? Quickest way to improve the environment I can think of is to flush you lot down the toilet.'

'What's he got against us?' Roth asked, as they pulled away from the barrier.

'Not us. Me. It was me got him chucked out five years back. Knut Haussner. He was on the take from a couple of whores on my patch and when one of them wouldn't pay up he razored her.'

'And I don't suppose he was kicking back your cut either?'

Becker stopped the car, looked across at Roth.

'Make one more crack like that and I'll pull your head off,' he said.

They were kept waiting again in a room strip-lit, with finger-marked venetian blinds, low plastic covered seats and couches (the plastic splitting) and glass-topped tables with the sort of magazines the management thought visitors might like to look at: *Auto-Motor-Sport*, *Playboy*, *Schöner Wohnen*. Forty minutes went by during which they consumed awful and overpriced 'coffee' from a vending machine; then they were shown into someone's office.

Someone? He was instantly forgettable and, despite the fact they were both supposed to be trained detectives, they forgot him.

'I have all the documents relating to the events of

Friday the twelfth, and photocopies prepared for you to take away with you, should you require them.'

Becker recalled that his voice was a touch squeaky, Roth that it was nasal.

'Let me take you through them. This is the record of the fire-drill we had at 14.25. This is Huber's request for a re-run of the test on container Bh 930312 K, asked for because it had been interrupted by the fire-drill. This is the record of the re-run. As you see the rads recorded are low, well within permitted limits.'

He twisted the file so Becker could read the top sheet. It was a deep ring folder nearly filled with A4 flimsies all apparently produced to the same pro-forma but with ascending numbers in the top corner. Becker checked that the numbers were consecutive, found that they were not.

'Why is one missing?'

'Because Huber asked for a re-run. That meant that the first document was superseded by the second. The handwritten note in the box called 'remarks' explains what happened.'

It was initialled A H.

Becker thought it through. According to Vesper, Huber had asked for a re-run and it had been refused. That meant that either Vesper was lying or the document in front of him had been faked. But if Huber had handled this document only ten days earlier then advanced forensic scanning would probably find evidence that he had. If he had not then probably the missing document in the sequence had been filled in by the machine, recording a high reading, just the way Vesper had described, but then it had been trashed.

'Right,' he said. 'We'll need to take that sheet with us . . .'

'Not possible. These files remain on the premises at all

times. Both Regional and Federal statutes say so. That is why I have prepared a photocopy for you.'

Handwriting, Becker thought. Analysis of handwriting has made enormous advances since every petty crook in the world has taught himself to imitate in ten minutes flat a signature on a stolen credit card. And the handwritten note in 'remarks' was three lines long—with an attested specimen of Huber's handwriting as control it should not be too difficult to decide whether or not this was or could be a forgery.

'All right, we'll take the photocopy.' He stood up. 'I think that's all we'll need.'

'I'm curious to know what all this is about,' said Squeaky. 'I mean, I do know Huber was murdered by a homosexual psychopath, but I don't see why this should bring the Eco-Cops down on us.'

"No, I don't suppose you would.'

Becker picked up the photocopy, put on his hat, pulled down the brim, turned to Roth.

'OK, let's go.'

Roth objected.

'But aren't we going to ask about the marshalling yard, about how . . .'

Becker turned, closed the gap between them, and slapped him. Not hard, his hand travelled no more than an inch or two. It looked like play, but it hurt. Becker was skilful in such minor deceptions. He looked back over his shoulder at Squeaky.

'Sorry. Pay no attention. My colleague is a junky, but he's almost over it.'

In the car he said: 'You cunt. You stupid, stupid cunt.'

'Why?'

'If Vesper's story is true, then Radwasthaus prevaricated when they told Huber that the originating reactor had made a silly mistake. It was a clumsy way out, thought up on the spur of the moment. They didn't know how much Huber told Vesper, and now because of you, you silly druggy shit, they have an inkling. It's a fence they'll mend, one they didn't even know for sure had a hole in it.'

Back at the office Renata looked at the photocopy.

'I suppose you did as well as can be expected. Trouble is I think we've been pre-empted on this. There's no example of Huber's handwriting at his apartment: it's been cleared. I suppose you can check out Vesper's, but I'm pretty sure that whatever else you may find there the one thing you won't find is a sample of Huber's handwriting.'

'His family?'

'He has none. He was from the East. His mother died from cancer in 1977 and he and his father tried to get through the wire shortly after. Dad was shot dead on the way but he got through. All we've got so far is his signature on the letter to the Greens, but this thing is only initialled. And like most people he made a drama of his signature, all whirls and loops, not like his normal writing at all.' She stood up, looked around. 'I'm sorry. I have an appointment.'

To buy an outfit that she could wear on Saturday at La Scala, Milan. Evening dress, semi-formal, but not too formal, Aldo had said. But above all stylish without too overtly seeking attention. That's a tall order, she thought, and not one I am likely to get right. However, a friend over in Hamburg had recommended a boutique that stocked clothes which were a bit more special than the ones the big department stores carried . . .

CHAPTER 10

'It was a real drag,' Dominic Stieffen cried. He was no more than eighteen, dark with curly black hair, wearing jeans and an Iron Maiden t-shirt which Sharon felt warm about. 'They carried on like an old married couple, in fact a bit like my mum and dad.'

'What were they arguing about?'

'Whether Albert should risk losing his job at that shithouse where he works, worked, by turning them in for some cock-up they'd made. Isn't that why you're here?'

'Of course.' Sharon thought about it. Yes, that was why she was there—up to a point. But like the rest of the Eco-Squad the murder interested her far more than the possibility that a reactor up-river and not all that far away might be suffering from what might turn out to be a mild attack of Chernobylia. The propaganda saying it could not happen had been part of her cultural background since before she was born and she had been at nursery school when the big demos and the debate of the mid-seventies made news.

'So how did it end?'

'We were in the Ganymed disco, Roger got drunk, lost his temper, and they split.'

'And what did Roger do then?'

'He came back here.'

Sharon looked around at 'here'. It was a neat 'studio', a bed-sit with cooking facilities and a tiny bathroom. All kept very tidy and with attractively presented drawings of machinery on the walls. She already knew that Dom-

inic was studying Promotional Art at the city's technical
high school.

'So he has an alibi?'

'No. I wish he had. I was a bit stupid.'

'How?' She leant forward towards him, she on a spongy
low chair which she suspected could be folded out into
the single bed he slept in, he on one of the two dining
room chairs, pine, simple, but decent.

'Well. We used to live together but got tired of each
other, oh about six months ago. Since then we had a
shag or two, yes, but just toilet stuff in discos like the
Ganymed. But when, the other night, he split from
Albert, I wanted him to stay here, and make it mean
something.'

'And he didn't?'

'No. He was worried about Albert. Really he loved
Albert, you see?'

From the tone of his voice, an inflection, a shadow of a
frown, she caught the presence of something unsaid. She
made a guess.

'Albert went off with someone else?'

'Yes.'

'Someone he knew?'

'I suppose so. Yes. Albert knew him.'

'But you did not. You did not recognise him. You did
not know who he was.'

'No.'

'Tell me what he looked like.'

'Do I have to?'

'It could help.'

'A warrior god. A Viking.' Rolling his eyes, camping it
up.

'But not part of the gay scene, here, in the city.'

'No!' There was resentment in his voice. 'It was the first
time I ever set eyes on him!'

'Sorry, just let me go over all this again and make sure I've got it right . . .'

'This is crazy, you know?' Stieffen stood up, walked round the room, ended up by the window where his long nails rattled on the pane. 'Why don't you just go down to the central police station and look up the files. They interrogated me there for six hours on the Sunday afternoon: it must all be there in their files.'

'I told you. I'm from the Eco-Squad. Serious Crime won't open their files to us on a case they're still investigating. Now, please, take me through, in detail, what happened at the Ganymed, just the last moments before Albert left.'

He sighed, as if to say I've done this already, too often. Then spoke like a bored adult speaking to a stupid child— to begin with anyway.

'Roger got really angry, started banging the table, then he said he was going to the toilet. Almost straightaway this big guy who had been sitting at the bar came and sat in Roger's place, you know, as if he had been waiting for the chance.'

'And Albert knew him?'

'Yes. But was surprised to see him.'

'So you're implying he knew him, but not as a gay, not as part of the gay scene.'

'That's right.'

Sharon stood up from the low soft chair, sat at the round table in one of the uprights.

'Come and sit down again, I can't talk to your back.'

Stieffen did as he was told, sat facing her, elbows on the table, chin in his hands. There was a bowl of fruit between them. She took an apple.

'May I?'

'Why not?' He shrugged.

She bit out a crunchy mouthful and through it said:

'Come on then, tell me what he looked like, this Viking god.'

'Not so much a god really. More like something out of Asterix.'

'Go on.'

'Tall, gingery blond, pocky complexion, the sort of moustache you could strain soup through. Like that Iraqi dictator's only fair. Big, and a bit overweight.'

'Age?'

Stieffen thought for a moment.

'Difficult to be precise. Older than any of us though. In his thirties. Maybe older. You get them like that every now and then. In the Ganymed. They're not gays really. Probably married, had a row with the wife, she's off sex or having it with someone else. They think they can go to a gay bar or disco and find a boy they can pay to ⸱ k them off. That's the sort I put him down as, anyway.'

'Clothes?'

'Polo-shirt with a collar, beige-coloured good quality trousers, broad belt with a heavy buckle shaped like a ram's head. I tell you one thing about him though.'

'Yes?'

'There was something about him said soldier, military. His build, his way of holding himself.'

'What did he say?'

'I can't remember the exact words, but it went a bit like this: "Hi, Albert. I've been looking for you. There's something we ought to talk over. Have you eaten?" Albert said, no. This guy said "Come on then, I'll buy you a meal," and took his arm. Albert looked frightened, looked as if he didn't want to go, but he went. Hans went with them. Then when Roger came back from the toilet, I asked him back here, but he wouldn't stay, like I said, he was worried about Albert.'

'OK.' Sharon lobbed the apple-core into a tin wastepaper bin near the door. It made a satisfying clang. 'Can you give me Hans's address?'

'I can, but it won't do you much good. Apparently as soon as they were out in the street Asterix told him to get lost. And because Hans didn't want to admit to us that was what had happened he went straight home.'

Sharon flipped back a sheet or two in her notebook.

'When my colleague Becker rang Vesper on Monday morning, a week ago, you answered the phone. At the time Becker thought you must be living there, but you're not, you live here.'

Stieffen blushed a little, looked awkward.

'Like I said: I used to live there, for a bit, about six months ago. We were ... closer then. Then this Albert thing started and I moved out, but I still had a key.'

'So why were you there on Monday morning?'

'There were some things there of mine, I wanted to get them back.'

She sensed he was withholding something.

'What sort of things?'

He was confused; he twisted away then stood up, went back to the window.

'Letters. Personal, you know? Letters I'd written to him.'

'Did you find them?'

'No. They'd gone. I knew where to look. He kept all his personal correspondence in a desk drawer, and it had all been cleared out.'

Including no doubt anything written by Albert Huber. Sharon thought: Sonnenberg had been right—samples of his handwriting were not going to be easy to find.

'You were jealous of Albert.'

'When it started, yes. Very.'

'Weren't you afraid the Serious Crime squad would pin his murder on you?'

'Yes. Of course. And I can't understand why they didn't, didn't try to. I can't understand why they think Roger did it.'

'But you didn't.'

'No-o-o-o.'

There was both anger and despair in the cry and either intense sincerity or an intense desire to convince her.

'Have you still got that key? To Vesper's apartment? I'd like to borrow it if you have. I'll get it copied and then send it back to you.'

'I don't think I should do that.'

'Do you want to get Vesper out of prison, off this charge?'

'Yes, of course I do.'

Which probably meant that it was true that he had nothing to do with Huber's murder. She went on.

'Then you should do what you can to help us. We are not investigating the murder, but we do believe it might be connected with the problem Huber was having at work. If we can clear that up we'll probably find out who killed him.'

Silently Stieffen pulled keys from his pocket and with some difficulty threaded a key off the sprung ring, handed it to her.

Back in the street she let herself into the passenger seat of the pool car, next to Meier, who was in the driving seat, just as she had left him. She sniffed, sighed.

'Alfred. You've been drinking. Better let me drive.'

Renata reckoned she'd found precisely the right outfit: a charcoal black crêpe silk trouser suit, very floppy, slightly see-through, sewn with hundreds of real jet beads. Trying it on in the boutique she realised that she had the height, stature and presence to be a top model, albeit a rather aged top model. But why not? She turned and twisted. Since few women, or their husbands, could afford clothes like this until they were at least her age, why not have them modelled by older women instead of by adolescent bimbos? And these days there was no shortage of women who kept themselves as lean and fit as she did. Meanwhile, the salesperson, as old as her but not in such good nick, assured her that the designer had worked for, or with, Armani for three years before quarrelling and going out on his own. His atelier was in Zürich so it was highly unlikely that anybody else would be wearing the same outfit in Milan. That clinched it, and she paid, well, signed a chit, for a guilt-searing amount of money.

No need to rush back. The weather had turned suddenly rather splendid: one of those freak warm days you get towards the end of March when waves of warm air from the south break gently over budding trees and spring flowers and suddenly you believe it is possible not just that winter might end but that it is actually over. Swinging the glossy red bag printed with gold she sauntered up the boulevards that line the east bank of the Aussenalster, the lake with its Geneva-like fountain. After ten minutes or so of this she discovered that it really was warm enough, at four o'clock in the afternoon, to sit by the flowerbeds filled with massed polyanthus, and take tea . . . outside!

She found a pavilion overlooking the lake with tables in the open air, and presently a waiter came to take her order. When it was delivered (English tea and plain biscuits) there was a carnation in a thin tubular zinc vase on the tray.

'Compliments of the management,' the waiter murmured. He looked Italian or possibly Spanish. 'You are our first customer this year who has chosen to sit outside.'

She was charmed, looked up and around, and saw not far away, almost on the corner of the road opposite, the Hotel Intercontinental. And at that moment she saw in the corner of her eye a young woman on her side of the road coming towards her. The woman checked, seemed ready to make a half turn, as if she did not wish to be seen by Renata, but thought better of it. She walked past Renata, without looking at her, choosing not to look at her, Renata thought, and trotted briskly across the busy avenue. She was wearing woolly tights beneath a baggy brown patterned jumper over a minuscule mini-skirt. If she had not checked Renata would not have given her a second thought. But now it came back to her.

Eight days ago, in that other Hotel Intercontinental, that strange presentation, that unlikely offer to ship industrial muck out of Germany and into Russia in a privately owned fleet of clapped out freighters, and this was the girl who had translated and lent sex appeal to the occasion.

And with the memory and her realisation that these people were here in Hamburg, came the answer to the question that had been nagging ever since she had heard Vesper's voice on Sonnenberg's tape describing how Huber's warning badge had glowed red in front of the cube container. It tumbled into her head like a shiny, new-minted coin. It was an epiphany. She knew, she was certain of it. Though every rational cell in her body cried against such a wild assumption on the very barest of evidence, a wild guess merely, and then making such an assumption a basis on which to act, she knew she would. The question had been: how do you dispose of a container holding objects dangerously radioactive? And the answer was: you employ Sheen Associates to do it for you.

What action could she take to capitalise on this sudden windfall of a perception? Twenty-four hour surveillance of the English quartet was out of the question: the expense and manpower alone would prohibit it; and anyway she'd never get a judge's warrant for it on the basis of a hunch. But there were other possibilities. Briskly she finished her tea, left a bank-note that even in Hamburg would cover the bill for a cup of tea and a free carnation, plucked the carnation from its vase, and hurried back to her car and car-phone. She put the carnation on the seat beside her and dabbed in her own office number.

'Get me Arslan please. Firat? Listen, a week ago yesterday a British firm called Sheen Associates gave a presentation in the Burg Intercontinental. Fifteen or so local businessmen attended. I want a list of their names on my desk by the time I get back. Oh, and don't be surprised when you find my name among them, it's not a mistake. How long? If I'm lucky with the traffic an hour and a half.'

That was a start. But what else? She holstered the phone, sat back in the black leather of her small red BMW, tapped her teeth with her fingernail. Send one of her people in impersonating someone with a similar problem. But who? Who out of the misfits that made up her squad could do that? Another option occurred and she phoned her office again.

'Has Arslan already gone? All right get me Becker if he's there. Andreas, get on to the port authorities in Hamburg, Burghaven and in Burg itself, and find out when any freighters belonging to the Sheen Star line are docking in or out during the next four weeks. I want the answer on my desk in an hour and a half.'

Again she replaced the phone, but this time turned the engine on and set the car moving through the early evening traffic towards the autobahn that linked the two cities. Stopping for petrol at a service station, she binned the carnation. The spicy smell of cloves was getting to her.

An hour later the Sheens' six-year-old Mercedes cruised along the banks of the Aussenalster towards an appointment with a demolition firm that was having asbestos trouble. As they passed the pavilion where Renata had had her tea El leant round her front seat to get Sheen's attention. She was now back in her secretarial uniform—the beige suit, the tights with seams.

'Harry?'

'Yes, El.'

'You know that woman who came to the presentation last week back in Burg.'

'The one who turned out to be the head of the regional eco-police?'

'Yes. Well, just now, when I came back to the hotel, she was sitting outside that café opposite, the one with the terrace overlooking the lake.'

'Are you sure, El?'

'Dead sure, Harry.'

'Shit.' But then he thought about it. 'Must be coincidence. I mean if she's the boss of her outfit she wouldn't be doing the leg work, would she? Still it might be worth mentioning it to Mr Ice Cream when next he gets in touch.'

Herbert drove on, out of rich sexy Hamburg, away from

the glitz and the port, into the hinterland of post-war cheap housing and huge industrial estates. Presently Harry cleared his throat and leaned forward.

'How are you feelin', El?'

'Pretty chipper, Harry. Why?'

'Important this one is. Gotta persuade them if we can.'

'Why's that Harry?'

'Well, it's no secret we an't done as well as we 'oped. And Sam reckons if we don't clean up four or five jobs by the end of this week, we oughta cut our losses and run. So be smart.'

'I always do my best, Harry. You know that.'

'Course I do, love. Course I do. But let them see a bit of leg up near the top, make those stockings hiss, give'm the old eye, make them feel the world's a better place since we blew in. OK?'

'Yes, Harry.' She wanted it to sound as bored as she felt, but she couldn't. He was a fighter was Harry, had come back bloody but unbowed a coupla times at least. Uncle Harry he'd been since way back, since he'd made her sit on his knee at family dos, Christmas and so on, and the hoarse whisper had come across his brandy-laden tongue that she was the loveliest little thing had ever come his way.

CHAPTER 12

Radwasthaus had been a door which opened too easily with apparently nothing on the other side. The Burghaven Reactor was a door that would not budge. By Wednesday evening Renata had had enough and insisted on an appointment, soonest possible, with the most senior official in the Regional Interior Ministry, Secretary Drenkmann. He could, she learned, find her a quarter of an hour at eleven forty-five the following morning. If she wanted longer she'd have to wait till Monday.

She did not like Secretary Drenkmann. And not just because she had inevitably heard too many rumours of cover-ups, faces saved, with hints of deeper corruption. Since he was at the top of a huge heap of which the police force was only a part, if one of the most important parts, it would be odd if such whispered rumours did not surface in bars and locker-rooms. Her dislike was more personal than that: he patronised her in a way he did not patronise men equal to her in status and rank; he was a great deal too close, in her opinion, to her former boss Hans Roehl of Serious Crime; and he was also, like Roehl, very, very fat; and finally, and almost worst of all, though it only mattered when she had actually to be physically close to him, he smoked a pipe.

Though his office was on the top floor of the building she worked in it might as well have been on a different planet. His personal assistant, a dour elderly woman who had never been known to smile, showed Renata into the presence at precisely eleven forty-five, indicated she should sit in a low, sway-backed black leather and chrome seat placed about half way between the door and his desk. This was huge and set in a sea of deep-pile carpet beneath a large and messy abstract painting done by an artist of international repute and entitled *Cohesion 3*. It was meant to symbolise institutionalised structural harmony but to Renata it pretty accurately reflected the institutionalised chaos in which she worked. The big man was, as usual, only to be perceived through the smoke clouds that enveloped his head, pierced occasionally by flashes of flame: no matter how much he puffed, he let the noisome thing out every three minutes or so and then had to rekindle it using a big chrome Zippo lighter. He had a pendulous lower lip, pendulous jowls and big tobacco-stained hands. His ash-strewn suit was always very dark grey with a thin stripe, and usually crumpled. In spite of all this she knew him to be devious, clever, and ruthless.

He had a small stack of printed papers in front of him. He scanned and initialled three sheets before looking up at her over half-frame spectacles.

'My dear, I shall be with you in half a minute, I promise.'

His voice was deep and resonant but flawed, a cracked bell. Because of the endearment her toes curled and she scowled back at him. Presently he dabbed a button, leant back, screwed the cap on his fountain-pen, spread himself, head on one side, in his big executive chair. A smile that was almost a leer spread across his face. Only when his dour assistant had collected the initialled papers did he speak again.

'I hear you have been making a nuisance of yourself.'

'I must be getting something right then. So who's complaining?'

'The Regional Vice-chairman of the Reactor Safety

Commission tells me you have been pestering him to disclose to you the log of the Burghaven Reactor. Is that why you have asked for this appointment?'

'Yes.'

'It is an extremely detailed and highly technical document. The readings from the instrumentation of five different systems are automatically recorded and computer-analysed on a two-hourly basis round the clock. It is not possible that any of it would mean anything at all to anyone in your team.' His thumb rasped, flame blossomed, was sucked into the bowl, the smoke thickened. Renata realised she might vomit and that the cost of replacing or even just cleaning more than twenty square metres of very expensive carpet would be high enough to be interesting.

'What is the purpose of this log?' she asked.

'Technicians also monitor the systems round the clock, but being human they are fallible. The log is there to be referred to if the human monitoring falls short in any way. It is also a record that can be referred back to after an incident, however small, to see if there was any indication however slight that something untoward was on the way and slipped by.'

'And of course it is a record of any incident.'

'Yes.'

'Mr Secretary, I have evidence that there was an incident at the Burghaven Reactor. It was never made public, but it produced high level radwaste which is being disposed of illegally.'

'You have no such evidence. You have the cobbled together gobbledegook of a homosexual on a murder charge who is trying to put together a defence based on the fiction that his murdered lover was killed because he believed Radwasthaus had accepted high level waste from Burghaven. In fact the murder had a homosexual background in which jealousy may have played a part, though there are signs that ritual sado-masochism was an element too.'

It was almost as if the earth had moved beneath her. Through an agonised moment or so she rushed the whole sequence of events through her mind. Why had she taken up this business, the defence of Roger Vesper? Because he was a witness in the case against Vereinigte Biowerke and initially she had suspected that his arrest might have something to do with that. Clearly it did not. Everybody seemed to have forgotten about Vereinigte Biowerke. But then came his second, taped interview with Sonnenberg and the possibility that Serious Crime was fitting up Vesper to protect the nuclear industry in all its manifestations, one of which had been responsible for Huber's murder. Renata was no Green—but she hated Hans Roehl, her former boss, and she realised it could well look to others, as indeed it now began to seem to her, that she had taken up the case in response to her obsession with a man she knew to be evil, that her actions had, after all, been less than rational.

Secretary Drenkmann watched her discomfiture and unusually set aside his pipe in a big copper bowl he kept for the purpose, leant forward over the nest his heavy fingers made.

'Renata. The Burghaven Reactor and the Radwasthaus plant in Burgdorf are extremely efficient, finely honed operations with a record of nearly twenty years of almost trouble-free activity. There have been hiccups with the nuclear programme, of course there have. But the record is far, far better than that of France, the United States, and of course, of Britain. The Vereinigte Biowerke case will not go by default because of this wretched Vesper business, I can promise you that...' he was reading her mind, and pretty accurately at that, 'but right now I should be very grateful if you would cease meddling in matters that are not really the business of DUK. After all, when all is said and done, nuclear power is the least polluting way of making electricity that has yet been invented.'

She gave that some thought.

'Wind?' she suggested.

'I beg your pardon?'

'Wind power. It can create electricity without even producing heat.'

He treated the suggestion with the contempt it deserved and returned to initialling the documents in front of him. She looked at her watch, saw that her allotted time was up, stood to go.

'So,' she said. 'I am not to be allowed access to the Burghaven Reactor log.'

The big head lifted, watery eyes searched the smoke from behind the spectacles.

'On the unsupported evidence of a homosexual with a record for making trouble in the past, and held on a charge of murder which at the moment looks watertight, no.'

But what he said had fired a memory: Sonnenberg's commitment to Vesper as his defence lawyer.

'You might just as well let me have it.'

'Why?'

'Dr Sonnenberg will get a court injunction to see it if you don't. She will make it a cornerstone in Vesper's defence.'

The eyes and the big head dropped again, and the big hand moved the pen once more across the right-hand bottom corner of the document in front of him. A dry cough from the dour secretary who had come in behind her told her that yes, really, it was time to go.

*

Back in her office she asked Sharon to bring in a coffee
and warn the others that she would want to see them
all in ten minutes. With the coffee she nibbled a muesli
bar. She noticed that as part of a promotion for the
product, the wrapper incorporated a tiny, self-adhesive
Mickey Mouse: collect ten, all different, stick them in an
album.

'Apart from Vesper, and the possible incident at Burghaven, what else are we coping with at the moment?
Andreas?'

Becker pulled his gaze back from the tops of the
greening trees he so much hated. He sighed.

'Market gardener out at Lindern using fertiliser in her
tomato greenhouses in concentrations which contravene
an EU regulation whose number I can't right now recall;
a farmer down near Neuenbrück who is draining wetland
of scientific interest in contravention of EU decision blah
di blah ... And of course a few loose ends at Vereinigte
Biowerke.' He yawned hugely, and not out of tiredness.

'Alfred not in today? Firat then.'

'Turkish importer of unpasteurised goat yoghurt, and
another who killed a sheep in the street at the end of
Ramadan. Helping Sharon with spot checks on car
exhaust emissions, and routine checks at petrol and
diesel pumps; helping Pieter with waste emissions in the
River Weser, that's of course in cooperation with the
Regional River Advisory Service ...'

And so it went on. Clearly they all had a lot on their
hands, and all were bored to death with it all.

'So. Plenty to be getting on with. You won't be disappointed to know then that the Burghaven Reactor, Radwasthaus, and Vesper are all now off our books.' She
looked around, trying to guess their reactions. Big Becker
and pretty Sharon both looked pissed off. Becker, she

supposed, because at last a case had cropped up which had a whiff of the evil he was used to, Sharon because she had worked hard, and done well on it. Neither Arslan nor Roth showed any emotion at all.

It was Sharon who raised a hand.

'Why? Are we allowed to know why?'

'Yes, I think that it's fair you should. On the one hand there has been no incident at Burghaven, and what Becker and Roth learnt at Radwasthaus—that the container Huber asked to have re-examined after the fire-drill was inspected again and found to be harmless—is now the officially accepted version. The story about it turning his indicator red in the marshalling yard is now thought to be Vesper's fabrication. And on the other hand Vesper himself and the Huber murder are a case for Serious Crime, and definitely and finally off-limits as far as we are concerned. All right?'

She tried to make it sound firm, but it came out harsh, abrasive, frustrated. Becker cleared his throat.

'I feel sure that break in the number sequence of the forms recording radiation was against regulations.'

'Andreas, it's a promising line to follow, I agree. But without a proper example of Huber's handwriting . . .'

'And now no hope of getting one . . . it's a dead duck.'

He sniffed noisily, brushed his big black moustache with the back of his hand, turned away. Renata was annoyed that he had interrupted her, even more annoyed at the barely concealed implication that she was a woman and had allowed herself to be over-ruled by higher authority more readily than would have been the case had she been a man.

'Andreas, you want to speak to Secretary Drenkmann about this, feel free. Sharon?'

'Huber wrote to the Greens on Friday. He was so worried he got the letter into the post in time for it to reach them on Monday. He wrote that letter before he met Vesper . . .'

'That letter is completely vague. It might have been about anything. It need not have been about the container and the fire-drill at all. And probably he told Vesper all about whatever it was about, and Vesper concocted his story out of his knowledge that Huber had written a completely unspecific letter. It's possible anyway.'

'And what about Stieffen? What about his evidence that Huber went off with a stranger who looked like Asterix?'

'Stieffen is in love with Vesper. He wants Vesper out of prison, free, especially now that Huber has gone.'

Sharon paused, shook her head, remembered how Stieffen had been puzzled that he had been let go when he had a far better motive for killing Huber than Vesper had. To him, and to her, it had pointed to Vesper's arrest as being a fit-up, as if Vesper was the target as much as Huber, killing two birds with one stone. She looked up, met Renata's eyes, found them stony, hard, admonishing. She looked away.

'OK. That's it. For now at any rate. Back to your routine jobs.'

They stood, shuffled, picked up the chairs they had brought in. Becker was the last, paused in the door, leaning on the chair he had been carrying.

'You asked for a list of Sheen Star sailings in the next four weeks. I don't know if that's anything to do with all this.'

She was suddenly conscious of stillness in the room, but of expectancy too, also of something lurking, dangerous. She gave a tiny shudder, a shake, as if dislodging an insect, a dead leaf from her padded shoulder.

'No, no it's not to do with it at all,' she lied, though she remembered she had no real grounds for believing it was.

'It's an entirely different matter. Incidentally I note that the first sailing you have on your list is of the MV *Eloise* from Burghaven at twenty-one hundred hours on Thursday first April. I want a manifest of what she's taking away with her on my desk, noon that day.'

'You're the boss.'

'Yes.'

She folded papers away into an envelope file, uncrossed her legs, looked up.

'Right,' she said. 'I'm claiming one of the days the Region owes me tomorrow. You won't see me again until Monday. Have a nice weekend.'

She waited until he had gone then ran through the routine security check she always followed before leaving the office for more than one night, ensuring that the numbers on filing cabinets were twisted well away from the combinations that would open them, that the drawers in her desk were properly locked. Then, as she often did, obeying an irrational and unpleasant compulsion, she opened the small drawer which housed her police issue Walther P38. She hated the ugly pistol, the power it represented, but every now and then felt the need to heft it in her hand, check the magazine, catch the unblemished whiff of refined machine oil. It was a symbol of the unacceptable side of policework, a side which, nevertheless, like the pistol itself, exercised its fascination.

Then, with something like a giggle bubbling in her chest, she thought: I'll show it, I'll teach it a lesson. She rummaged in her wastepaper bin, found the muesli bar wrapper, peeled off the tiny Mickey Mouse and stuck it in front of the finger grip on the breechblock.

PART II

CHAPTER 13

Through a bad week Renata had looked forward to her Italian break with an eagerness that matched her expectations when, at eighteen, she prepared for her first run down the Vallée Blanche on Mont Blanc. On that occasion, after the first magic of the ice tunnel and the terror of the knife-edge *arête* where, because of the wind, the guide had made them rope up and carry their skis, the actual run, twenty-three kilometres, had been fun but something of an anti-climax. Neither magic, terror, nor the mild disappointment of finding that something cracked up to be special turned out to be not just so special after all spoilt her weekend with Aldo. It was the tension of coping with his family.

She should have guessed, she told herself later. The Italians are strong on families. Everyone knows that. He had a wife, he had kids, they were going to Milan, Lake Como where the clan lived was just up the road. Wasn't it entirely to be expected that he would introduce her to them all, try to make her part of the family too? Of course it had never occurred to her that he would or even that he could. Lovers are a part of your life you keep separate from your marriage.

He shrugged hugely when she put this to him.

By then it was ten o'clock in the morning and they were south of Hannover, which was where they had boarded the Tiziano Express. Mixed forest, greening up, and pasture with flowers after the warm spell slipped by smoothly and almost soundlessly on the other side of the big window. Inside, the first class compartment was all theirs until they arrived in Milan at half past nine that night, including the pull-down bed, if they wanted it.

'Milano?' he said, when she asked him when they would arrive. 'Milano? But we don't get as far as Milano until tomorrow. Tonight we stay at my house on Lake Como. This train stops at Como at a quarter to nine. By nine we shall be home, where they are all waiting to meet you. And then we can spend the whole of tomorrow together before we go to La Scala.'

'All? Who are all? Who will be waiting to meet me?'

'My family.'

He was trying to be bold, face it out, pretend it was the most natural thing in the world.

'So?' She injected heavy threat into her voice. 'Tell.'

'My two sons, my two daughters ... they know all about you. They have expressed a great desire to meet you.' He ran his brown fingers, the hair behind his knuckles was black, through the greying corrugated hair of his head. Clearly he realised that a moment of truth he had been postponing was upon him. The track took a slightly tighter curve than normal and he steadied the octagonal green and gold coffee cups that had slipped an inch or so on the little table under the window. He took a breath. 'And Maria Incoronazione too.'

'Maria?'

'My wife.'

'Your wife? Your wife will be there?'

'Yes.'

She looked at her watch, picked up the file she had been reading (of course some of DUK's paperwork had come along for the ride), pushed the papers together, stood, and smoothed her hands down the sides of the cropped plum-coloured cord leggings she had chosen for the travelling part of the trip.

'In ten minutes,' she said, 'we arrive at Göttingen. And that's where I am getting off.'

'G'vanni, you're the last one. But you will be the hardest to beat.'
'Renata I don't think so. Jacopo is bigger than me.'
'But you are more fit I think.'
Renata stretched up, gave herself a second to take in yet again the blooming mimosa hedge whose frangipani scent drifted around her. When the gentle warm breeze off the lake puffed, little breaths of yellow pollen from the tiny pom-pom flowers gusted towards her. Beyond cypresses and a tall eucalyptus with swags of fresh leaf against its silvery shredding bark she could catch glimpses of the sapphire lake. Snow on distant alps glinted above it all. Then she dived, less perfectly than before, and lost the race, two lengths of the twenty-five metre solar heated pool, but only by a hand's breadth. That at any rate was Aldo's decision and he was judge. Personally she believed that she had won but that he had expected her to throw at least one of the races she had swum against his four children. The difference, she thought, as she towelled herself on the pocked dry deck, between Mediterranean and northern cultures: we must learn to lose some of the time, their children must learn to expect to win by their own efforts. She slipped the straps of her minimal one-piece costume and hugged the towel round her.

'So,' cried Maria Incoronazione from her wheelchair, 'the first prize for best swimmer goes to Giovanni, my second son. Come here G'vanni and let me give you a kiss.'

The youth, sixteen they said, an Adonis in Speedo briefs, came forward to receive it. Renata felt suddenly that this kiss was not enough. She had accepted the challenge from each of Aldo's kids to race her in turn in the pool, for a prize to be donated by their mother if any of them could win. She had expected that something more than a kiss would be on offer. She dropped her towel, ferreted in her bag, came up with a one hundred DM note.

'Here, take this too,' she insisted. And then was horribly conscious that she had committed some sort of enormous faux-pas. They had all gone pink. Why? Because she had offered money to a lad who had all he needed? Or because she was standing in front of them with a towel round her shoulders but with her top half otherwise uncovered? 'Buy something nice for someone you love.'

She pulled the towel to in front of naked breasts she was really rather proud of. She never thought twice about exposing them, granted the ambience was right: a beach, beside a private swimming pool . . .

G'vanni thanked her enormously for the note so it must have been her partial nakedness that had embarrassed them.

The feasting too was becoming a serious embarrassment. When they were dry, clothed and ready, they moved into a long panelled dining-room, with windows along one wall overlooking formal terraces that dropped to the lake. The furniture was heavy and old, the floor marble and the whole place echoed with the shouts of the children, the gossip and laughter of the adults (four guests, a business associate from Milan, a neighbour, with their wives as well, had also been invited) and the clatter of dishes and cutlery. And it went on for an hour and a half. Not my scene, thought Renata when the first plate was placed in front of her: tagliatelle lightly tossed in tomato sauce with an egg on top and garnished with thinly sliced white truffles; not my scene at all, when it was followed by carp poached in white wine, then ossobuco alla Milanese (especially for her she was told: every visitor to Lombardy expects ossobuco), and finally preserved peach halves stuffed with a mixture of crushed amaretti, egg yolk, maraschino and almonds. If she had taken it all on board with the wine as well it would have swallowed her entire calorie allowance for a month, let alone a week, and she was not prepared to do that.

'Simply delicious,' she murmured, tasting each dish as it came, savouring each mouthful with the care a dictator's food-taster might bestow, and leaving three-quarters of the rest.

The lady opposite her, about the same age as her, but ninety kilos of dark Italian beauty, leant across the table and asked her why.

'This morning,' Renata said, 'I swam against Aldo's children, and only Giovanni beat me. I want to stay that way.'

The Massive Lady dabbed her lips, swigged sparkling Ca' del Bosco from a tall Venetian flute, looked puzzled and repeated: 'Why?'

Renata's turn to look puzzled. Was there a language problem? She had understood that the lady spoke reasonable German and had some English.

'I mean,' the Massive Lady went on, but with a slight but cheeky grin hovering round her full painted lips, 'I mean why do you want to swim faster than a sixteen-year-old boy?'

Renata frowned a little, prodded the carp with her fork, put it down, offered the Massive Lady her brightest smile but said nothing. The Massive Lady forked in a giant mouthful of fish, chewed and swallowed enough to make speech possible. Clearly she felt there was a bridge to mend.

'My husband tells me you have tickets for La Scala

tonight. You are very lucky. As soon as we knew Pavarotti was coming we applied for every performance, but got nothing. Nothing anyway in the way of seats we would care to sit in. Are your seats good?'

'Middle of second circle I believe.'

'Not bad. Not at all bad. We could sit in those. So how did Aldo get them?'

'I don't know. Influence perhaps?'

'Influence? My dear, we have influence, believe me. Anyway. It's not such a great performance. The audience booed on the first night. And most nights since, I believe.'

A servant offered her a second slice of carp. She looked around, saw that most had finished, and waved him reluctantly away.

At the end of the meal, when they were drifting out of the room in small awkward groups, wondering how they would split up and what they would do next, Aldo took her hand for a moment.

'I'm sorry, but I have to talk business with my friend here for an hour or so. Would you very much mind spending some of the time with Maria, my wife, in her sitting-room? She would like to talk.'

'Do I have to?'

Aldo pressed her hand, looked solemn.

'I think so.'

CHAPTER 14

She knew where this sitting-room was, it was where she had been introduced, received perhaps would be the better word, the night before. Nevertheless another white-coated waiter, very dark (Libyan dark or just Sicilian?), led her down the marble passage with its busts of emperors on reversed obsidian obelisks, knocked with white kid gloved knuckles, and with a bow pushed open the door.

'Maria,' Aldo had said, the day before as the Tiziano Express whispered towards Göttingen, 'is five years older than me and eight years ago was far too old at forty-five to have our fifth child, who was stillborn. The birth was difficult. The doctors wished to save her life in an operation that would almost certainly have killed a baby who was already almost certain to die. Maria refused. She also refused a general anaesthetic since she suspected that they would abort, or rather intentionally miscarry, the baby if she were unconscious. The anaesthetist therefore tried to top up the epidural he had already given her some hours before. It was a difficult situation and we do not blame him for what happened. He left her permanently paralysed from the waist down . . .'

The Tiziano Express had begun perceptibly to slow as the fields gave way to the suburbs of Göttingen. Renata had sighed, had then sat down.

'Go on.'

*

Maria Incoronazione Nerone was a thin frail woman who looked at least fifteen years older than her actual age. Subtly tinted white hair frothed up above and around a face covered in wrinkled skin the colour of parchment. She had a striking high arched nose which seemed to suggest, if only by association with those pedestalled emperors, indomitable pride. Her dark eyes, set in deep, grey sockets, shifted constantly, were hardly ever still. Only the lines, especially those that started on either side of her nose and cut fissures almost to her mouth and down into her chin, spoke of pain.

Her electric wheelchair was state of the art, a bright stainless-steel frame on wheels, a throne for a science fiction empress in the twenty-first century. Finger touch controls made it as manoeuvrable as a monocycle ridden by a circus athlete.

The room she sat in was clearly her own, an eclectic mix of old and new, of high art and kitsch. Above a white marble mantelpiece a charcoal study for Dali's *Christ of St John of the Cross*, the foreshortened crucified Christ, hung in a matt steel frame. Looking around the rest of the room and picking up on a small Siennese quattrocentro triptych whose centrepiece was a sorrowing Virgin, Renata decided that it was probably not there to give pleasure or demonstrate wealth, but to stimulate devotion. For the rest, most of the colours were muted lavenders and mauves, the materials soft and silky, the furniture modern and light. There were a lot of signed photographs with personal messages, all in silver frames, including, and Renata recognised it was inevitable, not just one but three popes. One was John Paul I, which must have had considerable rarity value.

'Please come in and sit down.' The tone was not firm enough to be rude, but equally did not expect to be challenged. The voice had a slightly plaintive timbre much as if Aldo's wife had come to adult life with high expectations which had not been fulfilled. Thin white fingers flickered towards an upright armchair covered in chintz—dusty pink poppies on a pale mauve background. 'I want you to feel that you are my guest, and a welcome one, as well as Aldo's. Above all I do not want us to feel strained or embarrassed with each other.'

Neither was an emotion Renata succumbed to easily. She did, however, continue to feel irritated at the situation into which she had been introduced. She said as much.

'Of course you do. But really there is no need.' The chariot glided across the metre or so that separated them, and Maria put thin white fingers briefly on Renata's knee. 'When Aldo told me what you do I felt great relief: a person in that position, I thought, will be reliable and sensible and will keep him out of trouble. Poor Aldo is prone to trouble. Has he told you about his background, about our background?'

'A little.' That his father had been an engineer, that Maria on the other hand was pure *Almanach de Gotha*.

'It was a love match, of course. An accident.' Her laugh was like a wind harp made of fragile sea-shells caught in an unexpected breeze. 'My family would never have *arranged* such a marriage.'

'But they countenanced it.'

'Indeed yes.' Her German was fluent, but with an inflection, an accent Renata had difficulty in placing, the vocabulary occasionally quirky. Then she had it: archaic, well anyway turn of the century, top-drawer Austrian. 'You see I was the fourth child. With two brothers and a sister ahead of me it was unlikely that the family traditions would be left in the sole charge of the wife of a garage mechanic.'

Renata felt a sudden surge of sympathy for Aldo, a

warmth she had scarcely experienced since the Tiziano
Express pulled out of Göttingen with her still reluctant
self on board.

'As I understand it,' she said, 'shortly after meeting you
Aldo gave up a successful career working for Pininfarina.'

'However,' she ignored Renata's intervention, 'my two
brothers were drowned in a sailing accident, and my
sister elected to become a Bride of Christ.' She touched
the cross that glittered on the tight yellow skin of her
breastbone. 'An option I shall probably take once my
brood are all fledged.' She ended on a sigh.

Renata waited. She sensed there was more to this
interview than had yet been revealed, but felt it was up
to the one who had initiated it to bring up just what lay
behind it. Her hostess caressed the controls of her chariot,
and it whispered back a metre or so.

'Tell me,' she said nonchalantly as if making small talk
to fill in the gap, 'will this venture Aldo is now involved
in prove successful?'

'I have no idea. No idea at all.' Renata was taken aback.
'It's a field I have no knowledge of at all.'

'But as an environmentalist . . .'

'But I am not an environmentalist. I am a police officer.
As such I am required to uphold the law. At the moment
I work in a department that investigates breaches of laws
relating to the environment. In a year's time I could be
working in a totally different area.'

The dark eyes searched hers for a moment, then wandered away to examine some inner world. A world her
voice now came from.

'Aldo is very charming, is he not? And like most
charmers he is prone to self-deception. For him everything is for the best in the best of all possible worlds. He
assures me that this new venture will quite restore our
fortunes.'

Ah, thought Renata, and looked around, seeing the villa, palace really, grounds and all the rest of it, in an entirely new light: it would not be a comfortable place to be in if the brokers' men were knocking at the gate.

'I really do not know. I know nothing about his business at all.'

'But you would not actively seek to do it any harm?'

'What do you mean? Of course not. Of course I wouldn't.' What was this woman up to, what was she thinking of? Did she imagine that because she had found Aldo to be married, with a family, she might feel hurt, vengeful even? Then the truth dawned. 'Nevertheless, if it came to my notice that he was doing something illegal, against the law, I would break off the relationship immediately and take whatever action was correct and appropriate. But I am sure there was nothing like that in your mind.'

'Indeed not.' The motor hummed again and the shiny frame slid away from Renata, towards the window. 'Not at all. You see, Aldo has always had affairs, but he always comes home, to his children, to me. I quickly got used to it, even before my, our, tragedy. And they were not always with . . . sensible, yes sensible people.' She looked across the space she had put between them, and smiled. 'He can be so vulnerable. When you have so much to protect,' she looked around her and made a short but sweeping gesture with her right hand, 'so much to hold on to, people can manipulate you, make you do things you might not otherwise choose to do. But you will look after him. I'm sure you will.'

It was a commission, an order even, politely stated. It also, Renata felt, put her in a slot, in her place, gave her a role in the life of the household, a subordinate role. Concubine to a man whose wife could no longer provide sex. Concubine and minder. The voice went on, rose and fell, always with that slightly plaintive note.

'You must be tired: a long journey, all that swimming, lunch. Perhaps you would like a rest, a siesta . . . It would be a shame not to enjoy this evening to the full out of weariness.'

And like a servant she was dismissed. The audience was over.

It was not weariness that spoilt the evening but a growing sense that more lay behind this trip than she fully understood. Moreover Aldo himself seemed tired and preoccupied. She guessed that his meeting or whatever with the businessman who had come to lunch had not gone well. And the opera itself was a bit of a let down, once the first glamour of being in La Scala, of entering the fabled auditorium, had worn off. Through some silly quirk of the memory she had assumed that Pavarotti would be singing the tough role of Scarpia, the corrupt police chief, but that of course is a baritone's part. The tenor is Tosca's ineffectual artist lover. The garments she'd bought in Hamburg no longer pleased her though Aldo insisted they were perfect. They were too soft, too close to the harem, to the sort of role his family seemed to think she was playing.

And what, she thought, as Tosca plunged the fateful dagger into Scarpia's side, did his wife mean: 'You will look after him'? By keeping him on the straight and narrow? No chance. By using her position to protect him from the law? They'd better get that idea out of their heads.

They drove the forty kilometres back in a large Lancia Aldo kept at the villa. On the way she asked him:

'What did she mean: "restore your fortunes"? I have never in my life been so close to such conspicuous wealth.'

'Maria was born into a family which was enormously rich,' he sighed. 'Because her brothers died she inherited it all or almost all. She had no idea how much there was, but she believed it to be inexhaustible. The very very rich do tend to have that delusion: that the well is fed by a water-table and cannot dry up. But water-tables can drop. She gave most of it away.'

'Gave it away? Who to?'

'Missionaries. Monasteries. Leper farms. That sort of thing.' He sounded bitter. 'Almost anywhere where they would put up a plaque with her name on it and a pious little message in Latin.'

'I'm not completely sure about this, but I think she was asking me to turn a blind eye if it ever came to my notice that your business was bending the law. Aldo, you know I couldn't do that. Aldo?'

He drove on with lips set in a firm cold line for almost a minute, the lights of oncoming cars sweeping his tired, but to her still handsome, face. Then he stroked her knee with his right hand and smiled across at her. 'Of course I know that. I've known that all along.'

CHAPTER 15

On time, of course, at eleven twenty-eight precisely, the Tiziano Express pulled out of the small station of Bellinzona, mustard-coloured stucco with white edges and mouldings, cruised effortlessly into the climb that would take it up the long twisting valley, between ever closer cliffs of grey fissured rock, and into the darkness of the St Gotthard tunnel. Renata looked at her watch, looked at Aldo opposite her, felt her heartbeat rise as what she had been contemplating in a rather general way for an hour or more, almost ever since they got on the train, became more specific.

She had been quietly angry for most of the previous two days; she felt she had been manipulated and abused; and they had hardly touched each other through the entire time although they could have done. Some unspoken reticence about doing it under the same roof as his invalid wife and four children had got in the way. Now she was feeling sexually undernourished as well as angry. As the train climbed further into Switzerland she realised she was very sure about exactly what she wanted; had, in the three minutes during which the train had been stationary, worked out precisely how they would do it.

She shifted her buttocks on the soft leatherette upholstery to ease the pressure between her legs where already she felt tiny pulses and a glow of anticipation, leant towards him.

'I want to make love.'

He turned from the window in which he had been

watching her reflection, took her hands, came forward so their knees touched, grinned.

'Good. I'll get the conductor to make up the bed.'

'No. Just put the lock down on the door.'

He stood up, did so, swung the chromed hook so it dropped into its latch, looked round at the compartment: it was stylishly done out in grey with stainless-steel fittings, and with no windows into the corridor. The laminate panels above the backs of the bench seats were decorated with blown-up prints of eighteenth-century harbour scenes. Very tasteful. Switzerland trundled by on the other side of the big, sealed window.

'The blinds?'

'No.' She moved on to the edge of the seat, the armrests were folded into the back, and pulled her top over her head. 'There is no stop now until Lucerne, more than two hours away. Come on. Take your clothes off.'

'All of them?'

'Of course.'

He took off his jacket, hung it in the small closet by the door, undid his tie, sat down again and bent over his shoes to untie the laces.

'Don't look.'

It was the only thing she was sexually modest about, putting one foot on the bench and inserting her diaphragm.

'All right, now you can.'

He looked up at her and she swayed slightly as the train went into a bend and with a quick laugh she reached a hand to the rack to steady herself. Behind her, low chalets in green meadows with huge brown heavily uddered cows flowed lazily into the past. Nearer the telegraph poles and the gantries that supported the power cables flicked by more briskly. He pulled off his trousers and gallantly resisted the temptation to fold or hang them, just tossed them on to the opposite bench. They both looked at his penis, already rampantly erect, their eyes met and again they laughed.

'Lie down,' she said. 'On your back.'

In the recreation room beneath the Regional Police Headquarters back in Burg, Vesper conceded to himself that for the first time in two weeks he was, if not happy, then definitely enjoying himself. Sundays were easier than other days, brought small privileges like newspapers, a third course for lunch, and a full two hours in the large recreation room. There were fewer screws about too so the feeling of being constantly watched was not quite so oppressive.

There was only one table-tennis table beneath the harsh strip lights of the small rectangular hall, with ten stackable chairs down one side, a babyfoot machine and a dartboard on the other, and a coffee dispenser which did not work at the end. If there were more than four people wanting to play then the system was that at the end of each game (they just played games, not full sets) the winner stayed on the table, and took on the next challenger to have chalked his name on the small scoreboard. Vesper was now into his fifth unbeaten game in a row but looked like losing it. He quite enjoyed the prospect as it would release him to watch his opponent rather than the chik-chokking white ball.

Tuğrul Enver was seventeen, lean but not skinny, with a mop of glossy black hair stylishly cut. In tight t-shirt and jeans, he was the most beautiful person to come Vesper's way for a long time, longer than the fortnight he had been in custody. He moved with ease and grace, had a charming apparently untutored grin, especially when he won a point, and Vesper knew why he was there: the vice squad had picked him up on Friday night down a

dark alley with a Lutheran pastor's p.. k up hi. ..n.
That at any rate was what Vesper had been told by the
screw who took him down to the refectory where they ate.
In fact Vesper already knew him by sight: the Turkish
teenager had been hanging around the fringes of Burg's
gay scene for some weeks, was reputed to have fled a
sadistic lover in Hamburg.

Vesper retrieved an awkward spinning ball that had
just clipped the edge of the table from close to the floor,
but gave it a bit more air than was necessary thus setting
up the smash for Tuğrul to end the game at twenty-three,
twenty-one. The young Turk capered round the table,
fists in the air. Vesper laid the bat on the table, chalked
his name at the bottom of the list of future contenders,
found a tubular chair on the sidelines, settled back to see
how his opponent would manage against the next player.

This was a skin, a skin to his fingernails which were
painted a chipped black. The screws had kept his boots
and his studded leather waistcoat, indeed almost everything he wore since most of it could be turned into a
weapon of some sort or another, but they could do nothing
about the tattooed chain of swastikas round his neck.
Vesper feared that he would expect Tuğrul to lose to him,
and would kick the shit out of him if he didn't, but in fact
he played a reasonably straight game and lost without
grumbling, twenty-one–fifteen.

Maybe he was, beneath the paraphernalia of war on
society, a nice guy after all. Or maybe he felt that any
aggro he tried on would be repressed by the three other
young men in the room, all that were now left. As one of
them came up to take the skin's place Vesper wondered
who they might be.

They looked to be in their late twenties, were well
dressed in the sort of leisure clothes quite prosperous
young men who aspired to yuppiedom might wear, but

they had a latent toughness which Vesper found sinister. One of them was sitting near enough to talk to, and Vesper leaned across to him.

'What are you in for then?'

'What's it to do with you?'

Vesper shrugged, felt a frisson of dread.

'Nothing. Just trying to be friendly.'

'Don't get friendly with me, mate. Fucking perv.'

Aldo lay flat on his back so his toes touched the upholstery under the window and the top of his head was a centimetre or two short of the other end. But that would not quite do for Renata.

'Bend your knees a little, get your head down a bit.'

He did that.

'Now get yourself nearer the edge.'

He shifted so his right arm dropped and his right hand touched the cord-carpeted floor.

'I'll fall off,' bracing himself against the next bend as the train climbed into it.

'No, you won't.'

She hoisted her left knee over his face and into the space he had made, keeping her right foot on the floor. And she reached up with both hands to hold the rack above and then lowered her bottom towards his face.

'You know what to do.'

Tuğrul won the next game easily, so easily that he was able to wink and grin at Vesper as he made the points. This delighted Vesper who began to jump up and down on his seat. His big bony nose quested the air in front of him, he slapped his thighs as the lovely young boy stormed on, tormenting his opponent with slices that made the ball almost stand in the air in front of his flailing bat, and turning clearly signalled smashes into drop shots. At the end of the game (21–3) he chucked the bat on to the table, gave Vesper another wink and said: 'I need a piss.'

'So do I,' said Vesper.

When she began to feel that delaying her orgasm any longer was less fun than surrendering to it, she moved forward away from his head and holding his penis still firmly in her hand (if ever it had seemed to wilt she had manipulated it back to life) let it slip into her. Then she leant forward a little with both knees now on the seat, gripping his thighs, her arms straight and her hands flat on the leatherette on either side of his knees. By raising himself on his elbows he was able to add his thrust to the swaying of her pelvis. Pines clinging to rock and scree flashed by in front of her, grey water tumbled over lichened boulders. Until that day their lovemaking had been led by Aldo's skill, and that had been fine, he was better at it, understood better how a woman is in bed, than any lover she had had before. But now too, it was fine that she should take control, that she should decide how it happened. And it was funny, in both senses of the word, that all she could see of him were his lower thighs, his knees, his feet: parts of a middle-aged man that rarely inspire any emotion much stronger than amused tenderness. But the train and the rushing landscape were something else, almost she could believe she was alone with them, making love with steel, speed, and mountains.

She threw back her head, felt her hair caress the top of her back, how his palms closed over the soles of her feet, a trickle of sweat between her breasts, refusing to allow the pulsing heat between her legs to over-ride lesser sensations until it was impossible not to. High above them a motorway bridge spanned the chasm, the noise levels rose as the bogies coped with ever tighter turns. Then the two-toned klaxons bellowed, the Tiziano thundered into the St Gotthard tunnel and as the lights came on they came. But something shifted, shifted inside her.

In the prison toilet, a small space with stainless-steel fittings, a cubicle, a single urinal, wash-basin and hand-dryer, Tuğrul turned to face Vesper. He was already standing on the urinal step, with his fly unbuttoned. The extra height put his face almost on a level with Vesper's. He took Vesper's face in his hands and kissed him on the lips; then when Vesper's arms went round his neck, he dropped his and undid Vesper's fly, spread his jeans open, pulled out his penis. Vesper felt the young lad's hard and thin against his own, and against the bare skin of his stomach, and for a moment there was joy.

But then the door behind him slammed into his back, the horror started, and the pain.

CHAPTER 16

Nine hours of pleasant self-indulgence followed the St Gotthard tunnel. They had a long but carefully chosen lunch in the restrained luxury of the dining-car; back in the compartment they played a little gin-rummy, for a short time worked on the papers they had brought with them, shared a giggle or two over Pavarotti's performance as a barrel-shaped romantic lover the night before. Renata claimed that there had been more fervour in the top circles where the claques both for and against him fought it out with the vocal intensity of Inter and AC Milano fans. They dozed for a time, then ordered lemon tea which refreshed them. During the two hours between Frankfurt and Göttingen they made love again and the setting sun, low across the forested hills round Marburg, filled the compartment with a warm gold light. The final stage of the journey was the drive from Hannover to her apartment close to the centre of Burg. In Aldo's small sleek grey Ferrari it took forty minutes. And when they turned into her street and she was about to say that the day in the train had quite made up for all the earlier aggro and disappointments she saw instantly that something was badly wrong.

A small crowd, only six or seven people, but it was enough, spilled out of parked cars as soon as they heard and then saw the Ferrari.

'Stop here, let me out, and then get out, fast.'

But it was not as simple as that: she had two bags, and since the 250 GTS California is a two-seater, they were in the trunk behind. Aldo had to get out, open it, and by the time he was hoisting the large hold-all and document case with laptop they were around her. They scurried like rats about her feet as she surged the fifty metres down the sidewalk to the stoop in front of her entrance, arm thrown up against the spatter of flash-lights.

'Frau Fechter, is it true you swam nude in his swimming-pool? What's his wife like, Renata? What did she think of it all? Frau Fechter, who's the young lad in the pool with you, is he another of your lovers? Is it true you had a first-class compartment on the Tiziano Express and the door was locked all the way?'

She fumbled for her keys and then the numbered code that would release the secondary locks, turned, and pulled the two bags out of Aldo's arms.

'Aren't you going to ask him up for a night-cap, Frau Fechter? Aren't you going to kiss him good-night?'

For five minutes, alternately almost beserk with rage, and tearful with frustration and something not far from fear, she stormed about her four rooms, wringing her hands, chewing her knuckles, then just as the telephone rang, succumbing to a sudden tidal wave of exhaustion and collapsing into her big soft leather sofa. She reached out for the handset.

'It's me.' Aldo. 'I just got back. Are you all right?'

'No, I'm bloody not. What's going on?'

'I don't know. But I think there must have been a paparazzo somewhere in the grounds and he got a long shot of you by the pool.'

'Shit. But why bother? Why me? I'm just a policewoman, I'm not in that league. Not royalty or a top politician, not a super-star. Why are they hounding me?'

'Renata, I don't know. I really don't know.'

Suspicion flooded over her.

'Aldo, are you sure? Are you sure you don't know?'

'Renata, I just wanted to check you're all right. Look I'll be in touch.' And he rang off.

Gradually she calmed down but sleep was out of the question. She made herself coffee, drank some, regretted it, it should have been de-caff, warmed up a slimmer's soup, longed for the cigarettes she gave up fifteen years earlier. She racked her brains to see if she could come up with anyone she dare ring up, anyone she could trust to tell her the truth of what was going on. At last after an hour of this she realised that it was coming up to midnight, there should be news headlines on the hour: was the story big enough to make the final TV news of the weekend? She turned on the television and at first felt that no, it wasn't, it wasn't that serious. Yeltsin faced impeachment, a French general with the UNO was in a stand-off with the Bosnians as well as the Serbs, and at home, well, in the east anyway, demonstrations against unemployment. Then at the very end, just before the weekend sport and weather, it came.

'Amidst mounting demands for her resignation, Eco-Cop Chief Renata Fechter of the Burg Regional Police returned home this evening in the company of entrepreneur Aldo Nerone. It has been alleged that Frau Fechter spent the weekend with Signor Nerone in his luxury home on the shores of Lake Como ...' And the picture with it: a blown-up long lens shot of her standing next to Aldo's son, by his swimming pool, with a towel round her shoulders, a silly grin on her face and her breasts exposed. It was pasted beneath the dense gothic script of the local newspaper's masthead: *Die Burger Sonntagszeitung*.

As the commentary continued it was swapped for a flashlit snap of her about to get out of the low-slung Ferrari, in such a way that even to her her legs in the cropped leggings and neat black slippers looked undeniably sexy. In short it was a photo taken barely an hour before, yet it had already been fed into the national news.

'Kriminalhauptkommissar Fechter was brought to her Burg-Ring apartment an hour ago by Signor Aldo Nerone himself. Neither party would comment on the report. But demands for her resignation have already been made from both ends of the political spectrum. Signor Nerone imports and sells high performance cars which are often denounced by ecologically-minded . . .'

She snapped it off.

She refused the temptation to drink off the third of a bottle of brandy she had in her kitchenette, knowing that a hang-over was the last thing she needed, slept little and hit a particularly bad patch between three and four o'clock in the morning when loneliness almost swamped her. Since late adolescence when a much-loved father, a lawyer, ran off with one of his clients, she had eschewed any relationship with anyone that involved surrendering her own emotional independence, or the acceptance of another's dependence on her: the result was that out of a crowd of professional and casual acquaintance, many of them good friends, and a fair number of past lovers, there was no one she could turn to for comfort or reassurance. She slept at last, falling as healthy people are prone to do under such circumstances into what should have been a long, deep and healing sleep. But it was too late and her alarm shattered it too soon. Nevertheless she was still showering, hard pressure, alternating hot and cold, when she became aware of the telephone shredding the hiss of the water.

'Frau Fechter? This is the office of Minister Ilse Geller in the Parliament building. Minister Geller would like to see you here as soon as possible and in any case before you go on to the Interior Ministry. May I tell the Minister you will call in on your way?'

Renata glanced at a clock. Seven-thirty.

'Tell the minister I shall be at the Parliament Building by half past eight.'

Wrapped in a towelling bath-robe she made fresh filter coffee, added skimmed milk, cut a thin slice of wholegrain rye bread, and tried to assess what Geller's attitude to what had happened was likely to be.

Ilse Geller was the Minister for Women's Affairs, one of the two Greens in the governing coalition of SDP, Greens and splinter groups on the left. In the Regional Assembly the coalition had a majority of only four over the Christian Democrats, a majority which was additionally vulnerable because of the presence of two ultra-right members with whom the Christian Democrats had so far refused to ally themselves. There had been a lot of opposition to Renata's appointment as chief of the Eco-Cops, but Geller had forced through the Regional Cabinet's ratification, not because Renata was a Green, Geller knew she was not, but because she was a woman with an immaculate professional record whose promotion had apparently been blocked by male prejudice.

On the face of it Renata reckoned she ought to be able to rely on her support: female solidarity against the male-orientated right-wing tabloid press ought to be the line. But Geller was on the puritan wing of the Greens, an apparatchik dedicated to bureaucratic efficiency as the means by which the planet might be saved from ecological disaster, eschewing all truck with what she called the floral faction, beads, long hair and demos.

Renata finished breakfast, dressed quickly in almost the severest outfit she had, not the one she wore to police funerals but the one she kept for municipal church services, and scraped her hair back wishing either it were much shorter or long enough to put in a bun. Picking up her car-keys she felt properly grateful for the first time that the apartments had a basement car-park reached by an internal lift: at least she would be able to get past any media stakeout there might be at the front door.

CHAPTER 17

Geller was a tall lean woman, a year or two younger than Renata, with close-cropped black hair, above a large beak of a nose. When Renata was shown into her office in the post-war neo-Corbusier Parliament building which had been erected at the north end of the Schillerpark she was sitting behind a plain functional desk with newspapers, those of that day and the day before, spread in front of her. She did not offer Renata an invitation to sit down, but Renata did so anyway, feeling a sudden and unjustifiable surge of chagrin. The point very much was Geller's age. Some unreconstructed corner of Renata's female personality accepted the possibility of a male younger than her being in a position of authority over her, resented the fact that this time it was a woman.

Geller looked up, took off black framed spectacles but her fingers continued to hold them in readiness beneath the nose.

'Frau Fechter. The first thing I want to feel sure of is the accuracy or otherwise of these reports.'

'I have not read them.'

'They say that last Friday you travelled by train with Aldo Nerone to his family home on Lake Como. That you spent two nights there, going to La Scala with him on Saturday night. That on Saturday morning you were photographed by his swimming pool in a state of ... undress. That yesterday you travelled back here with him by train and car.'

'That is all true.'

'There is a very strong implication, never quite stated in so many words, that you are his mistress.'

'I object to the terminology. But yes, the relationship has a sexual content.'

The spectacles snapped shut.

'Frau Fechter. I must ask you to tender your resignation to Secretary Drenkmann as soon as you arrive at the Interior Ministry.'

Renata felt a sudden wave of heat flood up her torso to her face, a sickening lurch in her self-confidence. She drew in breath, counted slowly to five.

'I see no reason to do so. Nothing has occurred as a result of this relationship to interfere with the performance of my duties.'

'That is as may be. But there are other factors. One. This is, technically, an adulterous relationship . . .'

'Which his invalid wife condones . . .'

'Oh come on! You really had better read some of this muck.' The Minister turned a page and began to read: '"And what, we are entitled to ask ourselves, does the once beautiful Maria Incoronazione think of this affair, as she sits in her wheelchair and watches the healthy couple cavort before her very eyes? Is it possible to guess at the inner despair caused by this unfeeling pair . . .", and so on.' She smacked the desktop with her open palm: clearly she was very angry, had to wait for a moment to recollect what she had been saying. 'An adulterous relationship. In the last five years many churchmen, particularly Lutheran churchmen, have moved to positions on ecology close to ours. It is only a matter of time before they will swing many from their congregations with them. But not if they see the female holder of the first public . . . non-elective head of the first agency that exists because of our political clout, indulging in sex with . . . the sort of man Nerone is. And that brings me to the second reason for why I feel you have let us all down so badly.'

She leant back in her chair, tapped the spectacles on prominent front teeth which, if they had been Renata's, would have been subjected to pretty severe orthodontics at an early age.

'Do you know what sort of business Nerone concerns himself with?'

'He is a salesman of new and used luxury performance cars. He is attempting to create a facility out towards Burghaven which will be a sort of super-car supermarket.'

'And you see nothing wrong or questionable about any of this?'

'Not unless he breaks the law. And as far as I am aware he has not.'

Another deep, reproving sigh.

'Frau Fechter, I know you have no strongly held views about the environment, but like it or not, in the eyes of the media and the public in general your position identifies you with our movement. Your sexual, adulterous liaison with a salesman of the most indefensibly unecological motor vehicles there are can only do us harm. If you refuse to go of your own accord, you will have to be sacked.'

However, thought Renata, this hopelessly unlikeable person is not, after all, my employer. She stood up, smoothed her skirt.

'Thank you for your advice. I'm sure Secretary Drenkmann will let me know if he wishes to discuss my future with me.'

But Secretary Drenkmann had a problem. He had spent most of Sunday afternoon going over not only the newspapers which carried the photograph of his Eco-Cop's boobs exposed on or near the shores of Lake Como (and very nice boobs they were too), but also every scrap of paper he could get hold of relating to Fechter's attempts to investigate a possible incident at the Burghaven Pressurised Water Reactor which might subsequently have been hushed up. And at about half past seven, he decided that he had been right to close the case, she'd never get anywhere with it, especially not now with this albatross she'd fixed round her neck (he had studied the Romantic Movement in Europe at university and knew the Ancient Mariner well), and he might as well let her go. And at that moment the red telephone in the large library he worked in when he was at home purred insistently, warning of an emergency.

'Drenkmann here.' He had not asked who was on the other end: it could only have been the duty officer, one of his deputy under-secretaries, manning his desk in his absence.

'Sir, I have just had a report, and I must say I should have had it six hours ago and that in itself is worrying. A remand prisoner held at Regional Police Headquarters was very severely beaten by other prisoners at about half past one this afternoon, and is now in the City Hospital on a ventilator. The official report is that his condition is stable. The unofficial is that he has little chance of recovery from what appears to be, among other lesions, very serious brain damage.'

Drenkmann waited. This alone scarcely warranted disturbing his Sunday afternoon.

'The prisoner in question is Roger Vesper, held for the murder of Albert Huber . . .'

But Drenkmann had already guessed as much. Vesper's murder and the destruction of Fechter could not be coincidences. Someone somewhere with a lot of power and a lot to lose was in the shit, and flailing about in it too. Since he had been under pressure to prevent Fechter from looking into the Burghaven Reactor log, it looked as if it could be connected with the nuclear industry. It all had the evil whiff of a very serious scandal, a scandal which was bound to damage the Christian Democrats very severely indeed. And as his mind quickly and lucidly followed these logical stepping stones, Secretary Drenkmann felt a steady deep adrenalin rush: the excitement he lived for, the high that came from controlling the destinies of others, of being, ultimately, the man in charge. For the fact was that Drenkmann did not like the Christian Democrats, indeed he feared them.

Although he was a civil servant and not a politician, his job remained, as is the case in America, a government appointment which could be cancelled with a change of government. The socialists had controlled the Burg Regional Assembly for thirty years but almost always as the senior partner in a coalition, and Secretary Drenkmann had been at the top of the Interior Ministry for the last eight. Since he was fifty-seven years old, he expected, indeed intended, to remain where he was for the next eight. But elections were due in five months, he knew at least one corruption scandal involving his political masters was almost bound to surface before then, in spite of his efforts to suppress it, and that the problems of unification and immigration were, on balance, shifting the electorate to the right. If the extreme right gained say ten seats, then the Christian Democrats might well find the temptation to ally with them difficult to refuse.

He had sat at his desk for a further half hour, doing nothing but thinking, and occasionally making notes in a small personal notebook. Then he set his pipe and his pen on one side, and made the first of a series of phone calls, the last of which was that a request should be on

Fechter's desk when she arrived in the morning, asking
her to report immediately to his office.

'Before you say anything, Mr Secretary, I should like you
to accept right now my verbal resignation. As soon as I
get a chance I shall put it in writing.'

She stood in front of his desk, back straight, head up,
thumbs on the seams of her dark grey skirt, toes at forty-
five degrees. Very Nordic, thought Drenkmann, and felt
faintly repulsed. These were manners his generation had
fundamentally rejected, and for good reason. He did not
relish their return. He leant back and thumbed his Zippo
into flaring life, cleared his throat and then spluttered
through the smoke.

'Not accepted. Don't be a fool. Sit down.'

She did so.

'Secretary, I have just come from an interview with
Minister Geller. She has withdrawn her support for my
appointment . . .'

'Stuff. Neither she nor her ministry of harpies and
amazons has anything to do with your appointment. Now
listen to me . . .'

But she had to wait for a full minute until he was
satisfied that the pipe was going properly. Through the
smoke she studied *Cohesion 3* for a clue that might lead
to an answer to the riddles of the universe, or even the
organisation of human society since that was what it was
meant to be about. She found none.

'Last Thursday,' he said at last, 'following protestations
from the Regional Reactor Safety Commission that you
were making unwarranted enquiries into the running of
the Burghaven Reactor and Radwasthaus, I instructed
you to drop the case. Since then two new factors have
entered the equation. First, you were clearly set up to be
vilified in the press, which means you must have done

something seriously annoying to someone with a lot of money and influence, someone who wants your resignation. Second, yesterday afternoon Vesper was beaten up and hospitalised ... Ah. You don't know about that. Well. It happened. You'll get the details later but the poor chap is not likely to pull through. It is possible that these two events are linked, and if they are then the common factor is the Burghaven Reactor. Now normally I would not countenance such a theory. I have experience. A lot of experience. And one thing experience has taught me is that this sort of conspiracy just does not happen...' Embarrassed by the transparent hypocrisy, he cleared his throat again and leant forward, the bowl of the pipe clutched between podgy, stained fingers. 'But this time, well, it's possible.'

She waited, and, over the relief she already felt that for the time being at least she had a job, she felt a little surge of appreciation for the performance she was witnessing. In drag, she thought, this man could play Mother Courage.

'The nuclear industry is approaching a crossroads. As I am sure you are aware the first generation of reactors that went critical fifteen to twenty years ago are now approaching what was always intended to be the ends of their lives. A second generation is in the pipeline, but because of the economic situation it is hoped that the existing ones might be given an extended life of five years or so. After all, their safety and efficiency record has been, for an industry still in its infancy, remarkable, quite remarkable. Now, if a serious incident occurred right now, the whole debate that ran through the seventies would be re-opened and it is virtually certain that the old reactors would be decommissioned on schedule and that new ones would not be built to replace them. Consequently I do believe it is just possible that people who have an enormous amount to lose, both in terms of professional standing and hard cash, might just, just possibly enter into the sort of conspiracy you believe exists . . .'

'Mr Secretary, believe me, I have no preconceptions about this at all. I have evidence that a breach of the law has taken place in an area which falls within the brief of my department, and I have been investigating it. That's all.'

Drenkmann pulled back again and the lighter reappeared. Through the rasping and the flashes and the flames his grating voice dumped his final decision between them.

'Frau Fechter. I'm giving you a month. Prove there was a serious incident at Burghaven and a consequent cover-up involving murder and mayhem and I'll see that one day you make Chief Commissioner for the whole Region. Fail, and I shall be asking for that resignation you offered when you came in.'

CHAPTER 18

'I am very angry.'

Dr Sonnenberg, like a small grey tank, blazed away at her as soon as she finally made it that morning to her own office.

Renata was angry too, that her demoralised staff had allowed the tough lawyer through instead of making her wait, at least until Renata had had time for a coffee or tea, time to pull herself together.

'Yes, well. So am I.'

She swept round the room, got behind her desk, swung the chair in, plucked a pen from the black holder in front of her, tapped the desktop with it. Sonnenberg got out of the high-backed chair she had been sitting in near the window, came over to the desk, put her palms on the top, leant over her.

'You know why he's dead?'

'Is he dead?'

'Brain dead. He'll die when they turn off the ventilator, cut out the drip feed. He'll never speak again. And it's your fault.'

'My fault?' It was almost a scream: on top of everything else, this was too much. 'Why? Why is it my fault?'

'Because someone got hold either of the tape of my interview with him, or a transcript. Only that way could they have known how much he knew. And the only place they could have got hold of either was here, in this office.'

'Your interview at the remand centre could have been bugged. After all, they seem to have been able to murder him there, a little quiet bugging either way should not have been a problem.'

'There are very, very strict laws, as you well know, against bugging conferences between pre-trial remand prisoners and their defence lawyers. Laws which generally are observed since the slightest indication that they have not been will result in the judge throwing the case out. No. They got at the tape through your squad. You have a mole here, here in your squad.'

Renata looked up at the pale brown eyes set beneath tired lids in a square, lined face, held them for a full twenty seconds without flinching, willed the short, plain, tough old woman to back off, return to her seat by the window, as surely as if she had twisted her arm behind her back to make her do it.

'It is not as simple as that,' she said once Sonnenberg was sitting down again. She leant back, twiddled the pen between thumbs and forefingers of both hands.

'Why not?'

'I'll tell you in a moment. First, you tell me as far as you know, exactly what happened to Vesper.'

Sonnenberg sat up straight, her back as vertical as an old but thick and unyielding tree-trunk, but she looked out of the window.

'I persuaded him to use his recreational privileges. On Sunday morning he played table tennis with the other inmates, until three of the men who were with him saw him follow a young Turkish lad into the toilet. They suspected his motives and followed him in. He was, they said, attempting to rape the young Turk. They pulled him off and in the scuffle he fell, cracking the back of his head on the edge of the small hand-basin.'

'Oof!'

'Quite. But that is all they are going to tell us. Assault, even on a known homosexual attempting to bugger a minor, leading to serious injury and death is clearly Serious Crime . . .'

'And nothing to do with us.' Renata let the bitterness show.

'Precisely.' Sonnenberg sighed, turned back from the window, felt in a side pocket of her big old leather bag for a tissue, blew her nose. 'Now. Why am I wrong to think he died because someone heard what was on the tape I left with you?'

Renata sat forward, put her elbows on the desk.

'From Monday to Thursday my squad worked hard on the case, basing our tactics on the content of that tape. But on Thursday, at a quarter to eleven, Secretary Drenkmann closed the investigation down, officially closed it, denying me access to the Burghaven Reactor log, and no more work was done on it. Yet Vesper was attacked early on Sunday afternoon. There was no need. He was no longer a danger. Not, at any rate, because of anything either I or my squad knew. It could just be that Vesper was the victim of a homophobic attack by criminal thugs.'

Silence lengthened between them. Outside a big motorised mower trundled over the dull lawns, taking the top centimetre off the spring-grown grass, decapitating the odd daisy that had had the temerity to intrude and bloom.

Sonnenberg reached for her bag, put it across her knees, was clearly preparing to leave.

'So,' she said, 'that's it. Neither of us has any further cause, legal or official, to look into either of these matters any more.'

'Not so. I have just come from Drenkmann. Because of the media reports about my private life, which you have been kind enough not to mention, I offered him my resignation. But in the meantime he has been re-thinking the whole business, and by linking Vesper's death with what he sees as a plot to discredit me and get me sacked, he believes it is possible that something that happened at the Burghaven Reactor may lie behind it after all. He has given me a month to uncover whatever that may be. Moreover, during that limited period he has promised me whatever help he can lay on.'

'He will throw you to the wolves if you fail.'

'Of course.'

Sonnenberg stood at last, and with her case in her left hand came over to the desk. She thrust out her right hand.

'You'll let me know if I can help in any way.'

'Yes.' Renata took the hand, squeezed it briefly between both of hers, making it a gesture of affectionate solidarity rather than mere farewell. 'Of course. Of course I will.'

Renata sat in motionless silence for ten minutes or so, spent another ten minutes jotting notes on a pad. Then, using her intercom, she called the Eco-Squad into her office with the usual recommendation that the men should bring in chairs if they wanted to sit down. They shuffled in, for the most part embarrassed, avoiding her eyes apart from Sharon who offered her a smile that was almost charismatic in its attempt to offer, from below, intense support. Renata recalled the newspapers, the photograph, the television news of the night before. Clearly they were expecting her to announce her resignation; very probably they were speculating about what would happen next, about how their own lives would be affected by the upheaval.

Becker, large, heavy and ugly, swung the chair he had brought with him between his legs, sat with his elbows spread across the back: it looked like a gesture, a posture of separation, withdrawal, setting the back of the chair between them. Arslan had his beads out: the thirty-three names of God trickled slowly in an amber stream between the thumb and finger of his right hand. Roth's junkie pallor had returned, or so it seemed to Renata: the fingers of his left hand drummed a beat on his knee, occasionally his right shoulder twitched. And Sharon's patent adoration was, as always, a pain.

'Where's Meier?'

'Still off sick,' Sharon answered.

'Or he's forgotten where he's meant to be,' Becker remarked.

What a crew, Renata thought. What a crew.

'Right,' she said. 'We have a job to do. Secretary Drenkmann has reversed last Thursday's decision.'

She leant back, watched their reactions from behind hooded lids, over twined knuckles. The most discomfited was Becker—presumably because he had been so obviously wrong-footed. Sharon's reaction was greatest— two clenched fists framed an ecstatic grin. Roth looked unhappy, but he usually did; Arslan was suddenly attentive and tense. She went on.

'We are once again investigating the possibility that a serious incident occurred at the Burghaven Reactor, that it produced a body of high level *Radwast* which they attempted to dispose of through the Radwastwerk facility at Burgdorf and that Huber spotted what was going on. That Huber was murdered and Vesper, who knew what Huber knew, was implicated as his murderer. And finally that Vesper was, to all intents and purposes, murdered to prevent him from using the material he had received from Huber as part of his testimony in court. I must emphasise that the main thrust of our endeavours is to establish what happened at the Burghaven Reactor. We are the Eco-Squad, not homicide. However, solving the murders that are part of the whole business may lead us to the reactor. All clear so far?'

All four were properly attentive now, and their anxieties had shifted, were new ones.

'Right. The first, simplest and most straightforward thing to be done is that the log of the Burghaven Reactor must be analysed by an independent inspector, an inspector from another region. I shall set that up as soon as this meeting is over, and when I have Roth will look after him, escort him to the reactor, make sure that he is able to get on with his job without interference. I'll tell you the details later, Pieter, as soon as I have set it all up.'

That, she thought, should not be beyond the capabilities of a junkie.

'Next. Dominic Stieffen, friend of Huber and Vesper, testified to Sharon that Huber left the Ganymed disco with a character who looked like Asterix in the cartoons. We know they went to a Thai restaurant, the Golden Temple, because Serious Crime says that, according to the waiter they questioned, Vesper was there too, got violent with Huber and that they left together. It's just possible that Vesper knew where they were going and caught up with them, but that still leaves the Asterix look-alike. I want him traced, I want to hear his version of what happened. No, Sharon. Not you. Yes, Andreas? And before you speak, would you mind sitting on your chair properly.'

Cursing her beneath his breath for calling his childish act of rebellion, Becker turned the chair round, cleared his throat.

'I know the Thai scene. Prostitution of minors. Girls who are actually boys but take drugs to give themselves breasts. Drugs too. Opiate derivatives which they claim aren't as evil as heroin but get punters hooked on junk anyway.' He shot a hateful glance at Roth. 'Anyway. I

know enough about it all to break up anyone at that
restaurant so they'll tell me all they really can.'

'Good. Do that. Next. Vesper was our key witness. He
was arrested by Serious Crime for the murder of Huber.
His death, which to all intents and purposes has already
happened, is also being investigated by Serious Crime. I
need to know what they know, what the gossip is, what
the cover-ups are. I need you, Firat, to get on down there
and use all your wiles, everything you can, blackmail,
call in past favours . . . Look, I know the scene, I worked
there myself, I want you to find out what the people on
the inside track know about it all. I don't want hard
evidence. That can come later. I just want to know what
the spiel is down there concerning this whole can of
worms. Take Sharon with you.'

'Frau Fechter . . . Please?'

'Sharon?'

'I'd rather not . . .'

Renata thought: shit. It's bad enough that the men are
resentful, rebellious . . . but when this post-pubescent
chick starts chucking her weight about, where am I?

'You do what I tell you to do.'

Silence. The motor-mower was off in the distance
somewhere by now, but still there. An awful lot of land
had been enclosed when the Ministry reached out into
the countryside—the hidden agenda behind the move had
been the need to limit the over-production of milk and
dairy derivatives according to EU directives. And the
black girl, her face suffused with embarrassment, was
still not ready to shut up.

'Please,' she said, 'there is one aspect of all this that
has not been tackled by us, and I think I can handle it.'

'Yes?'

'Huber's body was found by someone. Who? Normally
one knows who found a body, who reported it. But there's

nothing in the records.' She repeated: 'I'd like to look into that.'

But Renata felt this was not the moment to give way. She knew she needed to reassert an authority undermined first by Drenkmann and then by the revelation, not of her boobs, but of the fact that she had an entirely unsuitable Italian lover.

'Sharon? You do as I say. Right. For the rest of this week we meet for briefing at eight-thirty in the morning, de-briefing six-thirty in the evening, yes you will be on overtime, and yes you will be paid. But if you uncover anything clearly significant you bleep me immediately on my personal number, not through the office.'

They left, and left her at her desk feeling drained and with nothing to do, nothing anyway she wanted to do, just telephone calls and then endless paperwork. She made the calls, setting in train the appointment of an inspector from the Regional Reactor Safety Commission of Hesse to look at the Burghaven Reactor log, then she made a start on the paper. She struggled for ten minutes, pushed it away, wondered if she should use her privileged position to take a swim in the Ministry pool at a time when it was unlikely anybody else would be using it, but felt no, that would not be right. She longed to be doing something, something practical, constructive, purposeful.

Sharon had a point. Huber had been found in the ground floor entry to his apartment block, just by the mailbox she had so sensibly rifled. But nothing in the reports indicated by whom. Renata found Sharon's filed report, wrote out the address, collected together the things she felt she might need, purse, bleeper, keys ... No. She'd not take her car. She'd travel on the public system, the first time for years. Why? it was an almost unconscious desire to be on the street again, an awareness that she had been out of touch with the ordinary world for too long.

That this was indeed the case was brought home all too clearly as she changed in the city square from the bus that had brought her in from the countryside to the tram that would take her to the station. The dark charcoal dress, the black silky coat with its discreet diamond clip on the lapel, dark stockings and court shoes, all put together to give an impression of sober restraint for her interviews with Geller and Drenkmann, attracted stares of curiosity and even hostility. She herself was not fully aware of how ritzy it was; which was silly since it had cost enough to feed, clothe, heat and house a family of four in tolerable West German comfort for a fortnight.

She looked around her from a bench seat near the exit: it had always been thus, she realised. It was just that she had forgotten—that the trams were used only by guest workers and their wives, people who looked like refugees from the East, the indigent and the old—who travelled free. The only ones who looked bright, approachable even, were the students from the technical colleges and the university. The bulky sweaters and jeans, the tasselled jackets and scuffed trainers reminded her of her own youth. Some even wore beads and 'jewellery' made out of leather, copper and feldspar. Had nothing changed? Or was this a self-conscious nostalgia whose purpose was to irritate teachers who had been real sixties people? There was also a group of backpackers from abroad, thumbing their guide-books and pointing out to each other the restored baroque of the Elector's Palace, the statue in front of the birthplace of Burg's nineteenth-century philosopher.

Trundling down Kaiser Wilhelm Strasse, the tram left the Ring that enclosed the cathedrals and palaces, the glittering department stores and boutiques, the familiar world of wealthy businessmen and industrialists, politicians and bureaucrats, professionals and technologists. Beyond the plane trees she could see first the Schillerpark with the Parliament Building beyond, where her day had started, then the boulevard sliced through the narrow alleys of the mediaeval quarter where Huber had lived, and presumably died.

Presently a recorded voice announced in the soothing tones of a funeral organiser that the journey would terminate at the station. Renata rose and then was swept out and down into the street by the backpackers, buffeted by their humps which thumped blindly into her shoulder and back as they swung this way or that to gabble at each other like squabbling gulls about the train they were about to miss. French, of course: no other nation produces youngsters with quite such boorish bad manners.

Out on the broad pavement she realised she did not know where to go: ask a policeman, she thought wryly, but instead found a large framed pictorial map of the area mounted in a vandal-proof armature. She made sense of it and set off along the route Sharon had followed less than a week before, but where Sharon in sweater and jeans had provoked only ritual appraisal of her sexuality, Renata was again greeted with confusion and hostility. Her clothes were too grand for a social worker, and the provocation they offered was not that of a whore.

And no one, she thought, as she turned the corner into the right street, is going to believe I am a policewoman, no matter how much ID I flash. So who shall I be instead?

'My name is Martina Huber. I am Albert Huber's mother. May I come in?'

The stout middle-aged lady with iron-grey hair, in a heavy cotton print dress, stood in her way like a bollard, dried heavy hard hands clutching a drying-up cloth.

'Albert,' she said, in heavily accented but tolerably accurate German, 'told us his mother died in the East when he was a boy.'

Shit, thought Renata, but quickly cast her mind back over what else she knew of Albert Huber's past. Father had died on the wire, Albert alone got across.

'I'm sorry. I should have been more careful. I was

Albert's foster mother, after he arrived here. He lived with me and my husband, and took our name. He, my husband, Albert's foster father of whom he was very fond, is also recently dead.' For the first time she was pleased with what she was wearing. 'We were very happy together for several years before he went to college ... We had no children of our own. For a time he was the son we had never had, but then ...' She shrugged, marvelling not so much at her own skill as the sense she had of enjoying all this. The Turkish woman took the bait.

'Yes. If I had been his mother, even his foster mother,' she muttered dourly, 'I would not have been happy about the way he lived. What do you want?'

'The police have told me almost nothing about any of it,' that at any rate was true enough, 'I just feel I want to know a little more about how he died, and why. I think it was you perhaps who discovered him?'

'No,' said now with relieved firmness. 'That was my sister-in-law, Ayla Muren.'

'Ah. Does she live here? Can I speak to her?'

'She lives here. But you can't speak to her. She's at the station. Cleaning toilets,' and she very firmly shut the door in Renata's face.

Renata retraced her footsteps, just as Sharon had, down the echoing wooden stairs and on to the marble-faced final flight. Like Sharon she looked down into the narrow dimly lit hallway, the mailboxes, the payphone on the wall. Sharon had done well with the mailbox, she conceded to herself. Maybe she is not quite the bird-brained floozy I take her for. And there, those are the worn black-and-white flags where Huber died. Not, she thought, that there is any proof at all that that is the case. That is simply what we have been told.

Out in the street again she thought through the next move as she made her way back to the station. It might be as well, when I meet Ayla Muren, to adopt a persona with a touch more authority ... but then, perhaps not. These people were rarely completely sure of their status as 'guests' in the country they serviced, most had some reason or other to fear the Immigration Service. She'll lie if she fears me. Woman to woman she may not.

Back at the station, in a sequence that Kafka would have been proud to have invented, Renata was passed *down* through four steps of the bureaucratic hierarchy from the Station Controller she had first approached, using her police department ID, through intermediaries to the Supervisor of Sanitary Cleansing who thought she was some sort of social worker. Tall, lean and tough, the supervisor had an office of sorts in the men's lavatories; little more than a lobby, it had two doors: one into the toilet area, the other into a passage where toilet rolls, mops, cleansing chemicals and so on were stored. It had a short staircase of its own to a locked door on the station concourse. It was through this that Renata reached the 'office'.

There was a table, a filing cabinet, two chairs and above the table a one-way window that looked over ranks of gleaming stainless-steel urinals, the laminated doors of cubicles. The most disconcerting thing about it was that many of the customers took it for a simple mirror and like fish in a tank swam up to it, almost put their faces against it as they combed their hair.

It's been said that no man is a hero to his valet: nor is he to his reflection in a starkly lit mirror. Without exception, they scowled, grimaced, frowned and turned miserably away, too conscious that no matter what they did their appearance would let them down. And they were right. Pocked, spotted with blackheads, greasy skinned, greasy haired, many with darkening patches from leaky willies in their groins, they represented the underbelly of Germany's manhood: the exploited, the no-hopers, the refugees, the drunks and the almost drunk, the ones who did not travel on trains for if they did that's where they would have had a free pee. But they haunted railway terminals. You never know what you might pick up at a railway terminal.

Renata turned away from this porthole on what men are really like, and looked across at Ayla Muren, a woman greyer, thinner, more evasive and self-effacing than her sister-in-law. They were sitting knee to knee in the two hard-backed chairs that almost filled the space they were in.

'Ayla, I know you have been questioned several times by the Serious Crime Squad and more recently by the Immigration Service.' She knew? Because the Over Director of Customer Services had told her so. 'Now I want you to understand that I have nothing to do with any of them. I am here because your case has been reported to us at the Regional Association for the Protection of Ethnic Workers' Rights, and I just want to check out that you are aware of your rights, and to make sure that these interviews you have had with other agencies have not made you feel threatened or that you have suffered anything approaching harassment.' During her time with the Serious Crime Squad, Renata herself had often enough been harassed by the Association — she knew what sort of line to take with Ayla. 'Do you understand?'

Ayla Muren, her eyes fixed on a point somewhere above and to the side of Renata's left shoulder, sighed, twisted a handkerchief between knotted fingers. Renata caught the uncooked garlic on her breath and repressed her reaction to it.

'Would you like to tell me a little about it all?'

'Is simple enough.'

'Yes?'

'They wan' me to change what I first say about the dead man I found.'

Her German was not as good as her sister-in-law's, less confident, more accented.

'Albert Huber?'

'That's right.'

'Would you like to tell me a little bit more about all that?'

'Do I have to?'

'It would help me to understand the whole picture, and the better understanding I have of it all, the more likely it will be that I can help you.'

Ayla sighed again and again the garlic came across, and her left hand fiddled with the edge of the black head-scarf she wore.

'They angry with me from the start. Because I phone them up from the entry without leaving my name. But they work out who I am. So I tell them how I come down the stairs, and see him lying there. How I can see he dead . . .'

'And what was it they wanted you to change in all that?'

'They say I misremember the way he lie. That I wrong to say his head toward the street and his feet on the stair, that he the other way round. And that I wrong to say cigarette burns on his wrists, and blood round his fingernails. They say he drug addict, and the marks on his wrist sores left by dirty needles. But I know they wrong.'

'How can you be so sure?'

Ayla Muren used the finger and thumb of her left hand to undo the small button that fastened the sleeve of her cotton dress over her right wrist, and pushed it up. She turned her arm over, exposing the inside. Between her wrist and her elbow there were maybe fifteen round or oval scars, bruise-purple, the skin puckered.

'These done by political police in Izmir. I remember how they look when they new.'

Renata swallowed, turned away, looked into the eyes of a young man who was pushing a metal comb through glossy wavy black hair. He straightened his black tie, turned. Beyond him a man in denims passed a package to a third man who handed him a sheaf of bank-notes, and then ran out of the area. The man in the black tie took the notes from the man in denims. Renata wondered if the Supervisor of Sanitary Cleansing was on the take, or if they just terrified her into silence. She turned back to Ayla.

'Why did they do that to you?'

'I official in the Textile Workers' Union. They want me give list of local members.'

'Did you come to Germany because of all that?'

Affirmative.

'And you do not want to be sent back?'

Head jerked up with a click of her tongue against her teeth. Turkish negative.

So. Albert Huber had been tortured, probably upstairs in his own apartment, and had been dumped in the hallway, probably already dead. One more question would confirm that.

'Was there much blood?'

'No.'

'But he had been stabbed many times?'

'At least three I see without moving him.'

The muted but steady gush of tiny waterfalls in the urinals, punctuated by the occasional storm of forced water in one of the cubicles, became a presence between them. Ayla shifted, sighed again. The smell of artificial pine overlay whatever other odours there were, but the garlic still won through.

'You're a police person, I think. Not from the Association.'

'Why do you say that?'

'I speak with the Association in the past. Over conditions of work here. They not like you. And the question about the blood not relevant to the rest.'

Of course. For all her grey slightness Ayla was intelligent and had a union past. People like that, thought Renata, never give up.

'OK. You're right. I'm sorry I lied. But I did not want you to be frightened of me because I come from the police. And I'll see that you come to no harm because of this interview. If they bother you again, the other police, call me on this number.' And she handed her her card.

Renata took a taxi all the way back to the Ministry. She felt excited, pleased with herself after her little foray back into real police work: two things had been cleared up, two areas of doubt clarified. Huber's murder was not the result of homosexual jealousy nor perverted sexual practices. Probably he had died during or after torture designed either to make him impart knowledge or possibly to coerce him. Possibly the stab wounds were inflicted after death to make it look like a different sort of murder. And the attempts to make Ayla Muren change her evidence clearly implicated the Serious Crime officers who had questioned her in the cover-up, even pointed to possible Serious Crime complicity in the murder.

What next? Well, that would depend on what the others brought in at the end of the day, but there still remained two nagging questions. Why had Vesper been murdered during the few days when the case had been closed? And why had she been set up to be vilified in the press during the same period? And then there was a third, the one she always pushed to the back of her mind, refused to address, though she knew she would have to face it sooner or later. Was Aldo involved? Had he known what he was doing when he invited her to Como, got her out in the open in her swimming costume?

As soon as she was back in her office she gritted her teeth for a moment, planned what she was going to say, dialled his number.

CHAPTER 20

'Scusi . . . momento.'

Aldo turned off the bleeper on his belt, walked across the concrete surface to his Ferrari, picked up his mobile phone handset. A tall woman, dressed in leather jacket, denims and combat boots, hung back with polite discretion, but not so far away that she could not hear his side of the conversation. Andromed Drenkmann was in her late thirties, her heavy good looks beginning to coarsen under the pressure of running her own firm of architects in a male-dominated profession.

'Si, no, si. OK. No. Yes, I understand, I understand. Of course, cara mia. But not now, on the phone. My place? All right. Can you make it eight o'clock? I have a full day and I don't expect to get away much before seven. Eight o'clock then. Ciao.'

He replaced the handset, locked the door. Andromed saw how he was suddenly pale, distracted. Until then he had been very jolly, bubbling even, as he went through the plans with her, working out a rough schedule for the works that would change this dingy place into a glitzy showcase for the best cars in the world. He had phoned her at ten in the morning with the news that the first banker's draft he had been promised from the consortium that was backing him was on his desk: yes, he could actually pay her for the work already done and make a start on mapping out the next stage.

'Bad news?'

'Not really.' He took her elbow, gave a sad little laugh. 'Anyway, not financial.'

'I think I can guess.'

She clicked her tongue at him with mock reproof and was amused to see him raise his eyebrows and pout the way one does when one is in a bit of a mess and in the company of a friend who knows it. As they walked on towards the outbuildings which would have to come down to make space for the miniature but luxurious motel she had designed she reflected that the newspapers had well and truly answered one or two questions she had had about Nerone.

They had known each other for five months, and got on very well, admiring each other's vision, talents, expertise. They had lunched together often, mostly working lunches out here at the racetrack, and almost always alone, and he had never made a serious pass, nothing beyond the sort of small gallantries politeness demanded. She had wondered why. And now, over the weekend, the newspapers had provided the answer: Renata Fechter. And he was seeing her tonight, eight o'clock, his place. She wondered if her uncle would want to know that.

'We may have a problem with the petrol storage tanks: I've been checking the EU directives and recommendations on the subject, and of course they're much stricter now, stricter than when this place was a car-racing track. Goodness. What's that?'

They'd turned a corner. Parked close up next to what had been a buffet-bar, and under an unkempt Corsican pine, the cube container on its transporter looked as alien as if it had arrived from outer space.

'Don't ask me, I don't know. I'm looking after it for a friend.'

Andromed pouted: 'Could be naughty?'

'Oh, I don't think so.'

But she remained bothered: as Secretary Drenkmann's niece as well as a struggling architect, the last thing she needed was to be caught up in some gross scandal involving drugs, arms, whatever.

He sensed her discomfort, gave a shy sort of laugh.

'Actually, I lied.' The charm of his smile would have sat prettily on the face of a seven year old with jam on his fingers. 'Two of the buildings were practically built out of asbestos. It costs the earth to dispose of stuff like that in accordance with regulations. Far cheaper to ship it out east where they're less fussy, and there is actually a firm that specialises in that sort of operation . . .'

And he remembered today was the day he was meant to ring up the Brits in Hamburg and check out the details of the shipment, so Kurtz could get someone to see to the routine paperwork Burghaven's harbourmaster's office required before they would let it on to the quays.

'Sheen Associates, Eloise Harman speaking.' She covered the mouthpiece. 'Harry, it's him. Mr Ice Cream.'

'I'll take it.'

Harry Sheen heaved himself out of the deep armchair by the window. He had spent much of the last two days in it, through the weekend when there was really nothing to be done, watching the pleasure-seekers strolling along the promenade above the Aussenalster, the tall white tumbling jet of the fountain, the little boats. He looked older, the contrast between the bruise-coloured skin round his eyes and the waxy pallor of his cheeks more marked than before. And he was virtually chain-smoking now, sending her out for pack after pack of German-made Senior Service. The plain fact of the matter was, as Sam said, laying it on the line, the gamble had not come off, they simply had not raised enough commissions to support their fleet of clapped-out freighters. That two of them had been impounded by the Rostock harbour authorities as not seaworthy, was almost a bonus: at least they could lay off the tiny crews.

'Sheen, here. Yes. I've got it. Are you ready to take it down? OK. Dockgate 6, quay D, MV *Eloise*. She docks Thursday, first April, 1315 local time. She'll start taking on cargo at 1600, and she'll sail on the tide at 2100.

'Yes, we've got a truck and a trucker lined up. What he'll need is a map for the proper route to your place from the motorway, no way he'll get that container out on the route we went in by, and of course the papers that will get him on to the dock and the container on to the boat. That includes our authorisation that he is moving a cargo on our behalf, and the stuff you promised. I reckon if you have it all round here by two o'clock, that oughta do. Now. Hang on a minute, don't hang up, not if you know what's good for you.'

He paused, cleared his throat, looked round at his three associates, raised his left hand, first two fingers crossed for luck. Eloise smiled nervously, smoothed her suddenly moist palms along the thighs of her cropped leggings. Florally printed, it was Harry's opinion they were made from a job-lot of furnishing fabric. Herbert, standing at the big window, caught his eye, flinched away. Fat Sam, with a calculator on his knee, froze with his ballpoint hovering above the per cent button.

'We've been like thinking this through. Me and me associates. And it's clear what we have here is a hot cargo, hot in more ways than one. So, we'll need another twenty K on the mat here before we move at all. Forty when she sails, and forty when we hand over to our Russian colleagues. No. I'm not arguing. This is non-negotiable. Yeah, do that. Do that.'

He recradled the handset as though it were dynamite, looked round again.

'He'll get back to us, he said.'

Herbert growled: "E would, wouldn' 'e? Reckon I might go private for a replacement hip if this works out.'

CHAPTER 21

KOK Becker parked his pool Opel in the multi-storey closest to Leopoldstrasse and took the lift down to street level. With black belted raincoat billowing about his burly figure and a hand securing his black brimmed hat and ignoring the subway, he swung across the six lane boulevard that separated the post-war town from the restored baroque area. He headed away from the town square and the cathedrals into narrower streets filled with boutiques and speciality shops selling flowers, chocolates, strange cheeses and even stranger sausages. Presently Leopoldstrasse became more shabby, the speciality shops gave way to small cafés and restaurants, many of them oriental. It was in fact a mini Chinatown spawned by the new freedom of movement within the EU which allowed Chinese from Hong Kong and Macao via London and Lisbon to bring their distinctive flavour into at least one street in every sizeable city in the community. Burg, just an hour or so down the motorway from Hamburg, its more cosmopolitan big brother, had been on the second wave.

Becker knew the quarter well, and two or three times acknowledged minutely raised fingers from shopkeepers or residents who remembered the days when he brought his own personal brand of rough but not corrupt order to the street, its basements and garrets. At least, they reflected, behind impassive faces, you knew where you were with Becker. But the Golden Temple had arrived after he had gone, taking over premises he remembered as a shop selling fans, slippers, joss-sticks, cheap silks and the like as a front for laundering gambling money from the unlicensed casino on the first floor. Becker himself had closed the casino, so presumably the shop, deprived of its real purpose in life, had followed soon after.

The Golden Temple was very much what he expected. The name was spelt out in gold lettering above the old shop-front window, the lettering contorted to look oriental. The window frame too had been reconstructed to look exotic. There was a lot of crimson gloss paint, and a lot of gilding. He looked at the menu posted outside and was surprised at the prices: they were way up higher than most of the neighbours', nearly on a par with some of Burg's best restaurants.

Of course, at eleven o'clock in the morning they were not yet open. He rapped on the door, rang the bell, and then turned his back, put his elbow on it. He could hear it ringing inside and he knew someone would come when the noise became insupportable. Three minutes later he heard and sensed bolts pulled back, locks withdrawn.

'Police.'

He flashed ID, and pushed past the lean twelve year old who had opened up. Boy or girl, you can't tell with Thais, he thought, but definitely ought to be at school. The ambience was muted, the small tables daintily dressed but of course the candles unlit, the tiny vases flowerless, and only a service light glowing at the back. Nevertheless he was impressed. Becker knew restaurants, could sense this would be warm, delicate, pleasant, and if the smells were anything to go by, the food, a spiced-up version of Chinese, Indian made subtle, would be good too, maybe good enough for the prices.

'The boss, please.'

And while he waited he rearranged his approach. He

had intended to identify the waiter who had apparently testified to the Serious Crime Squad that Vesper had been there with Huber and then lean on him even harder than the other lot had. But he realised that in this ambience a softly, softly approach might work better.

A woman, plump, dark, small and oriental, but to his western eyes more immediately pleasant and accessible than Chinese, Japanese, or Koreans, came out of kitchens at the back, stood behind the tiny bar and computerised cash register. Without saying a word she put down the cloth she was drying her hands on, eased the top off a tall bottle of Czech Budweiser, put it on the counter. Then she looked at him and added a glass.

'Saturday, the thirteenth. Just over two weeks ago. I want every scrap of paper you have relating to the customers who came in that evening. Credit card slips, Amex, Diner's Card, reservations. You won't have any cheques, I know that, but if your business is as well run as it looks, you'll have a record of numbers, names and bank-cards.'

'Well, we have reservations.' Her German was pure and careful. She hauled a big leather-bound diary out from under the counter, a page for each day of the year. 'Saturday nights, you can't get in here without a reservation.'

There were fifty names and he ran his finger down them. By each name a time, starting at six-thirty, ending at midnight, and the number of people in the party. By almost all of them an oriental squiggle which he guessed meant they had shown up. And near the bottom his finger paused on Hans Müller, ran on, and went back. Hans Müller might as well be John Doe, or Joe Brown, there were probably eighty of them in the phone book—which was why Knut Haussner had used it as a pseudonym when he worked on the Vice Squad. All the same . . .

'This one. Do you remember him?'

'No.'

The table had been booked for two people, and the table was numbered. Becker took a walk round the room, found the table in a small alcove. Very discreet. He came back to the bar.

'Even if he paid cash the bill must have the table number on it. I'd like to see it.'

Strong but delicate hands on the table, she gave him a long slow look out of dark eyes as unfathomable as mountain tarns.

'You are a policeman?'

'Yes.'

'Then you should know the police took all the records for that Saturday and they have not yet returned them. Because one of our customers was murdered later that night.'

'But not the reservation book.'

'No. People book in here up to three or four weeks in advance. So you had to let us keep it. That's why I showed it to you. I thought: that is the only paper they do not have, he has come back to look at it . . .'

'OK.' Becker turned his back on the bar, drank Bud, thought. Why had Huber gone off with Asterix? Surely, because he already knew him. Huber knew Knut Haussner, because Knut Haussner now worked as a security guard at the the Burgdorf Radwasthaus plant. Knut Haussner was large, fat, had a big ginger moustache and looked like . . . Asterix. He was also a fucking bastard. Enough. Surely enough.

He turned, put a five DM piece on the counter. Probably less than she charged paying customers for a single Bud, but still a fair mark up.

He left, not knowing how surprised, even shocked she was. A policeman paying for a drink? Was he really a policeman? She had heard though, that six months or so back, before the Golden Temple opened, there had been an officer on the beat who always paid ... not always the asking price, but what he judged was fair. Could this be him?

The Burg Brauerei was one of the two independent breweries left in the town, situated in a sidestreet behind the Police Headquarters. Serious Crime Officers used one large alcove with a long table and benches near the back as a sort of private lunch club. It was a big wood and brick barn of a place with much of the actual brewing machinery, huge shiny stainless-steel pipes with polished brass stop-cocks, visible but behind sheet glass filling one long wall. Waiters in long white aprons swung between the tables carrying round trays suspended from long central wooden handles, each capable of carrying a dozen straight-sided quarter-litre glasses of the light but heady brew. They whisked away empties, stood over you if you were drinking too slowly and marked up your beer mat with how many you had had.

At lunchtime waitresses pushed trolleys through the tables offering the two basic dishes the place served: whole hocks of boiled, skinned ham, or *Grünkohl mit Pinkel*, kale with smoked sausage filled with brain. Inevitably, day after day, the clients reminded themselves that outside north Germany *pinkeln* means not 'brain filled sausage' but 'pee'. Afters were huge technicoloured ice creams.

Sharon hated it, hated it so much that she actually set about itemising to herself what she hated. Item one. She was sitting on the fringe of the group, next to a grey man in a dark grey suit worn over a dirty blue polo shirt. He had thin, down-turned lips, small mean eyes, a bad complexion, halitosis. His hair was lank yet had the dry blackness, uniform all over, that tells you it is dyed and probably glued. He was, she knew, reputed to be adept at persuasion, persuading suspects to confess in such remarkably short periods of time no lawyer could afterwards claim the confessions had been coerced.

Item two, the food and the beer. Conscious that full jeans good, overfull jeans bad, was the rule, her usual lunch was skimmed-milk cheese on a thin slice of rye, an apple and Diet Coke. Item three, the way Arslan's five old buddies were behaving. He had taken her into the Brauerei, insisting, ordering her indeed, to act the part of his girlfriend. He had worked out that coming in on the arm of a hot sexy chick, a black at that, would give him the entry to male camaraderie that he needed if he was to fulfil Renata's commission—at least that was what Sharon assumed lay behind it.

'OK,' she had said, 'but just don't maul me, right?'

It had worked, she guessed. Anyway here they all were, sitting across the end of the long table, making a lot of noise, most of them with their jackets off, their shirt-buttons straining, their faces glistening and red, shovelling in great mounds of food and beer.

And beneath it all item four: she could sense how the camaraderie masked the way they despised Arslan, were manipulating him in several ways at once. First, they were taking him for a free lunch, which no doubt was why they were eating and drinking so much. Furthermore, they had read his arrival as an admission that he longed to be back with them, back with the big boys, and was ready to pay for an hour or so of being one of them again. They also despised him for being an Eco-Cop. What does an Eco-Cop do, one of them asked: chase round after old ladies making sure they use their doggy poopers properly, and thus obey the very new law that made their use obligatory?

And of course, finally, they despised him for being a Turk. Almost she felt sorry for him, but not quite: for he was item five. Ever since she had been shunted into the Eco-Cops he had patronised her, treated her like shit because she was a black and a woman which put her two levels below him, never mind the fact that he had rank too on his side, all culminating in that clumsy pass the other day, followed by the harassment in the lift.

And anyway there was no need to feel sorry. In the first place he knew, but his old mates didn't, that DUK would pick up the tab, and in the second he really did seem to be doing rather well.

'Vesper? Vesper! What a shit, what a wanker,' the one opposite him suddenly shouted, banging the handle of his fork on the table, then taking a long pull at his fifth beer. He had blond short hair, and a scar from his left cheek-bone to the corner of his mouth. He wiped his mouth on his shirt sleeve and went on: 'Of course it was bloody set up. Course it was. Listen. That pretty boy Tuğrul Enver, he's been on the take from us for the last coupla months, through him we pulled down that big hashish ring oper-ating through the Blücher Shopping Mall. He went in the book for soliciting Saturday night, released Monday, lack of evidence. But if need be he'll swear Vesper was raping him.'

'But what about the guys who beat him up?'

'Ossis. Ossi fascists. Ex-STASI they were, moved into the Rostock riot-squad. Got disciplined in Rostock for failing in their duty when the anti-immigrant riots broke out, in fact they joined in. So they quit and they've been hanging around us, hoping we'll take them on. Maybe now we will . . .' he laughed raucously, spewing sauer-kraut across the table. 'But probably we won't. Anyway, in the meantime, they do what we ask them. They were in on Saturday for harassing a tramdriver, threatening behaviour, you know the score, all fixed up so they would be where we wanted them on Sunday, released on Monday, for, yes, you've guessed it, lack of evidence on the tram charge. Vesper? No contest. They were saving Tuğrul from a fate worse than death.'

And again his horrid laugh billowed across the table.

Arslan looked at him, carved off a slice of sausage, spoke through it.

'But why? Who? Who wanted Vesper smashed?'

Scarface froze, fork in mid-air, and a sort of silence settled across the table.

'That's a fucking stupid sort of question to ask, my son. No wonder you're in the fucking Eco-Cops if you think you can ask that sort of question.'

The grey man next to Sharon touched her on the arm.

'I myself, I am not a fascist,' he said. And he looked around the Burg Brauerei with a moist nostalgic gleam in his eye. 'I am not a fascist. But my father was.'

Sharon had had enough. She opened her purse, took out her ear-buttons, put them on, put her Walkman on the table in front of her. Guns 'n' Roses. The heavy beat, the raucously shouted words, thrashed guitars shut it all out, then suddenly it stopped. She looked up. Arslan was standing above her. He had her Walkman in his hand. He snapped out the tape, dropped it in his pocket.

'Come on,' he said. 'I've had enough. You can drive me back to Gründorf.'

Five o'clock and Becker sat in his Opel, sixty metres from the gatehouse and barrier outside the Radwasthaus plant in Burgdorf and waited. Occasionally he could see Haussner moving about in the gatehouse, twice he left it and went into the reception building, three times he came out, checked papers and ID handed down from a truck cab, lifted the barrier. Becker had no idea when his shift ended but reckoned some time between five and seven was likely. He could have found out he supposed by getting someone to phone Radwasthaus and ask, but that would have alerted his quarry and anyway when he was a member of the vice squad sitting in a car and waiting had occupied at least half his working hours: it felt familiar, a blast from the past, he was used to it. He wasn't bothered that Haussner might spot and recognise him: he knew from experience just how far away you had to be to be unidentifiable in a stationary unmarked car.

At a quarter to six Haussner raised the barrier to a grey VW Scirocco, chatted briefly with the male driver. At six the same man appeared in the gatehouse wearing a uniform similar to Haussner's, and Haussner went into the reception building. At ten past six Haussner, now wearing a polo shirt beneath a check jacket and brown trousers held up by a belt with a ram's head buckle, got into a middle of the range Audi and drove up to the barrier. Becker started the Opel's motor.

He followed him into town, and on the way saw that Haussner was using a mobile phone. Telling the wife he had been held up at work? Becker could not remember whether or not Haussner was married. Half way round the Ring, the Audi took a left into the post-war grid of mainly residential building that closed in on that sector, but kept to the tree-lined main thoroughfare that sliced through it and linked with the motorway box beyond the suburbs. Becker wondered: is he heading off out of town? But presently Haussner pulled in and parked in permitted echelon under budding plane trees. Becker found another place about twenty yards on.

In the rear-view mirror he could see Haussner was on the other side of the road buying cigarettes from a kiosk. He looked in Becker's direction and then walked slowly back to the Audi, waited for as long as it took to light a cigarette, and then some. Becker got out, looked across the roofs of the cars between them. Haussner was using the phone again. Becker had no gun, no weapon at all, and since the Opel was a Ministry pool car, no radio. He got back into the Opel, and, just about certain he was doing the right thing, headed back to Gründorf, keeping to the main roads and driving carefully, always with an eye on his tail, and wary of side roads.

If Haussner had been involved in Huber's death, if Haussner had rumbled him and was now calling up muscle, it would be for one purpose only: to kill him before he handed in his report. Once he had reported, the need would not be so pressing.

He got back without incident.

CHAPTER 22

On her way through the outer offices Renata paused by Sharon's desk. There was an audio cassette tape among the papers. She knew Sharon often played a Walkman, and so long as her work did not suffer saw nothing wrong with that. But this tape looked as if it might be Ministry property, and that would not do. She picked it up, checked that it was, replaced it but resolved to speak to her about it.

Sitting at her own desk she looked out of her window at the fading light, the deepening sky and realised that it had been a near perfect spring day, and that she had hardly appreciated it at all. Most of us have a collection of mental tics, little refrains which the same stimulus always brings back. One of hers, in good weather, was her now mad not dead father's voice: 'On a day like this, you should be out in it, enjoying it.' Thursday, the last Thursday of the month, the day after tomorrow, she should visit him—she usually managed to—at Hearts' Haven. Meanwhile, a lot had been achieved and all in one day. One day? It seemed like a year ago, the day that had started with that awful Geller woman. And, with a lurch of her confident heart, she remembered it was not over yet. She glanced at her watch, Lord, as late as that? She picked up her personal phone and dabbed in the numbers.

'Aldo?'

'Yes.'

'I'm going to be late.'

'You already are.'

'Sorry. Give me another half hour . . . No, make it three quarters.'

'All right.' And he hung up. That, she thought, was a bit abrupt. But probably he's as uneasy about this as I am. More, maybe. She made suspicion scuttle like a big black spider to some inner recess of her mind, and began to tidy her desk.

For a start, not bad. Roth would take the Inspector from Hesse to the Burghaven Reactor at eleven in the morning. A lot depended on what he found, but at least she had been assured that the Hesse Inspectorate were incorruptible fanatics for nuclear safety. What else? Huber had been tortured, and the Serious Crime Squad had leant on the only witness outside the circle of police and forensic functionaries who knew that. And it was she herself who had rummaged that one out, albeit prompted by Sharon's perceptiveness. Becker had possibly identi- fied Asterix . . . It was odd though, the way he'd given up the chase—he had such a reputation as a bully over- ready to resort to violence. But perhaps that was just it: bullies don't take on odds . . .

And mentally she kicked herself, just as she had last week after taking a patronising tone with Meier over his alcohol problem. It's not only bullies who do not take on dangerous odds—policemen who survive don't either, nor do successful generals.

But Firat it was who had come up with the real goods: these three Ossi thugs, perhaps ex-STASI, trying to get into Serious Crime, they, and this Knut Haussner Becker had turned up, ex-vice Squad. Four ex-policemen. All bent which was why they were ex-. She shuddered. Rogue shepherd dogs are worse than wolves. And protected by Hans Roehl's Special Crime Squad. But why? Who for?

Nevertheless, a sense of it all was forming hazily in her mind, forces looming like shapes in the fog, the fog swirling a bit and a pattern, a structure coming through: like those weird poster-pictures, half science fiction, half neo-gothic fantasy, that were so popular when she was a student, twenty years ago. Fissured faces, weather-carved from rock or formed from dripped candle-grease, twisted into evil grimaces, tinted with the virulent colours of disease, yellow bile and acid greens, in darkness phosphorescent with decay . . . How many?

A hundred, no, a thousand or more people, from the very comfortably off well salaried managers and senior technicians, even those who specialised in making the whole loony business 'safe', no, especially them, to the contractors who had built and might build again new reactors, through to the bankers, financiers and share-holders, the politicians who had, for whatever motive, and few of them morally sound, legitimated the whole business, yes there were thousands of people out there who would suffer huge loss of prestige, reputation and wealth if a major incident occurred in one of Germany's reactors. Especially since, as Drenkmann had suggested, the whole question of a new generation of reactors to replace the old was now on the agenda.

Suppose there had been a major incident at Burghaven. Was it fanciful to imagine a group, even a quite small group of these people, might have come together to suppress it?

Would they ever be caught?

She sighed, looked sightlessly out at the now dark pane of glass that reflected more light than it let through. She shrugged. Probably not. Between them and the four thugs who had killed Huber and Vesper, there were at least two layers of middlemen. At the lower level conniving officers in DAMOK, Serious Crime. Well, she'd get them. Believing in law there was nothing Renata hated more than a bent lawman. But above them the organisers: the agents, the ones acting on behalf of what she now called in her mind 'The Syndicate'. Instructed by The Syndicate they thought out stratagems, procedures, and found the thugs on the floor to carry them out.

I should, thought Renata, as she realised her desk was almost clear, apart from two or three sheets of paper, be able to go that high ... And if I can, then maybe they'll crack and I'll get to the real rot at the top.

She glanced at the three sheets of paper. The information she had asked Arslan and Becker to get, phoning her instruction from Hamburg after she had bought that stupid trouser suit and seen the Sheen woman walking past the café. The smell of carnation came back to her and she shrugged it away. Drenkmann had closed the case before she could do anything about them.

Burghaven, 1 April, MV *Eloise*, 1315 local time. Loading commences at 1600, departs 2100 ... There were four other sailings Becker had found listed, two from Emden, one from Wilhelmshaven, one from Hamburg. But surely, if, and she had to remind herself it was a very big if, based on a hunch, an intuition, if Harry Sheen and his fleet of clapped-out freighters were involved, the Burghaven sailing must be the one. They'd want that container out of the country as soon as they possibly could.

And then the guest-list for the Sheen Associates' presentation. Why two lists? Ah. I see. One is a list of those invited with ticks by those who came: fifteen out of twenty-three. The other is a list of seventeen names—the fifteen plus two who had not been on the original list: Renata Fechter and Aldo Nerone.

Her heart lurched, a cold, nasty sweat prickled her forehead and her palms. That Aldo should have been there because he had been invited simply indicated that Sheen Associates had misunderstood the nature of his business. Converting a formula three racetrack into a

performance car hypermarket was hardly going to generate the sort of waste that needed to be shipped to other
shores. But he had not been invited—the second list
showed that. And she remembered now—how he had
been held up at the entrance, had had to show ID. Just
as she did, following him a minute later.

Her face fell forward into the palms of her hands, and
she rubbed them into her tired eyes. She did not know
what it might mean. But she knew she had to find out.

CHAPTER 23

She had her own key, on a keyring with a spare for the Ferrari he had not bothered to remove. It was something she had insisted on after her first visit: she did not intend to be left on the stoop while he got out of the bath or whatever to answer the intercom. In the mirrored lift, where the motionless air was spiced with sandalwood with a hint of recent cigar-smoke as well, she reflected she had only ever visited his twelfth-floor apartment on Saturdays staying over to Sunday mornings. Would it be different on a Monday? Yes, was the answer. The kiss he gave her as he opened the door was both perfunctory and wary, as if she might deny it or worse. His breath was tainted with alcohol, possibly cognac. There were no fresh flowers. Newspapers on the tables and the floor: of course, they, Aldo and Renata, were featured. And he was wearing a suit.

'I'm sorry. I really am sorry about all this.' He looked tired, ill almost, his normally sleek hair the colour of dark iron, lank, unkempt, his clothes more lived-in than they usually appeared. 'Would you like a drink?'

'Yes.' Surprised at the warmth of her own acceptance of unscheduled alcohol, she thought for a moment. 'If you're drinking cognac, I'll have one too.' She sniffed. The cigar smell again. 'You've not been smoking have you?'

The decanter he was pouring brandy from chimed.

'No. Visitor, business. He left ten minutes ago.'

She took the half-filled glass. It was heavy with a thick

base: he knew she hated the pretension of drinking brandy from a balloon. His hand shook, ever so slightly, but it shook.

'Aldo, I have not come here for sympathy, nor apology.'

'There's not much else I can offer. Except brandy.'

She sipped, cradled the glass in both palms, carried it slowly over to the dining table at the far end of the room. With its sparse but modern and elegant furniture, three small pieces of abstract stone carving, deep-pile carpet, everything in shades of grey from near white to near black, it was a place she had come almost to love for its understated luxury, and, in daylight, clean airiness. Now it seemed stark, hard. She put the glass on the black table top, moved out a chair and sat on it.

'I was set up. You know that.'

He shrugged, stayed in the middle of the room, in front of the granite but functionless fireplace, keeping the dove-grey hide of the big sofa between them.

'I suppose so. But I know nothing about it.'

'Oh come on!'

'Renata! You may have been set up, but not by me.'

But he flinched away, chewed on a fingernail, set his glass down on the stone mantel behind him, would not meet her eye.

She forced herself to be icy calm, suppressed overt anger.

'No one knew where I was going. I told no one. I did not write it down anywhere. As far as I was concerned when I left my apartment on Friday morning, you were the only person in the world who knew where I was going.'

'My family knew.'

'So one of them betrayed me? No. It won't do.'

He swung his head like a bull trying to dislodge banderillas. 'There are other possible explanations.'

'Yes?'

'The photographer might have been there on spec. There have been rumours, suggestions in the Italian press that Maria's fortune has gone. They know about, how . . . Damn it! They know she is crippled and that she condones my affairs, my mistresses . . .'

Renata had had a go at most sports and throwing the javelin was one. Her glass, shedding a slipstream of amber fluid, ricocheted off his forehead and smashed on the granite behind him. She had even guessed, correctly, that he would duck instinctively to the right when it came.

'I am not your mistress. This is not an affair.' It was not a scream: more a trumpet call, a challenge.

He dropped to his knees, plucked the handkerchief from his top pocket and dabbed the cut on his forehead, looked at the blood-stained linen and clapped it back. Nevertheless three drops splashed on to the thick off-white carpet.

She came to the back of the sofa, looked down at him.

'I'm not sorry about that. Not at all.'

He looked up at her, and began to mouth words, silently, with great emphasis. She did not know what they were. She didn't much care. She turned away: he'd live. Then the words came through, measured tones, a hint of a whine in them, striving to persuade.

'He was there on spec. He took the photo. He had all day to get it identified. They have libraries, these people, computerised, you know what computers can do these days, search and find, your face . . . You've been pictured in the papers often enough.'

Mentally she shut it all out. This was the routine, she knew, the routine he'd spent a lot of time on, working it out, rehearsing it in front of mirrors. There was going to be no shifting him from that chosen defence. She breathed deeply, forced a return to composure, turned on him, spoke slowly.

'Two weeks ago today you went to a presentation given by Sheen Associates in the Hotel Intercontinental. Why?'

She heard and recognised the squeak of hide as he hauled himself into the sofa. Recognised, because in the storm of lust that had overtaken them on her first visit to this apartment, they had been all over it and its squeaks, sometimes fart-like, had brought on storms of helpless laughter. She heard his long, quavering sigh.

'I was invited.'

She waited.

'I suppose they . . . I suppose they went through local directories, took bankers' advice, that sort of thing, and drew up a list, and I was on it. But why? Why do you want to know this?'

She felt the rage rise again, sought to control it.

'You are lying, Aldo. I know you are lying. I know you were not invited, I know that you went uninvited. I want to know why.'

She approached the sofa, looked down at his back, the back of his head, as he continued to dab his forehead with the blotched handkerchief. She saw for the first time that on the very crown of his head the hair was observably thin. He's going bald, she thought and then, I wonder if he knows.

He turned, looked up at her, and again mouthed soundlessly. Finally he said, and it was almost a whisper: 'I can't tell you. One day I will.'

Frustrated, exhausted, she turned from him, struggled to think out a new approach, another line, failed, shrugged, and left. The cigar smell no longer lingered in the lift.

In her red BMW she cruised the boulevards back north away from the expensive development where he lived,

eventually reached the Ring. It was almost deserted.
Lonely trams, like cattle that have lost the herd, trundled
empty and aimlessly. A couple of couples left the almost
empty cinemas ... who goes to the movies on Monday
night? Light rain glistened on the tarmac and the paving,
department store windows passed like cruise liners in
the night. She thought about Aldo.

She thought: I got all that wrong. Almost I love him.
Often, even if only for short spells, he made me ... happy.
Not satisfied, or pleased, or content, or triumphant, or
successful, but happy. Perhaps I have done the same for
him. Perhaps, if I went back not angry and frustrated,
and cheated, but as a lover who has shared happiness
with him, and we talk quietly about it all, about how his
business affairs and my job have somehow crashed into
and destroyed or perhaps only nearly destroyed our
relationship (silly, cold word), we might put something
back together, and perhaps too ... oh shit, was this not
Machiavellian? might he not actually answer my questions, and tell me why he went uninvited to the Hotel
Intercontinental two weeks ago, and why he got me
exposing my boobs for a hidden paparazzo? Might he?
Maybe.

Half way through her second circuit of the Ring she did
an illegal U-turn and cruised, just a little more quickly
than before, back to his apartment and again let herself
in without ringing first.

He was sitting on the off-white carpet, with his back
against the sofa and his head lolling on the big deep
cushion. Blood, almost black against the grey hide, had
leaked from a small hole in his right temple as well as
from the cut left by the glass she had thrown. His right
arm was flung out away from him and his fingers were
still loosely curled round the pistol that had killed him.

Without actually touching it she knew the gun was

hers. It was the police issue Walther P5 and it ought to have been locked in the small drawer of her office desk at Gründorf. She knew it was hers and not just one of thousands like it for there, on the breechblock, was the tiny Mickey Mouse self-adhesive label which she had put there in an attempt to neutralise the feelings of angst the gun carried for her.

For a minute or so she had to steady herself against the back of the sofa as a wave of exhaustion and despair swept over her. Then she moved back to the chair near the window where she had sat half an hour or so earlier and forced herself to think carefully, rationally.

She had seen sudden death before. Often. And once the body, her mother's, killed on a pedestrian crossing by a joy-rider, had been that of someone she knew and loved. She had decided then, identifying the shattered wreck in the hospital morgue, that a body had nothing to do with the life that had inhabited it. And so it was now. Maybe she'd mourn Aldo's shed existence another, better time. Maybe not. But now the body that was not him was a problem and a part of a much bigger problem. But for the moment she had to concentrate on the immediate aspect.

Her fingerprints would be on the gun whose number in any case would be traced to her. They were also on the broken shards of the glass she had hurled at him. No point in trying to sweep them up and get rid of them: she would not be able to make a forensically clean job of it and the fact that she had tried would be taken as evidence of a guilty conscience. She had motive too: a lovers' quarrel following the news story about them and that damn photograph. First the glass then the bullet, then the slightly clumsy attempt to make it look like suicide. She fought down the returning wave of despair as she realised how thoroughly she had been trapped.

It must have been done by someone he knew, someone

he had allowed in, someone who could get that close to him. Someone who knew her fingerprints were on the glass and on the gun. It was all too much. She felt midnight cold with it all. Inside her skull, exhaustion and despair fed off each other. She needed help, serious help. Only one person existed with the clout she needed: Secretary Drenkmann. After a moment's hesitation she got up and walked round to Aldo's desk where there was a PC, a fax machine, and a combined phone and answering machine.

She reached for it, but then remembered the homicide procedures she had been trained in, and pressed the redial button. Three rings then a recorded message, female voice.

'This is the private residence of Hans Roehl. Please wait for the beep and then leave your name, number and reason for calling.'

That was all, but with pulse quickening, she replaced the handset without speaking. With a little tremor of hope that the other side had blundered, left a crack in their defences, she activated the playback on the answering machine. There were three messages clearly relating to Aldo's conversion plan for the formula three racetrack and then:

'Signor Nerone? I need to see you. Phone this number after six pm.' A cold gravelly voice she knew well. And it was a stimulus too: it provoked hate spiked with Olympian distaste and it took the edge off the tired despair. Since it was the last message she then got the date and time stated by a pre-recorded voice: *Monday, 29 March, 1705, no more messages.*

She noted the number on the small square pad by the phone, tore off the sheet, and went into the big bedroom where there was an extension on the bedside table. She dabbed out the number, and, just as she had hoped, got the same recorded message as before: 'This is the private residence of Hans Roehl . . .'

It was a start, but not enough. She was still out of her depth, way out of her depth and in shit at that.

'I must,' and yes, she spoke aloud, was relieved to hear the normality of her own voice, 'think this through.'

She paused, and thought. They knew she had been coming to see Aldo that evening. They had already stolen her gun because they knew she was coming. She remembered the cigar smell. Had he, Roehl, been there all the time? In the kitchen perhaps? But no, the smell had been in the lift too, such smells do not linger long, it had gone by the time she left, but perhaps they, he, Roehl himself? Why not? had simply gone back out into the street, waited there in a car, waited until she had gone before coming back to kill him with her gun.

They would not have expected her to come back. This was the key, they did not expect her to come back. What did they plan to do? She was thinking almost aloud now, framing the words with her lips. Find some excuse, manufacture some excuse to get back in here tomorrow some time, or when it suits them, and then they find Aldo, apparently suicided, but actually murdered by me, and then they arrest me . . . and end of story. So what do I do now?

The answers became clear, a sort of a plan began to form, and appealing to Drenkmann was not, after all, part of it.

She took the gun from Aldo's hand, and shot him again, three times, in his chest and stomach, heaved his body over into an untidy huddle on the floor. She took the tape from the answering machine, then she wiped the telephones she had used, and the buttons she had dabbed, she did whatever she could to wipe out evidence of her second visit. Given she had been a familiar of this apartment for several weeks what she missed would be explained easily enough.

Outside she cruised the empty streets and boulevards until the sky began to lighten, until she was absolutely sure she had not been followed. Then on the bank of the Weser, at a spot where she knew the river was deep and the mud beneath deeper, she threw the gun with its Mickey Mouse sticker into the water. Almost—the hour, the battle, no the war she was fighting being what they were—she half expected an arm, a hand, clothed in samite, to catch it.

CHAPTER 24

Sleep was out of the question. Sitting at her kitchen table, in the growing light of day, she put pencil to paper and drew up an account, debit and credit, of where she now stood.

On the debit side Sonnenberg was right: there was an enemy in her camp, a spy, a mole. He, or she, had stolen her gun. What else? Ever since the murder of Huber he or she had reported back to Roehl just how far she, Fechter, was getting in her investigation, and at some point had alerted Roehl to the fact that she was far closer to the truth than was safe. Which of the successful lines she had been pursuing had gone that far down the road? Desperately she thought back over the last few days, and finally she decided that the turning point had been her instruction to Becker and Arslan to find out all they could about the docking of Sheen's ships, with later her instruction to Becker that she should have a copy of the *Eloise*'s manifest on her desk, midday on the day she sailed. At the time she had been playing a hunch, but the fact that Aldo had gone to the presentation uninvited, and then lied about it, had proved to her satisfaction that the hunch was a good one.

She herself had lied when ordering the manifest: she told them all that it was nothing to do with the Burghaven Reactor. It did not matter whether or not the enemy believed the lie: what they knew was that nine hours before the *Eloise* sailed she would know that a cube container, the same size as the one missing from

Radwasthaus, would be on the dock waiting to be loaded.

What else on the debit side? Well, she was up against a ruthless enemy, who not only had a spy in her camp, but had huge resources of money and manpower to back up a will that would stop short at nothing: torture and murder were already routine. If they thought it would serve their purpose they would be quite capable of launching a rocket attack on her office or her apartment, nothing, but nothing could be ruled out. She shuddered at the thought but pushed back the cold wave of fear and loneliness that threatened again to break over her.

There was no point in mystifying the forces she was up against: they might represent or be part of what was most evil in human nature, but they were nevertheless finite, material, there was nothing inherent in their nature which said they had to win. So what did she know about them? She had earlier proposed to herself a syndicate, a board of people who stood to lose enormously if the German nuclear programme was halted or reversed. These were the paymasters, the clients. Who were the agents, the executors of the paymasters' will?

Clearly Hans Roehl was one and beneath him other officers in the Serious Crime Squad. But they were adept, that little clique, at concealment, at covering their tracks: she knew only too well just how clever they were. Roehl himself would have received no unexplained payments, no, probably not even into the proverbial Swiss bank account. He was a year off the first retirement option: who better to be put on the board of some company or agency connected with the nuclear industry as a security consultant? The pay and perquisites would be commensurable with the responsibilities of a job he might do for several firms he had 'helped' in the past ... And meanwhile, beneath him, there were perhaps tens of officers in his department who would do whatever he said out of fear or greed, but probably fear. And at the bottom of the heap bent ex-cops like Haussner and the three ex-STASIs.

So Roehl himself never actually carried out anything concretely, provably criminal. Except, possibly, the murder of Aldo. But nor was he the boss, the brains, of that she was sure. She knew him well, had worked under him for years. He was capable of almost anything, but not of masterminding a complex operation of this sort, dealing with widely divergent areas at once. Yes, he could set up a murder or two, but spiriting cube containers out of existence, chartering cargo space on a freighter, fixing documentation in such widely differing places as a harbourmaster's office, a plant like Radwasthaus and who knew where else were beyond his range. Somewhere there was a general, a mastermind.

Suddenly she recalled the tall, grey, cadaverous man who had stood at Roehl's side at the Schippbauhaus reception. That could be the man she had to bring down if she were to survive. And again she shuddered.

And on the credit side, the pluses? First, she knew where the container with its radioactive contents was hidden. Clearly it was on Aldo's racetrack. And they did not know that she knew. Secondly she had scotched the attempt to frame her for Aldo's murder. When would they choose to find his body? Why, when she again became something that had to be stopped. And what would they find? Almost nothing of the elaborately prepared scenario that had been set up to incriminate her. This would wrong-foot them to start with at any rate.

With this perception came a dawning sense of where and how she had gone so badly, so tragically wrong in the twelve hours or so after Drenkmann had given her the green light. She had gone at it with ruthless energy, making no attempt at all to disguise the fact that she was in business again. She had gone a long way, uncovered a lot, but she had alerted the enemy: they knew an inspector would be in Burghaven the next day; Becker had been to the Golden Temple, had possibly been spotted by Haussner; even Firat's lunch at the Brauerei might now look like what it was—an attempt to find out what was going on inside Serious Crime. Perhaps they knew even that she herself had interviewed the woman who found Huber and still insisted that he had been lying as if he had been dragged downstairs from his apartment rather than in from the street. And always there was the mole, the spy, who would feed most if not all of this information back.

Suddenly she felt tired, properly tired. She pushed aside the paper she had been writing on, went into her bedroom, threw herself on the bed. For a moment, as she looked through the window into the blue of a rain-washed morning sky, she mourned the death of Aldo: but then recalled that he had initiated the relationship knowing who she was. She turned away from the window and shut out the light and the hollow bitterness that might undermine her, dwelt instead on the developing presence of a strategy.

She slept, for an hour or so, and when she awoke she knew how she should proceed. She would move now with the guile her adversaries used, but with an added advantage—from now on they would be one step behind her, instead of the other way about.

PART III

The Duke of Wellington used to say that as a strategist he was flexible, his plans were made up of ropes like a harness: if one broke, all he had to do was tie a knot. Wolfgang Kurtz, aka Heinrich Herz, of Alterlog, Zürich, was an admirer of Wellington. He was also learning a grudging respect for KHK Renata Fechter—nothing Hans Roehl had ever said of her had led him to expect in the first place such tenacity, and in the second an ability to improvise which he felt was almost as good as his own.

He turned from Aldo Nerone's now crumpled body and walked to the window.

'Why did she come back?'

'Who knows? We don't even know it was her.' Roehl sat on the end of the hide sofa, with his big hands hanging loosely over his knees. He gave the dead man's head a casual kick. 'We can arrest her anyway. She may still have the gun. I can cobble enough together to hold her for twenty-four hours.'

'She won't have the gun. And Drenkmann will have her in front of a judge and out on the loose again by lunchtime.'

The tall dark cadaverous man slid a sliver of grapefruit fibre from his interrupted breakfast (strictly vegetarian from the Hotel Ramada on the motorway box out of town) from between a canine and a molar, dropped the shivered toothpick he had carried away with him on Aldo's off-white carpet.

'This is serious, you know?'

Roehl, who did not like anybody and had learnt over the last week or so to dislike Kurtz rather strongly, looked back and up at him over his heavy shoulder. He heard the reproof, the laying of blame all too clearly in Kurtz's voice, saw it in his manner.

'Why don't I just get her wasted? Pushed under a tram. Stabbed resisting a mugger. That sort of thing.' Among the many things he disliked about Kurtz was the to him unnecessary elaboration that he brought to assassination. He felt the canny, uncanny Swiss relished too much and too irrelevantly the elegance of his cunning: Huber and Vesper both removed by making it seem one had killed the other. The same with Fechter and Nerone. And neither had worked.

'I don't think you understand.' Kurtz delved into his black gaberdine to an inner pocket beneath, pulled out a cigarette case and a lighter—both slim and gold. Roehl turned his head away, fighting an urge to gag on the foul smell that was coming. Kurtz did not smoke often, but when he did the cigarettes were mentholated. 'Fechter somehow made the connection between Sheen Associates and the container. I think we have to assume that a similar leap of imagination is not beyond her and that she will realise the container is parked on Nerone's land outside Burghaven. Once we knew she was going to check the MV *Eloise* manifest we were going to do a switch anyway. But I now think we have to make it today. Indeed in the next few hours. If we can bring that off . . .' he looked at his watch, 'in the next couple of hours, we shall have avoided the worst that might arise out of this . . . débâcle. And we shall have given ourselves a day or two to work out what to do next. Come on.'

He swept from the window towards the door, leaving Roehl struggling to get out of the deep sofa, struggling to get to the door not too far behind him. On the landing he buttoned his full double-breasted jacket over his barrel-shaped corseted torso, boarded the lift just ahead of the closing door.

'You did not ask me to keep a watch on this place after Nerone had been shot.'

The tall Swiss looked down at him, breathed noisome smoke across his balding pate.

'Do I have to think of everything?'

Wellington had the same problem. He had to think of everything.

CHAPTER 26

Renata drove, Becker sat beside her and resented the fact that she drove—not least because this was no small Opel from the Ministry pool but an executive Toyota: he wondered gloomily at what backhanders had been handed out to ensure that the Interior Ministry's departmental heads got the use of classy Japanese cars instead of the BMWs everyone else drove.

She had a good reason for driving while Becker sat at her side.

'Andreas,' she had said, just as soon as she had cleared essential paperwork from her desk, made a handful of phone calls, 'shut the door and sit down.'

He did so, but angled the chair so there was no direct confrontation.

'I am not going into details,' she had continued, 'but I want you to understand two things.'

He looked up at her warily, wondering what was coming next.

'Three actually.'

He realised she was very tired, had taken less care than usual with her appearance. She was wearing a simple undecorated denim top over black leggings cropped to her calves, and what looked like little more than black pull-on slippers. Her normally luxuriant dark chestnut hair was roughly clipped back with the sort of grips you buy for your pre-teen daughter. He knew about such things. He had a pre-teen daughter he was allowed to see one weekend each month. He thought it was disgraceful that an officer senior to him should feel able to come to work dressed like that.

'I want you to understand three things. One. I am going to crack this Burghaven Reactor business. Find out the truth that is, whatever it turns out to be. Two. There is a spy in this department. I am going to find out who she, or he, is, and . . . bring him to book. Finally. I am not going to be killed. As a result of . . . working out, making these other things work.'

Yes, he thought. Yes. She is very tired indeed. He waited.

'And so from now on you are going to be my minder. You are going to stick close to me day and night. Everywhere I go you will come too. And if I do get killed, then I want to be sure you go down with me, preferably ahead of me, that they have had to kill you before they kill me. Is that understood?'

Which was, he supposed, why she drove, and he rode shotgun. Almost literally except it was his police issue Walther that threw out the line of his suit.

She was driving fast, up the autobahn towards Burghaven, through rain heavy enough to keep the wipers on intermittent, and, he had to admit to himself, she drove well. She was now wearing a lightweight but full and belted white mac. Presently she shifted her buttocks, leant forward a centimetre or so, gripped the wheel a shade tighter. Sensing the movements he glanced at her face. She was biting her lip.

'Andreas, tell me, who is the mole, the spy in my department?'

Very slowly he eased his big back into the soft leather behind him.

'Christ knows. They're a rotten bunch.'

'I know.'

'Roth and Meier are the two most vulnerable. Both

with habits they can't kick. Someone in Narcotics could be feeding Roth with whatever he's on. He'd do anything not to have to pay for the stuff.'

'Not Meier, though. He phones in sick so often he wouldn't be much use. What about the others?'

'Not the black girlie. She's not got enough between her ears to manage that sort of double life.'

Intermittent shafts of distant sunshine caught the distant mantis-like tops of the hoists on the nearest of Burghaven's docks. She flicked the indicator switch, took a slipway signposted 'Burghaven Docks, South', made it in effect a left turn by taking the option that led her back under the carriageway she had left. Then another left took them from the main road on to a minor one, a concrete thread through dense but managed forest.

'Arslan?'

'Ali Baba?' He pushed derisive air through pursed lips. 'First, I'd have to know who you think this mole is working for.'

'The people who are hushing up what looks like an incident at the Burghaven Reactor.'

'You mean money? Ali Baba doesn't need money. He's got a rich dad back in Ankara.'

'Not that rich. Commissioner.'

'Rich.' Said dryly, the implication was that in a country like Turkey if you were that high up in the police you were rich.

'Andreas, if you were the mole, what would you do it for?'

Again the pushed snort of derision.

'Need you ask?'

Renata drove in silence for a moment, with half an eye on the right hand fence and grassy bank that separated the road from the forest. Foxgloves in heavy bud. No, she thought, I do not need to ask. But I might as well answer.

'You'd do it to get your old job back.'

There it is. The spur that led to the formula three racetrack. She glanced at the dash: 11.17., and then at him. He would too.

'We're too late.'

'What are we looking for?'

'Three metre cube container of course.'

'There's not one here.'

'No.'

They'd been over the whole small dilapidated site. Fairly extensive demolition had been begun on the smaller stands on either side of the main one. Most of the more or less intact buildings behind lacked doorways big enough to take something four and a half metres high, which was the height needed with the cube on a trailer. The three repair shops, which had once had hydraulic ramps above pits and could have perhaps taken it if the trailer had been broad enough to straddle them, were open to easy inspection through shattered windows.

Renata looked round and then up the high brick rear wall of the main stand to the row of windows on the top: the hospitality suites, in one of which she had spent a strangely subdued afternoon drinking ice-cold Frascati and listening to Aldo talking up his grand design for a hypermarket for hypercars. She felt heaviness descend on her like the thickening cloud which was now low enough to drift through the tops of the tallest pines. The rain was not so much a drizzle as falling mist.

'There are tracks off into the forest. They need not have taken it far.' She thought of the sleek Toyota bouncing and sliding down muddy rides and fire-breaks. And provided they knew her schedule, the ways in which she had been delayed, and there was every likelihood they did, there was no point. They could have shifted it one kilometre or a hundred. She turned back towards the car and Becker followed, hooded eyes warily checking out the receding vertical geometry of tree-trunks.

'Hallo, what's this?'

Coming towards them through the mist the low circular lights of a low-slung black Jaguar XJS convertible. It pulled up ten metres in front of Renata and Andromed Drenkmann unfolded herself out of the low bucket seat and on to the concrete. She gave herself a shake much like a pony released from a horse-box. She was dressed as she had been the day before, in denims and leather. By the time she was out Renata was by the wing of the car, waiting for her.

'Hallo. You must be . . .'

'Renata Fechter of the Regional Police. And I know who you are.'

'Yes. I . . . I. Frankly I did not expect you to be here.'

Where did she expect me to be then, Renata asked herself, noting the inflection.

'No? Why are you here? I did not expect you either.'

'I work for Signor Nerone . . . was working for him. I heard the news on TV. It occurred to me that the police might want to . . .'

'The news. On TV?' Renata struggled to keep sane, dug nails into her palms, fought off the swimming sensation in her head.

'That he's dead. Possibly that he killed himself. Surely . . .?'

'Yes, yes of course. I simply did not expect them to release it so soon.'

She was so damned tired, but yes, she'd hang on, she'd stay in control. She went on:

'So why are you here?'

'It's not easy to explain . . .'

'Try.'

'Well, it seems almost certain that the project I was working on with him won't go on. But the designs I did for him are really good, and, if nothing else, if I can salvage them I can exhibit them, maybe persuade someone else to take them up. And two of the originals are here, only photocopies back at the office.'

'You felt there might be delays if you went to the police and asked them to release them now.'

'Yes.' Andromed smiled gratefully at her.

'All right. Do you have a key?'

'Yes.'

They walked together up the greasy grass slope to the side of the stand and then scaled the terrace to the hospitality suites at the top. Becker padded behind, but always scanning the areas beneath them. Andromed found a key. Once they were in Renata closed the glazed door, leaving Becker on the outside. She moved along the picture windows which faced across the cleared area, gave a view of most of the old track. Andromed rustled through rolls of paper she extracted from cardboard tubes, found what she wanted.

'When were you last here?'

'Yesterday.'

'What . . . is there anything different today?'

Andromed stuffed a roll of drawing paper into a tube.

'Up here?' she asked.

'Anywhere.'

'There was a container, on a trailer, not far from where your car is parked. It's not there any more.'

Inwardly Renata breathed a sigh of relief, a relief spiced with bitterness that her suspicions about Aldo were proving to be justified.

'Did you . . . you and Aldo talk about it at all?'

'First he said he was looking after it for a friend. Then he said it was full of asbestos from the old buildings here, and he was having it shipped to the east. It would be cheaper than disposing of it here.'

'Which was true?'

'The first. The amount of asbestos he would have found on a site like this would not have been a problem, not that sort of problem.' Casually she opened the big refrigerator, glanced in. 'He gave himself, and whoever else was here, such good working lunches.'

'Yes.'

'I suppose someone will come along and clear it all out before it goes rotten.'

Particularly she was looking at a plate of large Dublin Bay prawns covered with cling-film.

'There's half a bottle of that lovely wine he used to drink. Shall we finish it?'

'Why not?'

Renata was almost dizzy now with tiredness and delayed shock, but as the other woman found and rinsed glasses she forced herself to think.

'Listen. I would like you to tell your uncle about that container. But you absolutely must not tell anyone else that you saw it. All right?'

'Goodness. That sounds serious.' Andromed poured the wine.

'It is. Aldo did not kill himself. He was murdered.' She added, knowing it was foolish, but she could not help herself: 'and not by me. And then I think you should leave the country for a week or so. Until I or your uncle say you can come back.'

She took the glass. For a moment they looked at each other, then clinked glasses: no need for either of them to make the toast that was on their lips. They drank.

'You look awfully knocked up.'

'I am.'

Faced with sympathy she knew she was going to weep.

She let Andromed take her in her arms, let her cheek drop on to the soft leather of her shoulder, let the flood of sobs go. Some minutes later she pulled back.

'I'm going to get the bastards. You know that.'

'Yes. I expect you will. Good luck anyway.'

Andromed took an open box of tissues from a shelf, handed it to Renata, who added:

'Don't forget what I said about the container. It's important.'

Outside on the terrace Becker turned his back on them with disgust. He had not been able to hear what they said, but the sight of them drinking and weeping had been more than enough.

CHAPTER 27

Sharon King found Tuǧrul Enver through Hans Graf, Vesper's ex-boyfriend. The 'out' gay scene in Burg was not that extensive, numbered less than a couple of hundred who socialised in no more than five or six bars and discos. She correctly guessed that Hans, the most promiscuous of Vesper's circle, would know where the young Turk could be found.

Graf's address, which she got from Dominic Stieffen, was an apartment inside the Ring: his mother's, though he was not often there at night. The block was one of the few apart from the central square and the cathedrals that had had its original nineteenth-century neo-baroque stucco restored. Perhaps through some chancy fluke of backdraught or whatever it had escaped Butcher Harris's firestorm more or less intact. Inside, the apartment was a memorial to a departed culture or fashion and a shrine to the man Sharon took to be Graf's father.

Frau Graf ushered her through a narrow dark corridor hung with paintings of dying tulips and gangrenous lilies into a salon that had high ceilings and big windows. The colours were predominantly orange, yellow and black. There was a key pattern frieze in orange and black above a dado hung with paper printed with a geometrical pattern of interlocked triangles. The furniture was nineteen twenties art deco as were the ornaments: predominant among them was a matt aluminium statue, not far off life-size, of a lean smooth nude nymphet carrying what looked like a marble globe on upstretched arm high above her head. A netball she was about to score with? Frau Graf stooped to a wall-plug and the globe became a lamp: the nymphet was after all nothing but a lamp-standard.

Frau Graf was a thin, alcoholic sixty-five, dressed in long straight pleated chiffon, patterned with lavish scarlet poppies. She wore lipstick the way whores do in paintings by Schiele and she chain-smoked Marlboro Lites through a long jet holder.

'I am not sure if Hans is awake,' she croaked, and waved Sharon into a deep chair, printed in the style of the paper. 'He told me to expect you, but then ... I'm sure he had not realised you are a black.' Her voice became vague and she left.

Sharon waited in the silence conferred by double-glazing. She found the atmosphere at first oppressive, then more positively disagreeable. The aroma of schnapps and harsh Virginian that moved with Frau Graf like an aura had gone with her: the basic odours of the apartment flooded back in her wake. A century, perhaps more, of boiled pig and cabbage. A clock, its brassy innards exposed, ticked and wheezed, loaded each moment with doom. Above the granite mantelpiece there was a large oil: a *fête champêtre* recalling Manet's, though the landscape was sunny, Mediterranean. As in the Manet the men who reclined among picnic baskets, bottles and so on, wore clothes but the women were naked. One of the men, no more than a boy really, wore a pale yellowish uniform with a swastika armband. The painting was indecipherably signed but clearly dated: 1936.

To the right of the fireplace, the inner corner of the room was a shrine. The base was a heavy quarter-circle table, black lacquer inlaid with nacre and ivory, which supported at the back a large silver-framed photograph of a young handsome man in SS uniform. He could have been an older version of the youth in the oil painting. Around the photograph, on the walls behind it and on the surface of the table were medals, including an Iron Cross, second class, a shiny steel dagger with a hilt bound with silver wire, more photographs, some personal belongings: a gun metal cigarette case, a lighter, a small black pistol. Suddenly new odours overlaid pig and cabbage: the full range of Paco Rabanne—shower gel, talc, after-shave.

'Papa. A difficult act to follow.'

Sharon turned. Hans was, it was to be expected, wearing a dark silk robe woven with gold dragons, but he was, physically at any rate, not quite at one with the ambience. Short, no taller than her, thickset, almost chubby, he had small eyes set in a rosy complexion beneath very pale blond hair cropped very short. She thought for a moment.

'They must have been quite old when you were born.'

'Yes. 1968. He was fifty, she forty. For fifteen years he was presumed to be infertile following privations at the end of the war and the eight years he spent in prison as a minor war criminal. During which he was frequently kicked in the balls. Twenty-five, no twenty-six years ago, he underwent fertility treatment and the result was me. Papa died, possibly of shock, ten years later. You want to speak to Tuğrul about how they killed Vesper?'

'Yes.'

Hans turned to the door he had come through.

'Tugsie, I know you're there. Come on in. Nice young black lady wants a word with you.' He turned back to Sharon. 'He's quite pretty but a tart— basically just a tart.'

Pretty? Sharon's heart gave a lurch when he came through the door. Tuğrul was slim, had olive skin which glowed with health or from the shower he had possibly just shared with Hans, and a lot of it was on display. He was wearing tight white briefs, and a white towelling bath-robe which was short and he had not bothered to fold it over and tie the belt. His thick glossy black hair was cut behind to make a bullfighter's tail and was still wet; his cheekbones were high but his eyes large and very dark. His brick red lips were full but well-shaped and his teeth were very white. His nipples were brown. He had long fingers and long toes. He sat himself in a small chintz covered armchair, stretched out long hairless thighs and well-formed shins, crossed his ankles, and grinned.

Sharon pulled a chair round in front of him so its back faced him, sat astride it, spread her arms across the back.

'Tell me,' she said, 'what happened when Roger Vesper was beaten up.'

'Why?' he grinned again, but unease was evident.

'Because I am a police officer.'

Tuğrul glanced across at Hans who leant against the doorjamb close to his father's shrine. Hans smiled, and nodded.

Tuğrul pulled the robe over his chest and folded his arms above it, drew in his knees and leant forward a little.

'I've already told the police.'

Sharon shifted, lifted a buttock, took ID from the hippocket of her jeans, flashed it.

'Tell me.'

'I went to the toilet. I had just finished peeing when he came in. He stood behind me, undid the top of my jeans and the belt buckle, pulled my jeans down so they were round my knees. He put his hand on my prick, balls and all, squeezed so it hurt, hurt very bad. I could feel his prick, very hard pushing into my bottom. He was very strong...'

Hans reached into his father's shrine, picked up the shiny dagger. He came between them and knelt in front of Tuğrul, forced his knees apart, wrenched down the briefs enough to expose his genitals.

'Tuğrul,' he said, 'I suppose they said to you that if you did not swear to their version of what happened they would put you on an immorality charge and ship you back to Anatolia. If that happens then I promise you you will go back to Anatolia without your balls. Now tell the nice black lady what really happened.'

CHAPTER 28

'Vesper's dead.' Renata sat back in her deep chair so her face was out of the light cast by the desk-lamp. She looked to Sharon like a ghost of her usual self: dark shadows round her eyes, somehow frailer, thinner. Becker stood by the window, facing out, big solid hands behind his back, fingers occasionally twitching. 'Whether or not they pulled the plug on him, or he just died anyway, I have no means of knowing. Sit down.'

'I'm sorry.' Sharon had never met Vesper, but knew him to have been a good man, and brave too, deeply loved by his small circle of friends. 'But at least I do now know what happened.'

'Go on.'

'Tuğrul Enver was picked up by Serious Crime the night before, Saturday. He wasn't doing anything particularly wrong at the time, they just went into the Hallöchen Bar and took him down to Central. There were the usual threats, the worst being deportation. All he had to do was get Vesper into the toilet with him, and later swear attempted rape. In the toilet he provoked Vesper into a close embrace, then the three men came in. Tuğrul did not stay long, but he's seen police beatings before, both here and in Turkey, and he reckons these were professional, very professional.'

'Could he identify these men?'

'He reckons so. But he won't unless he's found a regular job, preferably in a bar, with prospects good enough to get Immigration off his back.'

A knock on the door behind her as she finished. She half turned, saw Arslan come in. Renata looked up at him, but noted the distaste on Sharon's face.

'All right, Sharon. Thank you. You did well.'

Sharon got up, left, Arslan took her chair.

'OK, Firat. How did you get on?'

The tall Turk crossed his legs, leant back. Pretty well, Renata guessed was the answer. Smug bastard.

'Otto Hochberg lives at 1129B Singerstrasse. Unemployed, eighteen years old. He was in when I called at 1415 hours,' he flipped open a small notepad. 'For ten minutes or so he displayed marked hostility, but eventually calmed down enough to make a statement . . .'

'Sweet reason, Firat? Or did you slap his wrist?'

'A bit of both, Frau Fechter.'

He grinned white teeth in a sallow complexion. But before he could continue with the report of his interview with the skin who was the last person to play table tennis with Tuğrul before Tuğrul enticed Vesper into the toilet, they were interrupted. Sounds of the approaching storm penetrated the glass divisions that separated Renata's office from the rest of the suite as Dr Sonnenberg pushed aside protests from receptionists and secretaries. The small, stocky, middle-aged woman in her old-fashioned clothes and sensible shoes flung open the door, marched across the space between and smashed a cased audio cassette on to the black top of Renata's desk.

'Get a player, and play that.'

'What is it?'

'You'll see when you play it.'

Clearly there was no point in asking her to wait until Arslan had finished his report. There was a moment or two of bustle, the cassette was slotted into a player. The intro to Guns 'n Roses' Paradise City filled the room. Renata snapped it off.

'What is this?'

'I have no idea. No idea at all. But I do know one thing. It is not a copy of the interview I had with Roger Vesper eight days ago.'

'Dr Sonnenberg, you had better explain. Firat, give her your chair.'

Sonnenberg sat, smoothed her grey pleated skirt. Her head came up, proud, enquiring, determined.

'At two o'clock this afternoon I heard that Vesper had been murdered . . .'

'Murdered?'

'He could have remained clinically alive for years. Somebody switched him off. Probably the Serious Crime Squad policeman who was sitting at his bedside. Anyway, as soon as I heard that he was dead I felt I should play back that interview. Don't ask me why. I am not always rational. I came over here, made my request and Meier brought me out that cassette. You will see that the casing is labelled, but not the cassette itself . . .'

'Dr Sonnenberg, I don't understand. Surely what we have here is a copy of your tape. You took your tape back to your office.'

'No.'

'Why not?'

'I left my tape here to be copied for your archive. I also asked for a transcript to be made. Presumably both those tasks were carried out. What I want now is for you to find the copy, recopy it and let me have one of them.'

Renata pressed a button.

'Tell Alfred Meier I want him in here immediately.'

It took an hour to make some sense of what had happened. Most of the evidence seemed to indicate Sharon was at fault and possibly deeply guilty too. But Arslan could not escape suspicion either. First, Sharon admitted the cassette was, in a sense, hers. The office had a stock of blank cassettes: occasionally she filched them to make copies off friends' tapes.

'But why?' Renata asked. 'I am surprised you cannot afford the originals. But certainly you can afford to buy your own blanks.'

Sharon shrugged miserably. What she could not admit was that throughout a deprived childhood and early adolescence as one of three children of a single parent, black at that, such practices had been natural to her. When the opportunity to repeat them occurred, she reverted: not out of need but out of a sort of respect for the person she once was.

The next question was why no copy had been made of the original tape. Here there was confusion. It should have been Meier's responsibility, but he made mistakes with the machinery, and had formed the habit of asking Sharon to make the copies for him.

'But why was no transcript made?'

No one was prepared to come up with an answer. But in the end the overworked clerk who had been given the job admitted she had shelved it until that very morning, and then she found she was transcribing Paradise City. Not wishing to get involved in what she sensed was going to be a major row, she simply replaced the cassette and hoped it would all go away or never happen.

But at the end of it all Sharon stood up, turned round, pointed a finger at Arslan.

'You took that cassette off me yesterday. In the Burg Brauerei. You took it out of my player, and put it in your pocket.'

He looked back at her, eyes harsh with hate and scorn.

'Yes,' he snarled, 'and when we got back here, and I found it in my pocket, I tossed it on your desk.'

Renata stood up, palms on the desk, head flung back.

'Enough. This has degenerated into farce. Meier, King, Arslan, all three of you are suspended on full pay until a proper enquiry has worked out what happened. Now get out and stay out. Stay out until I send for you.'

When they had gone, all except Becker, Sonnenberg stood, smoothed her skirt: 'You realise now it's as if that interview with Vesper never took place at all. It's the last shred of evidence we had that the Serious Crime version of Vesper is a pack of lies.'

'What do you mean?'

'They've put out a press release. They regret Vesper's death, but they have now closed both enquiries, both the one into Huber's death and into Vesper's.'

'They can't do that.'

'They can. And they have the backing of the State Attorney. Vesper was a psycho who went in for anal rape on young men. That's the story, and they're sticking to it. You see, Renata, they *know* my tape no longer exists, or at least not outside their headquarters.'

Renata looked at the door through which the three suspended officers had gone.

'One of them?'

'Maybe.'

'Which? Becker, which one of them is it?'

The big policeman from Vice half turned, looked over his shoulder. Throughout the meeting he had kept his eye on both the door and the outside, taking his role as minder with relentless seriousness. Now he shrugged.

'Maybe I'm wrong about the girl,' he said. 'She's not as stupid as I thought.'

CHAPTER 29

An hour later, at about six o'clock, Harry Sheen's oldish hired Merc with Herbert driving and Eloise as usual along to map-read and interpret cruised down minor roads and lanes north-west of Burg. They were all nervous. The phone call demanding a meeting and announcing that the place of the meeting had already been left at the hotel desk with a map showing the route they would need to take to get there, had been abrupt and peremptory.

'Count me out,' Sam had said, replacing the phone, 'that is someone up whose snout you have definitely got, and since a ton gets you a pony they're a dodgy lot, I'll stay home and mind the shop.'

That had been just after four o'clock. It had been a long drive from Hamburg down the motorway then right round the south of Burg before heading back up north-west past Oldenburg. Nearly two hours later, and with the bright spring sun now well in their eyes, they found the slipway and then the minor roads that led into a featureless but well-drained fen. Water-meadows filled with Friesian cattle alternated with stands of regimented timber and fallow fields, the whole intersected by waterways and canals. Not all were to do with drainage. Presently they crossed one, ruler-straight and narrow, but along which thin but very long barges trundled as close to the banks and to each other as subway trains.

Sheen peered between the two front seats, eyes in a grimace trying to make sense of the occasional signs.

'It can't be long now, can it El?'

'I reckon not.'

Presently she told Herbert to take a left on to a raised causeway metalled evenly enough with stone, but no tarmac. On their right a big square field whose bluish-green crop suggested rye rather than wheat, on the left and below them a hedge of pollarded willows, a ruler-straight dike and a marsh of reeds that looked as cultivated as the rest and probably was. A flight of three shelduck cruised above it, banked and disappeared behind the reeds a couple of hundred metres away, presumably on to open water.

'Are you sure you've got this right?'

El sighed.

'Every landmark and direction has been precise so far,' she said. 'Why should I have got it wrong this time?'

'What are we looking out for then?'

She looked at the third of three pages torn out of a ring-bound notepad.

'A stand or windbreak of . . . oh shit. What sort of a tree is *pappel*?'

'Poplars?'

'Yes. You're right. How did . . .? Oh, I see. OK. Go to the end of them, turn left, you'll come to a canal, and there we are. Journey's end.'

After the poplars a final stretch of track, rutted and far bumpier, but short, brought them on to a long concrete quay, fifty metres wide and a good two hundred long. At the far end there was a black creosoted clapboard barn with high gables and, tucked up against it, the container, still on its trailer, they had last seen at the disused car-racing track. In front of it there was a Mercedes, but very new, and a less new middle-range Audi. To their right a canal: not as wide as the commercial one they had crossed earlier, but definitely more than a dike. The sun was now only five degrees above the horizon, the sky in this flat country immense and apart from a criss-cross of vapour trails, empty. The shadows from the trees behind them lay stark across the concrete. Herbert drove them down the quay but stopped thirty metres short of the other two cars.

El shuddered. 'Sam was right to stop at the hotel.'

Three, four, finally five men stepped out of the cars, approached theirs, stopped five or so metres away from it, surrounding it. Three of them were young, wearing windbreakers and jeans. The fourth was older, wore a tweed suit, had gingerish fair hair, and a big ginger moustache. His ears stuck out, like, El thought, Prince Charles's. Nothing else about him was like Prince Charles. But it was the fifth that caught their attention, though he hung back behind the rest. He was tall, wore a dark baggy suit beneath a long lightweight black unbuttoned raincoat. His high forehead was streaked with the black thinning hair he had plastered across it; tinted glasses or shades sat beneath it and above prominent cheekbones.

'I think they want us to get out,' said El.

'Wait,' said Herbert. 'Make them make the first move.'

The big ginger-haired man with the moustache came up to the passenger door at Sheen's elbow, wrenched it open.

'*Raus.*'

It was half-way between a grunt and a shout. Sheen moved across to the other side and got out, thinking to himself: this guy has seen too many war films. Ginger, wrong-footed, lumbered round the back, caught Sheen's elbow. Sheen angrily shoved him off, and got a push in the shoulder that nearly had him on the floor.

'This lot are out of order,' Herbert murmured, 'way out of order.'

Wincing with the stab of pain from his arthritic hip, he almost bundled himself out of the driver's seat to get to Sheen's aid, but the others had seen the move and the three younger ones were in line between him and Sheen.

'Two of you I reckon I could handle,' he said, in English of course, 'but maybe not three.' He stayed where he was, with his hand resting on the wing of the Merc.

The tall man in the dark coat moved closer, stood in front of Harry. He looked at him, his cold eyes slightly narrowed behind the tinted glasses for a full twenty seconds, then he took a step closer and hit his face, backhand, forehand. Then he peeled off the single black glove he was wearing and put it in his pocket.

'Mr Sheen, you were ill-advised to attempt blackmailing me into paying more than the very generous offer I had made for your services. It has put our relationship on a different footing. The basis of mutual trust has gone. You will now do what I want because you are afraid of me.'

A touch scared, Sheen admitted to himself. But fucking angry too.

'Nevertheless. My original offer still stands, though you will have to work a little harder for the second and third payments.'

He turned, walked slowly towards the barn. Ginger gave Sheen's shoulder a gentler push, enough to make him follow.

'As you see, the situation has changed.' The tall thin man gestured towards the container. 'Not only have I had to move the cargo, it has also become necessary to abandon the sailing from Burghaven the day after tomorrow. However, you have two boats arriving at Emden on Monday fifth of April, one at midday, the other at three in the afternoon. You will instruct the master of the second boat not to dock at Emden but to proceed up the Ems estuary to Leer. This canal joins the Ems at Leer. You will arrange for the container to be shipped by barge to the Leer dock to arrive there shortly before your boat and you will arrange to have it shipped to the original destination, as arranged. Is that clear?'

'It's clear. But it's asking more than we might be able to achieve in time.'

The tall man turned abruptly, came back towards Sheen, passed him, spoke brusquely to the men who still faced Herbert by the car.

Eloise saw two of them peel away, head round the front of the car towards her door—she fumbled for the locking catch, but too late. She tried to anchor herself to the inner handle but the first was too strong for her: the wrench he gave half pulled her out and the second of them caught her upper arm, dragging her almost head first on to the rough concrete. Suddenly she felt outraged that this should be happening to her, outraged and incredulous, then the pain came as they bumped her shoulder into the side of the car, banged her head into the wheel-cap, and then hauled her upright by twisting her arms into her back. She screamed, kicked and even bit at them for a moment, but clearly they were trained in man, or woman-handling. Skilfully they hustled her over to the barn, turned her, slammed her backwards into the clapboard.

Inevitably Herbert made his move. He blocked the chop the third man aimed at his neck, smashed a heavy punch into his midriff and then backhanded his ear. Clutching his now sprained right hand he went for the other two but checked too late when he heard the slick click of switch-blade. The knife slashed the air in front of him, laid open his cheek with a three inch gash which instantly filled and spilled. He turned away, dropped to his knees, hauled his shirt out of his waistband and pushed the material into the wound. The man he had felled got up, kicked him in the head. The one with ginger hair gave just a glance at Harry Sheen, checking there was no fight in the older man, went over to Eloise.

She looked into his narrowed piggy eyes, saw a sly grin spread his lips, then his hand flashed backhanded across her cheek. In her head it was a percussion like a thunderclap, it was bright yellow flashes in her eyes, and then it was pain, and before she could duck or kick, back it came, forehand, backhand, forehand. She felt her knees give, she rolled to the side, but pulled herself into a huddle as she went down, arms over her head, and inside she pleaded silently that he would stop, she'd do anything if only he would stop hitting her.

And he did. But just as she was about to risk raising her arm enough to peep out she felt a short spurt of warm liquid play over her wrist: with a cry of disgust as well as fear she realised what it was, and she rolled away from it, but more fell on her neck. She caught the briefest glimpse of him shaking a fat uncircumcised penis over her, before shrugging enormously, and zipping it away. The grin was now huge.

The tall man turned to Sheen.

'Clearly we had not frightened you enough, but perhaps now you will realise just how dangerous we are. If anything goes wrong,' he continued, 'then Knut will find your young girl and demonstrate to her what else he can do with his prick. And maybe the others will take their turn. Meanwhile, there are one or two details I shall want you to observe. Are you listening?'

Herbert could not drive until his wound had been stitched and dressed. Sheen, his psychological as well as physical condition compromised by years of nicotine and alcohol abuse, not to mention the fact that he was pushing sixty-

five, was not in any state to drive either. So El drove in
spite of swelling bruises that threatened to close her eyes.
And as she drove, asserting control over their three lives
and thus re-establishing a psyche badly disturbed by
shock, fear and humiliation, the distress she felt modu-
lated quite quickly into rage.

She followed the signs to Burg's general hospital, found
it, parked, led Herbert who still clutched his now blood-
soaked shirt-front to his cheek into Casualty, then sat on
a black leatherette banquette in the waiting area. Presently, and unasked, a nurse or orderly who looked Indian
invited her into the privacy of a cubicle and gave her a
small bag of ice cubes to hold against her now savagely
aching face. Moved by this unsolicited kindness in a
world that had suddenly become as brutal as the media
would have you think it is, though on the whole you don't
believe them, she wept a little. But soon the anger burnt
up again.

Which was why, when Herbert emerged from the
casualty area half an hour later with thirty tiny black
stitches exposed beneath scarlet mercurochrome all down
one side of his face and wearing a striped hospital pyjama
top instead of his shirt, which was now wrapped in a
plastic bag, she was ready to assent when he said: 'We'll
make the buggers pay for this, our El. We'll make them
pay.'

'Sure we will.'

She followed as he trotted briskly, swinging his bad
leg, through the automatic doors and on to the tarmac of
a car-park street-lit now beneath a night sky. 'Herb, you
had your shooter. Why didn't you use it?

'There was four of them El. Clint Eastleigh could have
taken four out sharp-shooting with one shooter before
any of them got to him, but not me.'

'Clint Eastwood, Herb.'

'Him too. Anyway I still got it.'

'What?'

'Me shooter. I'd a lorst it, if I'd tried to use it. Gi' us the keys.'

'Are you sure you can drive?'

'Sure I'm sure. What's the matter with Harry?'

Sheen was slumped back in the corner of the rear passenger seat, head thrown back, mouth open. He looked frail as well as elderly, but he was all right. As Herbert opened the door for her, they heard him snore. He woke with a start as they got in, coughed, cleared his throat.

'OK then Herb?'

'Fine Harry. Right as rain.' He started the engine, let out the clutch. 'Hamburg then, is it? Pick up the signs for me El.'

Harry Sheen cleared his throat again.

'That should not have happened.'

Herbert glanced in the mirror at his boss.

'No.'

'We'll do what the bastards want, and then fuck off home. I'm well pissed off with Kraut-land. Should never have let that happen. Especially to a young girl like El.'

Herbert drove in silence for a minute or so, found the motorway spur.

'That's not quite how we see it, Harry. Is it El?'

'No way. And there's no call to be so fucking sexist, Harry. Herbert got hurt a lot worse than I did.

'He can take it.'

'I can take it, Herb. You better believe it.'

The big car rumbled on.

Harry Sheen cleared his throat.

'What we goin' to do then?'

'We'll think of something, El, won't we?' Herbert glanced across at her.

'I already did. Not the first exit, Herb. That takes you back to Burg. The second.'

'Got it, El.'

He began to hum, and diddle-diddle-diddle under his breath. It sounded like the Ride of the Valkyries, but then it shifted to the theme from Holst's Jupiter: *I-I vow to thee my cou-untree* ... Presently he glanced at Eloise again.

'What's this plan of yours then?'

'You know that bit in the paper this morning. Italian businessman murdered in his apartment, you know who he was don't you?'

'Mr Ice Cream Man?'

'Right. It said he had business troubles setting up a supermarket for performance cars on a disused racetrack. That's where he met us. And now here's the big one. He's the same guy made the papers on Sunday for getting his leg over the chief of the Eco-Police, the lady we saw at the hotel in Burg, then again in Hamburg.'

'So, she's bent. Mixed up in it with the rest.'

'I don't think so. Paper editorial hinted it was all a plot to get her to resign.'

'So what's the plan?'

'Well, I think we should arrange to meet her. Renata her name is. Nice name. Second name Fechter: that means Fighter. And I got something on offer.'

'What?'

'The number of that stretched Merc.'

'Look, El. This has got to be done good. It's got to stick. Any of them bastards still around when the dust settles, they'll come after us later. We'll need more muscle than we got...'

'Herbert, I've been thinking about that...'

'Listen.' Harry's voice from the back. She felt his hand on the back of her seat as he hoisted himself forward.

'Listen. Herbert's right. Nutters like that. The tall boss one in black, and the fucker that wee-ed on you, you don't mess with. You waste'm or you leave'm be. Believe me. I know. But muscle can be arranged.'

'Here in Hamburg?'

'Why not? Jace and Ash. What do you think?' Harry glanced at Herbert who said nothing, but drove on. The streetlighting as they went under each standard gleamed on the glossy threads of his stitches, so it looked as if a thin centipede was crawling down his cheek. The distorted colour of the lamps made the mercurochrome look like blood. Then he nodded.

'Yes Harry. Jace and Ash could do. They could do nicely.'

Hearts' Haven rest home for elderly people with mental problems was on the coast twenty kilometres beyond the Burghaven Reactor. After dealing with the more important things on her desk, including a fax, which demanded personal attention, from the Intercontinental in Hamburg, Renata announced that she would take in the reactor on the way and get a preliminary report from the Hesse Inspector. Becker again came along as minder, but when they got there she made him wait in the reactor's car-pound.

The Inspector, Franz Jäger, turned out to be a tall very lean dark-haired man in his mid-forties. His hair was wiry and unruly though cut short, there were deep lines in the pale skin of his cheeks, his eyes were dark and as watchful as a hawk's. Oddly they put Renata in mind of a certain sort of football player, the sort of striker who plays little part in the general run of the game but lurks mid-field in the opponent's half, ready to make a sudden tactical run into neglected space to receive the well-placed pass he can score from. Renata did not watch nor know much about football, but, under Aldo's enthusiastic guidance, had discovered aspects of the game that fascinated her. They had spent several Sunday afternoons watching the televised Italian League.

She met Jäger in an office which had been allocated to him on the first floor of the administrative building. Outside, a quarter of a kilometre away, she could see the slightly domed roof of the seventy metre cylindrical containment vessel which held the reactor, coolant pumps, pressurisers and the steam generator. It was a neat uncluttered structure in comparison with the sheds and hangars beyond which housed conventional generators, turbines, heat exchangers and chimneys, all knitted together with a macaroni-like web of giant pipes stitched with gantries. Presumably, she thought, the white vapour is not radioactive. Screens of tall, fast-growing poplars had been planted round the whole site. Now twenty years later, they were mature and as high as all but the largest of the structures.

'How much do you know about Pressurised Water Reactors?'

'Not a lot.'

He had placed her in an office swivel chair at a high glass-topped round table rather than at the desk he actually worked at. He sat in the quadrant next to her, and spread a large sheet of draughtsman's paper in front of her. On it there were three labelled diagrams with titles: *Schematic layout for a PWR*; *PWR pressure vessel and core*; *PWR fuel assembly*. They looked very complicated.

'These are, of course, very simplified,' he said. 'But you ought to have a general idea of what's going on if you're going to have any sort of understanding of what I'm going to tell you.'

He offered her a smile which was both shy and rueful: she sensed that he did not really expect her to understand what he was going to say. Then he unfolded bi-focals with heavy black frames and took a silver pencil from the inside pocket of the dark jacket which hung from the back of his chair.

'First, the overall system as it exists inside the containment vessel.' He prodded at the first diagram. 'This is the actual reactor containing the fuel core. This is the pressuriser, and this the steam generator, and this the coolant pump. All are linked by water pipes. The water, ordinary water, acts as a neutron reflector when it passes down the outside of the core, as a coolant as it goes back up through it, and finally it is the first step in the heat exchange process which powers the generators. It is a sealed system, there are no leaks, because the water that flows through becomes highly radioactive from the moment the process is initiated.

'We start with the pressuriser. This puts the water under pressure which means it can be heated to 315°C without boiling. It then passes through the reactor where the fission processes, which I shall return to in a moment, heat it to close on that temperature. It then passes into the steam generator where the tubes that carry it are in contact with tubes carrying a second stream of water. The heat from the pressurised water heats the second flow to steam, which is then fed off to drive conventional turbines to generate electricity. All right so far?'

She supposed so, and nodded. He turned to the second diagram. Its basic shape was that of a fattish cylinder, but the outside part cut away to reveal a horribly complicated interior. *PWR pressure vessel and core.*

'I'm not going to explain everything to you, just the simplest basics. The lower half, beneath the inlet and outlet nozzles, is filled with fuel assemblies, which I will explain to you in more detail in a moment. For now it is enough to know that they are clusters of fuel rods containing uranium pellets, part enriched. This is an unstable radioactive substance which emits radiation. When large amounts are close together, in a critical mass, the speed at which radiation takes place is enormously speeded up, a chain reaction sets in, fission processes take place and produce thermal energy which produces the heat that brings the pressurised water up to 315°C.

The fission process is controlled by control pins made of a
neutron-absorbing substance, in this case boron steel.
When the control pins are lowered into the fuel rod
clusters the fission process ceases because the mass is
thus rendered no longer critical. As they are withdrawn
it restarts. All clear?'

'Not really. I don't understand what radioactivity is, or
radiation or neutrons. But I think I've grasped the
mechanics.'

'Really, for present purposes, that'll do. Moving
upwards the top half of the vessel holds the control rods
when they are withdrawn, the very complex machinery
that raises and lowers them, and several systems working independently and together to make the whole thing
as safe as possible.'

'As safe as possible.' She phrased it flatly, not a question but a doubt. He understood.

'No such man-made system can ever be completely
reliable. However, the belief is that the effects of any
malfunction can be limited to acceptable levels of safety
by incorporating several complementary systems, with
back-ups and so on. It is presumed that a serious incident
is not possible because it would involve an almost impos-
sibly unlikely conjunction of random malfunctions occurring at the same time.'

'Is there any particular sort of way in which things
could go wrong that I am likely to be able to understand?'

'I think so. Since TMI2 in 1979 . . .'

'I beg your pardon.'

'Three Mile Island, Unit Two . . . when several feed-
water pumps failed the water coolant produced hydrogen
which exploded. The reactor got within sixty minutes of
melt-down which only failed to occur through what the
inspectors later called 'dumb luck'. But lessons were
learnt. Since then the chances of anything of the sort

occurring during normal running really are acceptably low, assuming there is no major outside intervention like a bomb attack or being hit by a low-flying aircraft, or whatever.'

She spotted the emphasis. *During normal running.*

'But if things are not running normally?'

The pencil stabbed at the third diagram: *PWR fuel assembly.*

'Or not running at all.'

'I don't follow that.'

'There are one hundred and ninety-three fuel assemblies inside the reactor. As you see each unit is a rectangular cuboid frame, and if we refer back to the second diagram you will see that they are stacked throughout the lower part of the pressure vessel. Each assembly contains two hundred and eighty-nine fuel rods placed on a seventeen by seventeen grid, and into each a cluster of sixty-five control rods can be inserted, spaced strategically across the grid. Each separate fuel rod is filled with pellets of uranium oxide enriched to a few per cent U-235 and cased in zirconium cladding. The full capacity of the reactor is over three and a quarter thousand fuel pins giving a total weight of ninety tons of uranium.'

'I had no idea so much uranium was in use in one place at one time.'

'No. Most people don't. Of course the tonnage is minuscule compared with the amount of coal or oil that is needed to generate the same amount of electricity, but then . . .'

'Coal and even oil are more or less stable substances and not in themselves dangerous.'

'The nuclear industry would argue that all sources of thermal energy are dangerous if mishandled. And that includes oil spills in the sea and acid rain. Right now that is not the sort of discussion we want to get into.'

'No. Go on.'

'As the fissile process continues the nature of the fuel changes and eventually the rods become what the industry calls 'spent fuel', which implies it is used up, inert, like ash from coal or exhaust gases from oil. This is not in fact the case. What actually happens is that as the process continues the composition of the reactor fuel grows increasingly complex and it becomes increasingly difficult to keep track of all the competing processes taking place. Fission products occur. Some are gases like krypton and xenon which exert pressure and try to break out. The intense neutron flux can damage the crystal structure of the fuel, the cladding, even whatever is used in the control rods. Sooner or later it is necessary to take out the 'used' fuel, and replace it. And in a PWR that means shutting down the whole process. Are you with me?'

She thought back desperately, trying to recall what he had said before. A sudden awareness of her own ineptness in an area like this flooded over her and she began to feel as if she were breathing and thinking through cotton wool.

He prompted her: 'If things are running normally, it is now generally accepted, and this is something that I, as a professionally trained devil's advocate accept, the risks of serious malfunction, serious that is to the environment in the widest sense, are acceptable.'

'Yes. I remember. If things are not running normally then all these fail-safe systems will take care of what is wrong. But when it is not running at all, in other words during refuelling, when the whole process is shut down, then what . . .?'

Jäger suddenly stood up, loped to and fro across the big window. Renata recalled this time, not a striker in a football game, but a caged wolf in a zoo. He came back not to his chair, but to the point on the circumference of the table exactly opposite her. He put his palms flat on the table and, substantial though the table was, she felt the surface beneath her forearms respond to the pressure.

'I was sent here, at your request, to examine the log, to see if there was any evidence in it that the sort of incident that might have produced unscheduled high level waste had occurred. It is actually quite a speedy process, as several months of normal activity can be checked both on the computer itself and on the relevant printouts quite quickly. It is speedy simply because an anomaly, a blip, an unexpected event would stand out like a, like a banana in a coalbucket. And there was none. There were a couple of clusters of slightly variant readings back in January which would need very close analysis to explain, but on the other hand one would be suspicious if there were no minor blips at all. Under normal circumstances I would not worry too much about them.'

'But the circumstances were not normal?'

'They are not normal for two reasons. One, they are not normal because the highest authority in this Region has called me in to look at the log. But there is another reason. At the beginning of February the annual shutdown commenced, the shutdown when one third of the fuel assemblies are replaced. Now during that time the log which I have been examining is also shut down and other recording procedures are run instead which I have not yet been given access to. But already two factors present themselves.'

'Yes?'

'One. The shutdown was started six days ahead of normal schedule. Two. Instead of the routine seventeen days the whole process should take it took twenty-five bringing us almost to the end of February. Management warned me that this was the case almost as soon as I entered the perimeter.'

'And?'

'I was told that the early start was necessary because one of their most experienced operatives was ill, cancer of course, and not likely to return to work for several months if ever, and a second had unexpectedly taken early retirement at Christmas. This meant that the whole operation had to be carried out with at the top men with little experience of leadership, and at the bottom men whose experience did not go beyond theoretical training under simulated conditions. Since the team is quite small anyway, this is important. Aware of all this, management put forward the time of commencement and allowed the extra days.'

'Is all this feasible?'

'Perfectly.'

'So?' She felt a second wave of despair flood through her veins.

'All I am saying so far is this: that if an incident occurred which some judged should be hushed up, an incident which produced high level waste beyond what one would normally expect, then this is the area, the time-span we should be looking at.'

'Then that's where you'll be concentrating.'

He pulled out the chair he was leaning over and settled into it, made an arch of his forearms, rested his chin on his knuckles.

'It's not as easy as that.'

It wouldn't be, she thought to herself.

'The whole business of refuelling is very, very complex and potentially very, very dangerous. First of all you have to be sure that the shutdown is complete, that all the control rods have carried out their function. Then the core has to be cooled, the radioactive water pumped out into cooling tanks and more coolants run through the system which also have to be handled carefully. Then the vessel is drained and the lid is taken off, and with it the mechanisms that manipulate the control rods which are now safely inserted among the fuel rods. A long series of complicated operations follow, most automated but not all. This process rarely follows a completely predictable pattern and this means that the records of what happens are complex, humanly adjustable, and conceivably deceptive unintentionally as well as intentionally. To analyse them would require a full commission of enquiry, very expensive and you won't get it unless or until . . .'

'Unless or until?'

'You find unscheduled, unexplained high level waste that can be shown to have emanated from this plant.'

'Catch 22.'

'I'd say so.'

He swung round the table, clicked back the point of his silver pencil, and rolled up his diagram.

'Sorry,' he said. She wasn't sure whether or not he meant it, guessed he could have conflicting views on the matter. And she wasn't sure either whether she was glad or not that the fax from the Hamburg Intercontinental had led to a phone call from which she had gathered that the Sheens believed they knew where the missing high level waste could be found.

CHAPTER 31

Becker waited until she was out of sight, then shifted over into the driver's seat, found his knees were jammed against the bottom edge of the dash, slipped the seat back half a metre and spread himself. His eye wandered briskly over the controls: to his prejudiced eye they looked somehow flash and insubstantial, not like those of the large solid BMWs the senior officers of all the other forces drove. He turned the key she'd left in the ignition, fooled about with buttons for a moment or two like a kid with a new toy until he had the window where he wanted it, the radio playing the sort of accordion-with-brass beer garden music he liked, and propped on the steering wheel a pocket format photo-strip magazine with strong porn 'n' violence content.

Presently, he sensed rather than saw the arrival of Pieter Roth: caught a flicker in the wing mirror, heard above the muzak the tap of leather on tarmac, smelled the sour stale odour of the man. He dabbed a button, released the lock on the front passenger door and the ex-narc, thin, grey, with a heavy jaw, slipped in beside him.

Roth, ignored, drummed fingers on his knees, twitched, ran a finger round his shirt collar, caught the middle of it between thumb and finger, lifted it.

'Funny,' he muttered, 'these changes in weather. Seasonal I know, but who would have thought it would be as warm as this, as this. I mean yesterday it was quite brisk. The breeze off the sea.' He paused. 'Nice music.'

Becker turned a page, but the way the corner of his

heavy mouth stretched a little showed he was enjoying the torment.

'You did bring it, did you? I mean you've got it with you?' Roth's agitation made him rock on his buttocks.

Becker's grin spread a little. He folded the magazine away into the side pocket of his suit jacket, then his big hand delved into his inside breast pocket. He pulled out a tiny flat heat-sealed plastic bag of white powder, let it rest in his left palm.

'Shit. Is that all?'

'Come on! Fifty grams? You know better than I do what that costs on the street.'

But already Roth was calmer. Moses on the mountain, looking over Cana, probably felt no hurry to get down, once he'd seen the Land of Milk and Honey. An alcoholic is content to take his turn at the counter, once he's in.

'Where's it from?'

'Colombia, I believe.'

'Oh shit! I don't want coke!'

'Oh boy, are you out of touch. The Colombians are diversifying. They can actually grow the poppy in their own country whereas they have to import coca-base.'

'Is it any good?'

Becker picked the sachet from his palm by one corner between his right thumb and forefinger, swung it in front of Roth's nose and let it drop into his lap where anxious fingers were waiting to catch it.

'Try.'

Roth's fingers now moved with surgical precision, tore a tiny triangle from a corner of the sachet, made a fist of his other hand with the thumb on top, tipped a few grains into the hollow above the bottom joint of his thumb, slowly hefted it to his nose and sniffed. He shuddered.

'Not good then?' Becker asked.

'Don't know yet. Wait for the hit. But it's bitter, and that's a good sign.'

The muzak played on and presently the ex-narc smiled, leant back and relaxed. 'It's OK. It works.'

He delved in his pockets, found a small roll of sticky tape, put the sachet on the top of the dash. Then, working methodically with steady fingers, he tore off a half centimetre of tape, sealed the corner he had opened, tucked the sachet in his top pocket, patted it.

Becker put his hands on the lower rim of the steering wheel where they fidgeted for a moment.

'Right. So what's happening here? What have you found out?'

Roth now spoke slowly, rationally, professionally.

'There's a very nervy atmosphere among the ordinary workers, guards, cleaners, the ladies in the canteen and so on.'

'Yes?'

Becker split a match, used it to excavate from between two molars the meat that had been bothering him since breakfast. It was something you didn't feel you could do in front of a woman who happened also to be your boss. Roth went on.

'Something happened, they don't know what of course, back in February during the annual shutdown. It's impossible to get details: no alarms went off, no evacuation, nothing dramatic. But some unusual decontamination procedures were implemented and a helicopter ambulance shipped someone out. They don't know who but a senior technician everyone liked hasn't been inside the compound since. That's about it really. The rest is just rumour. The union convenor went to management, said that the work force felt under-informed, and therefore probably exaggerated amongst themselves the significance of what had happened. Everyone would feel much happier if they actually knew, actually knew what happened.'

'And they told him it was nothing serious, and there was no way ordinary folk would understand anyway.'

'Yes.'

'I expect they're right. They know what they're doing.'

Silence lengthened between them, then Roth shifted uneasily.

'That's not the attitude you had at Radwasthaus. You were keen enough to get to the truth about that container, and the relevant documentation.'

'Just doing my job.'

'Yeah. Well, that's what I'm doing here.' He opened his door, swung his legs out. 'Ciao. Thanks for the gear.'

He tapped his pocket again and walked back to the admin building.

The land became flatter, poorer, much of it fen or heath, broken only with occasional stands of poplar, and market gardens— many with glasshouses smashed. Year round salads grown under plastic in Spain and Holland had ruined the local industry years ago. The sky, however, was brighter, lighter as they approached the sea. Presently Renata used her right hand to scoop up a pair of smart but unassertive shades from the shelf between her and the windscreen, slipped them on. Although the sun was behind them the reflected glare and the sea light were intense.

'Did Roth have anything to report?'

'About the plant? No. Nothing.'

She glanced at him, almost without moving her head. Becker had his head turned slightly away, his right elbow on his left forearm, chewing the nail of his right thumb. There was a bead of sweat on his left temple.

'Are you too hot? I'll open your window if you like.'

'I'm fine.'

Nevertheless she turned up the airconditioned cool flow a notch, fished a tissue from under the dash, dried one palm and then the other.

Stunted pines, a sand-dune some ten metres or so high covered in coarse squeaky grass and sea-kale not yet in flower, a gap in the dune and the sea beyond, sparkling white wave crests racing in above water deep blue and steel grey. She drove the Toyota through the gap and on to a short promenade of small hotels, cafés, beach shops, most still boarded up and empty. The resort had been developed in the late thirties and most of the architecture was from that period. For brief decades both before and after the war it had flourished but then the combination of a sea polluted by the rivers that flowed into the bay and the opening up of the Mediterranean virtually killed it. But if the water was no longer as healthy as it looked, the air seemed fine and two or three of the hotels had converted to Homes for the Elderly, the Insane, and the Terminally Ill.

Renata's father qualified under all three headings and was spending his final days in the care of the doctors and nurses of Hearts' Haven. It was the largest and most expensive establishment and used exclusively by men and women who had reached the top of their professions before age and illness had reduced them to the wrecks they now were.

Renata directed Becker to a windswept car-park to the side. Swinging her legs out she realised he was about to get out too, on the other side.

'Wait here,' she said.

They faced each other across the car roof. The big man buttoned up his jacket, straightened his tie, wiped his big moustache on the back of his hand.

'I'm your bodyguard, I come in with you.'

'You didn't back at the reactor.'

'You wanted me to see Roth, and anyway there was not much chance of anyone attacking you there. But this is a public place and a lot of people know you come here, are here today.'

'Andreas, I don't want you with me. You'll upset my father.'

'Look.' He waved his arm up at the dune that lay behind the ex-Hotel. 'Even now a sniper could have picked you off from up there.'

'Then I had better get indoors. And you had better get back in that car.'

She turned on her heels, walked away briskly, making her straight tall back a statement: I'll bust you if you try to follow me. He watched for a moment, frowned, bit his lip, shrugged and at last, as she turned the corner, got back into the car.

The main building was large, thirties functional, and dull: uniform smooth pale grey stucco, streaked beneath the windows, covered the whole façade. The windows themselves were broader than they were tall and framed in painted metal: the paint had flaked almost as soon as it was on. An attempt had been made to soften one semicircular wing with virginia creeper, but at that time of year it looked tired and ill. The daffodils in the beds were almost over, they looked like used yellow paper handkerchiefs; the wallflowers and tulips were still in bud. North facing seasides in these latitudes are not kind to plants.

The interior was much better. A big entrance hall floored with an orangy parquet, highly polished, silvery-grey walls with big paintings of tropical flowers, and ferns flanking the bottom of a long sweeping staircase with chrome rails did indeed recall the luxury hotel it had been forty years earlier.

Dr Liszt, the senior doctor and senior partner, was waiting for her by the reception desk. He was tall, had a mane of silver hair, wore a perfect light-grey suit that set off the golden brown of his tan. He exuded professional bonhomie, an air of studied calm, made you feel that it would be a pleasure to die under his care. When she first met him Renata's reaction had been one of revulsion, but over three years she had come to feel that faced with the horror of Alzheimer's and/or Parkinson's one could do a lot worse.

They shook hands, and Dr Liszt indicated that she should go up the stairs ahead of him.

'How is he?' she asked.

'Fine. I understand he's sitting in his wardrobe with a very important client and does not want to be disturbed. He can't understand why you want to see him unless it's to borrow money. After all it was only yesterday that you were here last.'

Renata felt a wave of irritation. She was no longer fond of the man who had deserted her and her mother just as she was about to go to university.

'Maybe I shan't bother then.'

'Up to you.' They were now at the top of the stairs. Dr Liszt indicated they should head off to the right. 'I've put the lady in number twelve. It's empty at the moment.'

He opened the door for her, discreetly closed it behind her.

Renata had the briefest impression of a light-filled room, furnished in shades of cream and beige, and empty of any personal belongings or even touches. Then the woman, girl really, who was sitting at the dressing-table near the window, stood and turned. Renata recognised her. She was tall, had brown hair, fashionably short and stepped, wore a baggy woollen mottled grey top over the briefest of skirts and black woollen tights. Her face was dreadfully bruised and she had two puffy black eyes, the colour of a thunder-filled sunset.

Renata could not restrain a sort of half cry, half commiserating laugh.

'Oh dear,' she said. 'Who did that to you?'

''That,' said Eloise Harman, with grim determination, 'is just one of the things I hope we'll be able to work out together.'

They shook hands—Renata found Eloise's palm unacceptably moist, but by and large she felt ready to listen to her.

CHAPTER 32

Most of the vehicles, and there were many of them, including official limos, a dark green and very utilitarian bus, a couple of small armoured cars, and an empty container trailer, remained parked against the stand of poplars. Their green leaf shoots, almost fully out of their chestnut-coloured casings, glowed bright emerald in the morning light. A Mercedes water cannon, which had possibly not been used since the demonstrations against PWRs twenty years earlier, and was now deployed to provide instant decontamination, trundled to the front of the small procession which was forming up on the rough track in the shadows cast by the trees. Slowly it all began to move in due order round the corner and on to the quay towards the clapboard barn and the cube container tucked away in its lee.

There were even a couple of launches from the harbour police on the upper and lower reaches of the canal.

There was something almost mediaeval about the scene, the mixture of costumes, the strict order of precedence compromised by considerations of safety. At the front, behind the water cannon, Franz Jäger led three colleagues clad like champions in armour in cumbersome white and silver suits with perspex visors. Then came technicians, also protectively clothed but not so thoroughly: men from Radwasthaus (though not from the Burg branch), the nuclear safety commissions and so on, equipped with warning discs, radiation meters and other tools of their trades. Then, at a discreet distance, came the nobs: Secretary Drenkmann with aides; Fechter with, as always, Becker in attendance; and a small, worried man who was the Acting Director of the Burghaven Reactor—the Director was attending a conference in Stockholm; and finally, deployed in skirmishing order, a section of Federal Frontier Guards, paramilitaries in green uniforms with walkie-talkies and sub-machine guns. Above them a helicopter rattled along in slow sweeps checking visually and by radio with the road-blocks that had been set up behind them.

'If,' Drenkmann murmured to Renata, 'this turns out to be what you think it is, then presumably my niece can come back from Corfu. If it doesn't, you'll be looking for another job.'

They were turning the corner of the poplars and Renata involuntarily threw up her arm against the still almost horizontal sun whose beams flooded uninterrupted across the fen, bounced back from the surface of the canal.

'I think she should wait,' she said, 'until it's all wrapped up. She'll be needed as a witness, and we want to be sure anyone who might want to get to her is locked up before she reappears.'

Drenkmann frowned.

'That's impossible,' he grated. 'And you know it. I can't lock up the entire nuclear industry.' He stopped. 'That's it then.'

'That's it.'

They were still two hundred metres away, still on the track with the quay ahead and the canal gleaming to their right. The three-metre cube was hard to make out against the black of the barn, and the harsh glare of the sun which was almost above it.

'Doesn't look much, does it?'

'But I don't think they want us to go any further.'

The water cannon had stopped. The four men in front,

the ones most comprehensively protected, went beyond it, took readings from the meters attached to their suits, consulted with each other. Presently one of the lesser technicians in white overalls walked back almost to where the main party had come to a standstill. He produced a spool of red and white plastic tape from a webbing bag slung over his shoulder and ran it from one of the last of the poplars to an old grey mooring post. The slight breeze was enough to make it flutter prettily. The Acting Director looked even more miserable.

While all this was happening a new vehicle arrived in the area behind them. Becker looked over his shoulder, saw that it was a Ministry Opel. His mouth clamped into a rictus of doubt, even fear, as he identified the two men who got out but remained standing by the car. He touched Renata's elbow, cleared his throat.

'Meier and Arslan are here,' he murmured.

'I know.'

She did not turn.

'But they're under suspension.'

'Not any longer.'

Something buzzed and one of Secretary Drenkmann's aides handed him a mobile phone. Drenkmann turned the volume up, held it so Renata could also hear Jäger's voice as the four men in their space-age suits lumbered on towards the container.

'The readings we have already taken suggest there is highly radioactive material in the container. We are now going to proceed towards the container with the purpose of opening it.' The voice was dry with a forced refusal to become emotional. 'Since the opening faces across the canal and the door itself opens in your direction, there should not be any appreciable increase in danger to you provided you remain where you are. If there is you will be notified and asked to return to your vehicles.'

Drenkmann handed the phone to Renata. His big hands pushed into the wide pockets of his jacket and came up with pipe and pouch. It occurred to Renata that she was more likely to get cancer from the fumes that swirled round them than from any gamma rays that might be coming their way. Jäger's voice continued.

'We are now peeling off the tape that was used to mask the labelling on the container and the locks. My colleague from Radwasthaus Dortmund has confirmed to me that this is a Radwasthaus container. The serial number is upper case B, lower case h, 930312, upper case K...'

Through his smokescreen Drenkmann's unkempt eyebrows signalled a question to Renata but before she could give the answer Jäger had provided it.

'... my colleague confirms that this corresponds with the number of the container their employee Huber questioned at the Burgdorf plant. We can now feel certain that this is that container. My colleague is now releasing the locks: one electronic lock and two manual.'

Across the space that separated them Renata could hear a high squeak and then see first of all a steel beam swung clear, then the door itself swung out to face them. Then two of the four figures rounded it so the door concealed them.

They heard on the phone the inrush of breath, but almost a minute elapsed before Jäger spoke again.

'I am looking at four fuel assemblies of the sort used in Pressurised Water Reactors. The fuel rods are clearly spent, indeed from their condition, that is there is marked swelling, they are discoloured, I can already detect with the naked eye cracks in the cladding which is covered with crud, from all this I would guess, and at this stage it is only a guess, they should have been changed during last year's refuelling or even that of the year before. In short they are very severely corroded. This corrosion has spread to the control rods and the control rod assembly including in the one I am looking at, the hold-down spring. One effect of all this could be that withdrawal of these fuel assemblies, which is normally fully automated, jammed. If that was the case then withdrawal would have had to be carried out manually under conditions of heat, possibly approaching boiling point, and toxicity. One moment please. There is something else . . .'

The silence lengthened, but broken by sounds of heavy breathing, and the sort of clanks and thuds one might associate with the manual movement of heavy metal structures. Incongruously Renata was put in mind of the iron-pumping room in the Ministry gymnasium. Then the voice again, and this time the hysteria was audible.

'Right. Behind the fuel assemblies we have found two suits of the sort we are wearing. Only one of them appears to have a body inside it . . .'

A new sound, nearer and nastier than any they had yet heard. The Acting Director of the Burghaven Reactor was vomiting up what must have been an unhealthily large breakfast. Drenkmann's big, black-shod feet almost twinkled in their effort to get out of the way.

Becker turned on his heel, pushed his way through the men who were behind them, almost ran back up the track towards the Toyota. At first Renata was not aware that he had gone: when she was she broke through behind him, but was still way behind him when he got to the car. He pulled open the driver's door, reached for the phone, punched in numbers, straightened. Firat Arslan supported by Meier faced him.

'Becker, give Meier that phone. Good. Now I want you to understand that I have a warrant here for your arrest and the first thing I must ask you to do is hand over your police issue hand-gun.'

Becker looked from one to the other and then at Renata

who had now joined them to make a semicircle closing him in with his back to the car. His heavy broad face crumpled, he lifted it to the sky and squeezed out a short sigh. Then his right hand went to his left armpit, while his left hand pushed back his jacket to reveal the Walther P5 in its sprung holster. So far the movements were slow, but as the gun jumped into his hand he moved with the speed of a snake-strike. His left thumb released the safety catch, the right pulled back the hammer. Arslan leapt forward, got a grip on the big man's right arm. It was not enough to stop him. He still managed to get the muzzle into his mouth. Squeezing the trigger was not a problem.

When the mess had been cleared up, and Renata had recovered from a fit of shaking and gasping that had almost overwhelmed her until one of Drenkmann's aides arrived with a hip-flask of brandy from the Secretary's inside pocket, Meier gave her the phone Becker had handed to him. With hands still not completely under control she pressed redial, and heard once more the already over-familiar tones:

'This is the private residence of Hans Roehl. Please wait for the beep and then leave your name, number and reason for calling.'

CHAPTER 33

'For how long have you known Becker was the spy?'

'It seems like for ever, but actually it was Tuesday morning, the day before yesterday. Naturally I'd hardly slept at all, but eventually I did. And when I woke up it was clear to me. I should have got there ... at least twelve hours earlier. Oh God, I'm tired.'

Partly it was the warmth of the big official car as it cruised down side-roads towards the motorway that would take them back to Burg. But its smells, its whole mobile ambience too: Secretary Drenkmann had been using this car for seven years—the leather had been cured for a second time in rich pipe smoke with more than a hint of the marvellous cognac he had made her drink when she found the shaking would not stop. It was as if she were being driven in the lounge of an expensive all-male club, or the waiting room of a very classy brothel. He had insisted that there was no question of her driving the Toyota, and added that he needed to speak to her privately. She had looked at Meier—he was the senior of her two staff there—and, refusing to compromise, had been blunt.

'Are you drunk?'

'No.'

'Have you been drinking?'

'No.'

She had tossed him the keys and he had caught them neatly.

*

'How did you know, what was the clue?' The voice beside her now rumbled on.

She sighed, rubbed the balls of her thumbs in tired eyes. It was an effort to think back, to remember.

'I think,' she said at last, 'you came under pressure to take me off the case because I had guessed that the Sheens were being used to get the container out of the Region. Because of that I asked for lists of all the Sheen sailings, and Becker told them that I had. But then, the next day, on your instructions I closed the case, before I went to Italy, and told them to get back to routine work. But then I asked for a manifest of the MV *Eloise*'s cargo to be on my desk by midday on the day she sailed, and that alerted the spy to the fact that while they were off the case I was not.'

'But they were all still there?'

'No. Only Becker. The others had gone. That's what I should have remembered earlier than I did. If I had I might have saved Aldo ... and lots of other things would have worked out better.' She choked on tiredness and grief, but went on. 'So when all the business of getting the fact I was having an affair with an environmentally incorrect businessman into the tabloids went ahead, through to framing me for the murder of Aldo, it was plain that they knew I was not about to let go after all. And only Becker had known that, had been able to tell them that.'

'But you made him your bodyguard ... Ah, I see why. That way you had him always beside you, you knew what he was up to, you could use him to feed disinformation to the other side, and so on. Very clever. Very, very clever.'

This made her feel absurdly warm. She was no fool, had read the books, understood herself quite well. What she was getting was praise from Daddy and that was something which had always been in short supply when she had needed it from her real father.

'Becker was good too. He maintained his cover extraordinarily well.'

The enormous eyebrows next to her lifted—at least a centimetre.

'Really?'

'Oh yes. He went about his duties with complete professionalism, even to the point of identifying Knut Haussner. The way he saw it, the way perhaps his Control saw it, was that that way we'd never suspect him. It would have to be up to them to clear up any damage he had done them. At least they'd know where they were.'

Drenkmann thought about it, nodded with satisfaction: he appreciated the symmetry, what, had it all been a challenging puzzle or even a detective novel, he would have called its intellectual elegance. When Drenkmann felt pleased he felt for his pipe. Renata knew it, and contrived by facial expression and body language to make him pull his big hands back out of his pockets and on to his knees.

'But why? What did he want? What was he after? Money?'

'No. He just wanted to be back on the Vice Squad. He actually said as much to me.'

'Ah.' The rich voice was suddenly benevolent, as understanding of human frailty as Jove. 'The perks. Free meals. Free booze. The backhanders. Even, should he have been so inclined, free pokes.'

Renata was startled. Was this the limit of Drenkmann's own ambition? No, of course not.

'Not at all. Like you, he wanted to be in charge. Rulers of the Universe. He had his Universe, you have yours. He had been deprived of his and he wanted it back. He was no mean copper there either. He did a good job. Bent a few rules, knocked evil guys about a bit more than he should have done, but he kept the patch tidy. If I'd understood that a bit better, and actually worked towards getting him back there, then probably he would have stayed straight. Probably.'

Drenkmann brooded for a moment: possibly over the interdiction on pipe-smoking.

'And your suspension of Meier, King and Arslan was a blind?'

'Yes. Dr Sonnenberg dreamt that up. They've been working away at it all on the quiet. And since Becker was always with me, the opposition never knew.'

'The opposition. Who are they?'

'Well, Hans Roehl for a start . . .'

'He nearly had you closed down, you know. On Tuesday. Tuesday evening Supreme Public Prosecutor Schreider asked to see me at home. He said that Roehl had just about enough evidence to justify charging you with the murder of Aldo Nerone and, privately, off the record, he wanted to know what I thought about it. It was a tricky decision to have to make. Especially since that arch-harridan Ms Geller was gunning for you too. If the murder weapon had been there and they had been able to tie it to you I would have had to concede. As it was they knew your police issue pistol was not where it should be, not in your desk . . .'

'Becker again?'

'I suppose so. And they knew that the bullet that killed Nerone was fired from that gun or one very similar. It really was not an easy decision.'

'You can't have really thought I would shoot Aldo.'

'Why not? They knew you had been there. There was evidence, substantial evidence of a fight . . .'

She recalled with a shudder how she hurled her brandy glass at Aldo when he had bracketed her with earlier mistresses, just another girlfriend approved by his crippled wife.

'And the missing gun was a poser. You see, I argued to myself that if they were trying to frame you they would have left the gun, your gun there to be found. Or they would have returned it to your desk so they could then impound it and do forensic tests to show it was the gun that killed Aldo. But the fact that it had disappeared rather implied that it was not a frame-up . . .'

Renata felt herself go cold: these were lines of argument that had not occurred to her when she threw the pistol into the Weser.

'So why did you ask Supreme Public Prosecutor Schreider to hold back?'

'Because you sent Andromed to me. Once I knew that there really was a missing container and where it had been hidden at least for a time, I felt you were on the right track. And if you were, then they'd go to considerable lengths to stop you. I took a chance. I was right. I suppose. Unless you did kill Aldo?'

His throaty laugh expressed unease.

'No. They killed him. But I came back, took the gun and threw it in the river. They don't know that I did that.'

She looked out of the window. They were on the autobahn now, approaching Oldenburg. They would soon be back at Burg and she felt a tremor of angst at the thought. This enclosed, sheltered journey in the big warm car was a sort of time out of war she needed, but she needed it to be longer than it was going to be.

'Roehl, then. Who else?'

She was confused for a moment, had forgotten what his original question had been.

'The opposition? An ex-Vice cop called Haussner who works for Radwasthaus and almost certainly killed

Huber. Three thugs, Ossis, ex-STASI, who killed
Vesper . . .'

Drenkmann showed impatience.

'At the top. Who's organising it?'

'It seems it's a man called Wolfgang Kurtz, also known
as Heinrich Herz. We traced him through the Mercedes
he's hired from Euro-Car. Same source as led us to the
container gave us the car number. He's been at the
Ramada for the last two weeks, and he's been visited
there by Roehl. If he is Herz, then he owns and largely
runs a firm called Alterlog with an office in Zürich. As far
as we can gather from Interpol Alterlog specialises in
clearing up difficulties for big corporations when the
difficulties can only be solved by serious law-breaking.
Including, apparently, murder. The problem though is
that since he never seems to work inside Switzerland, the
Swiss police won't cooperate in investigating him.'

'And who is paying him?'

'I have no idea.'

The big car purred on inexorably. BURG 50kms. Drenkmann was silent for a time and when he did speak his
voice was quiet, almost meditative, saying things that
were the result of experience and rumination.

'The trouble with nuclear energy,' he rumbled, 'is not
the processes themselves, the dangers they inevitably
entail, the problems of waste and so on. What's wrong
about it is that it is run by human beings for profit,
status, high salaries and so on. No one in the industry is
there out of a high-minded desire to produce cheap, clean
electricity. It's not human error I am talking about, it's
human greed, human fear of loss of income and status,
that sort of thing . . . When we give the military guns and
bombs the circumstances under which they may use them
are carefully circumscribed by democratically elected
politicians and their civil servants. But we hand these

terribly dangerous systems over to businessmen and
technicians and we say "make them work—or else". Or
else you will be sacked, or else you will make no profits.
So if something goes wrong they do not cheerfully own
up; if something turns out to be more expensive than
they expected they do not concede that they cannot after
all fulfil a contract within the financial parameters that
had been set. They conceal, they do things on the cheap.
And accidents happen and they try to pretend they have
not happened. "Or else!"'

He paused at last, put his big hand on her knee. It was
a gesture filled with unlikeable content, for she did not
feel he would have made it if she were a man—though in
fact he would have done. Nevertheless she accepted the
sympathy, albeit paternal and, possibly, sexist, that lay
behind it.

'Renata,' he continued, 'I want to know who is paying
this Herz or Kurtz. Can you find out?'

'I think so. I have a plan.'

'You know you must do it on your own. Rounding them
up is a matter for Serious Crime and DUK. And since
Serious Crime is so heavily compromised . . .'

'I understand. We go it alone . . .'

In spite of the warmth of the sealed car, she shivered.

CHAPTER 34

A knock on the door. El opened it. On the threshold in the hotel corridor two men. Both were lean, had a hunky well-trained toughness about them that their loose windbreakers could not conceal. Their dark hair was cut very short with widow's peaks, their teeth even and white, their complexions tanned by wind and cold as well as sun. They were, clearly, twins. Both carried black instrument cases—big enough to hold dismantled soprano saxophones.

'Uncle Harry here then? He's expecting us.'

'You must be Jason and Ashley.'

'Jace. And Ash. Can we come in?'

'Of course. I'm Eloise. El.'

She was suddenly conscious of the mess her face still was.

'Nice to meet you El. Shame about the boat. Don't worry though, we'll sort the fuckers out for you.'

They spoke in turn, with scarcely a breath between them and with intonations precisely identical, as though only one of them was speaking.

'Boys, it's good to see you, glad you could make it.'

'No problem, Harry. Family's family, innit?'

'How's business, then?'

'Busy, Harry, but not so we have to be in the shop every minute of the day. Or night.'

Sheen turned to El.

'They're good lads these two. Got discharged for breaking up a class joint just off the Reeperbahn. So they borrowed some pelf off of me and bought the place. Best investment I ever made. Herbert, the honours please.'

'What sort of joint?' El asked while Herbert busied himself with Johnnie Walker Black Label.

'Usual fing. Bum and tit show for starters. A Lezzie act. Hostesses . . .'

They settled into the armchairs with scotch in their glasses. Presently Jason, or Ashley, opened his instrument case and pulled out the three components of a small machine pistol which he began to wipe over with a cloth, squinting down at them, and every now and then buffing up a spot which was to his critical eye less than perfectly clean.

He grinned up at El.

'Burp gun really.'

'More like a fart gun,' said the other. 'Lotta noise but not much lethal over fifty yards.'

'Puts the frighteners on, though. Poli use'm. In fact these are police issue—like they went missing.'

Sheen intervened again.

'Boys, how long can you give me?'

'As long as it takes, Uncle. As long as it takes.'

He sighed, bit his lip, nodded at fat Pratchard.

'Right, Sam. Let's go for it.'

Sam hauled himself out of his chair, stood by the repro eighteenth-century table and the telephone with speaker attachment. He dialled.

'I should like to speak to Herr Doctor Kurtz.'

'Who shall I say is calling?'

'Sheen Associates.'

Sam Pratchard covered the mouthpiece with his podgy hand and beamed round at them.

'They speak English—they always do in these posh hotels.' He moved his hand. 'Hallo?'

'Mr Sheen?'

'No. A representative for Mr Sheen.'

There was a long pause, then:

'I should prefer to speak to Mr Sheen personally.'

'I'm afraid that's not possible right now. He's tied up in a meeting . . . Shit! He's hung up on me.'

Pratchard pressed the redial button. Harry took the opportunity to reach across to the mini-speaker. He turned up the volume a notch, looked round at El, Herbert, his nephews, gave them all a nod, settled back in his armchair. Then stretching across the arm for the pack he shook out a German Senior Service and lit it from the stub already there. Thin nicotine-stained fingers shook, but not so as you'd notice.

'I think he'll speak to me,' Sam was saying, 'when you tell him the goods we are trans-shipping for him are emitting curies at a rate that our gamma counter could not cope with.'

He grinned again, waited. What eventually came was a small explosion.

'Listen. I do not know who you are, but it was very foolish of you to make a statement like that on an open line. I demand to speak to Mr Sheen personally.'

Although Kurtz normally spoke the sort of perfect English with simple vowel sounds, not diphthongs, that only educated foreigners and the Welsh can achieve, guttural crispness had now crept in.

'Listen darling, like I told you, he's in a meeting.'

Again, a longish pause. Then, more slowly now:

'Just what is all this about? No wait. First, I want to know your name and how you found out mine, and how you could reach me.'

'My name, Dr Kurtz, is immaterial. And as to the other questions, well you will just have to be a man and face up to the fact that Sheen Associates is rather bigger than you thought, with resources you cannot possibly know of.'

Again the grin. Harry Sheen began to splutter, had to stuff a handkerchief in his mouth, waved with his free hand at his two nephews.

'So just what is all this about?'

Sam's voice took on an unctuous whine, though for those in the room with him the grin remained.

'Well, quite frankly Dr Kurtz, we're not sure we want to handle this one. Quite frankly we feel a tip-off, anonymous like, to the authorities is in order. I mean, you never told us like it was fucking radioactive, did you? And we do have a responsibility to our employees, I mean exposing them to that sort of radiation for the time it takes to get that boat through the Kiel canal and up the Baltic . . . I mean, you know, they could sue us if they got radiation sickness, cancer and all that . . .'

Again the pause, then the voice, lower, and hoarser.

'How much?'

'What was on offer, plus a million DM.'

Longer pause.

'I'll get someone else to handle it. You're not the only squalid little firm of shit-shifters, you know? There are others.'

'Language, Dr Kurtz, language. There's one more thing you need to know. We like decided, you see, that where it was that container comprised a public hazard. Kids fishing, pleasure boats on the canal, that sort of thing. So we moved it.'

'And there's one thing you're forgetting. What happened to your friends the other day . . .'

'Ah yes. Now that was not nice. And we admit if we'd known you could be that nasty, and that silly, we'd have had some friends along too. Listen. Anything Alterlog of Zürich can put in the field, we can match. You gotta realise that . . . You still there, doctor? Righty. I can see you'll need to give this some thought, and when you have, say in half an hour or so, give us a bell. Or else someone in the Regional Reactor Safety Commission will know where that container is before you do.'

Sam put down the phone, beamed round at all of them.

'I enjoyed that,' he said.

CHAPTER 35

El, with Jace and Ash, arrived at the racetrack just as the setting sun touched the tops of the tallest firs in the forest. Ash parked his red Escort Si cabriolet in the space where the pits had been. First they checked that Fechter had arranged for delivery of the container, or one very like it, back to where it had been when El first came to the track; then they climbed the terraced stand to the hospitality room Nerone had used as an office.

'Neat joint,' said Jace, opening the big refrigerator door, scanning the contents. 'How long we got?'

El glanced at her watch. 'KOK Roth should be here in twenty minutes. When he's here then we move into the second stage. Since they'll be coming from Burg we'll still have forty minutes before anything happens. Call it an hour.'

Ash turned from the big glass screen that overlooked the track.

'This really was a formula three track?'

'Yes.'

'What's *Trüffel*?' asked Jace, holding up a small labelled tin.

'Truffles. Sort of mushrooms I think.'

'If it's OK with you I think I'll give the wheels a spin. Not often you get the chance to let the old girl have a proper whirl.'

'There's eggs, a pan, a gas-ring. Fancy a nice mushroom omelette?'

It was the first time that they had revealed to El that

they did after all have different personalities, different tastes.

Twenty minutes later, with Ash somewhere on the far side of the track in the middle of his seventh lap, and Jace readying himself to slip beaten egg into a smoking pan, an Opel came cruising down the final straight.

'This'll be Roth.'

But it wasn't. A black, or blackish girl, in sweater and jeans that she might have had trouble fastening, got out, locked the door, and trotted up the tiered stand towards them. El slid back the glass door, called when the girl was still six tiers below.

'Just stop there a moment and tell me who you are.'

The girl pulled ID from her hip pocket, held it in front of her.

'KOK Sharon King.'

'We were expecting a guy called Roth.'

'I know. But he didn't show so they sent me instead. Listen, there's a mad fucking son of a bitch out on that track damn near shunted me. He must have been doing close on two hundred, maybe more. I know what I'm talking about, I used to be with traffic . . .'

'That's my bro, always fancied himself as a bit of a Mansell.'

'And you got the papers, the warrant and all that?'

'Sure. Hey that smells good. You some sort of chef or something?' Sharon asked.

'When I get the time. Here he comes again. Somebody'd better do the chequered flag bit next time round and tell him supper's up. There's a reasonable fizzy Asti in the fridge if someone would care to ease the top off . . .'

Out in the countryside, south of Burg, the red sun dipped into river haze, became a raspberry lollipop: the giant cedars of Lebanon on Drenkmann's lawns shifted from blackish-green to greenish-black. He turned from the big window, reached across his desk, snapped on a light. His big head swung like a tank turret, took them all in: first Renata Fechter, now wearing a track-suit and trainers; then Firat Arslan whom he quite liked, the Turk had an air of menace about him and communicated an ability to be ruthless. Since Becker had topped himself he was the only one in Renata's team with balls.

Meier, of course, did not impress—old before his time, dandruff on his shoulders, and he fidgeted. For the first time Drenkmann really and deeply regretted that Fechter's squad was such a mess. An error of judgement and to some extent his own. Then the two Engländers. One thin, tired, with huge brownish circles round his eyes and his fingers eternally clamped on a cigarette that emitted sandpaper for the throat, and the big burly fellow, also oldish, with the hectic cicatrice down one cheek. What a crew, he thought. Is it possible they can bring this off?

A phone buzzed. His hand, momentarily and unusually uncertain, hovered: but it was Renata's mobile. She swung her knees to the side to reach for it and he relished the turn of her waist beneath her breasts. She listened, murmured, listened again, closed it down, looked up at him. She caught her breath before speaking: even at a time like this the bastard's eyeing me up.

'KOK King is in place.' She turned to Sheen. 'Apparently one of your nephews has cooked them a truffle omelette.'

Sheen poised his cigarette over an ashtray on the floor beside him.

'That'll be Jason,' he rasped, then coughed. 'He fancies himself as a galloping gourmet.'

The worm of ash missed the ashtray but fell on the carpet without breaking up.

Not knowing and not wanting to know what a galloping gourmet was, Drenkmann looked at his watch. Thin as a crêpe but gold.

'She'll be in touch with Haussner. Forty minutes and he'll be there. Run it through once more before you go.'

Renata lifted her head, ran her long fingers through the hair pulled back off her temples, straightened her knees.

'Firat takes Mr Sheen and Mr Doe to the Schillerpark. Meier and I follow. They climb the knoll to the Monopteron, Firat stays close but not too close. Kurtz, and whoever else he brings along, joins them there. They wait for Haussner to phone in that the container is out at the racetrack, has the right serial number and so on. Kurtz then hands Sheen the money, and Firat moves in and makes the arrest. Meanwhile, over at the track, Sharon King, supported by Jason and Ashley Murdoch, arrest Haussner and whoever is with him . . .'

'Why not Roth? Why King? Why a young woman . . .'

There he goes again, she thought.

'She's very capable. More capable than Roth right now. He phoned in from his home—he was stoned, badly stoned and paranoid with it. God knows what he's got hold of this time, or where from. Anyway . . .'

'Anyway, then we offer Kurtz limited immunity if he agrees to testify against his employers.' Drenkmann heaved out pipe, tobacco pouch and the rest. He stuffed the pipe and looked over it and rasped his Zippo with his thumb. Through clouds of smoke he added: 'It might work. It might.'

Renata shuddered, looked round.

'We leave in ten minutes. If anyone wants a wee or anything, now's the time.'

Meier pulled himself to his feet, excused himself.

*

Not so many kilometres away, on the autobahn box also south of Burg, Dr Kurtz folded the last of his silk shirts on to the top of his third suitcase, pulled the elasticated tapes across it, linked them, looked round at the suite in the Ramada Hotel where he had lived for a fortnight. Roehl, his backside too big for the upright armchair, eased himself along the bed.

'All packed up then.'

'All packed up. Apart from the toiletries.' Kurtz went into the bathroom.

'What time's your flight?' Roehl raised his voice.

'Twenty thirty. Check in an hour before.'

The lean fingers scooped the unopened packets of hotel soap, the mini-shampoos, even the shower-hat into his bag along with his own things. Waste not want not. He glanced at his cadaverous face in the mirror, took off the tinted glasses, gave them a polish, replaced them, ran a silver mounted pocket comb through his thin tinted black hair. He went back into the bedroom, squeezed his toilet bag into the side of the case, closed the lid, the catches, gave the combination wheels a turn or two.

'You'll miss the finale.'

'It'll be in tomorrow's papers.'

Roehl chewed a thumbnail.

'Is this business in the Schillerpark going to work?' he asked. Yet again he felt that the solution Kurtz had come up with was too fancy, too clever by half. Always there was this attempt to achieve two different ends by one complicated means—in this case the wasting of the Engländers coupled with the final blow to the Eco-Squad's credibility.

Kurtz looked down at him with something like a sneer. It was as well Roehl was using his canines as manicuring tools and could not see it.

'I hope so. It will be pleasant if it does. A joke, a game.'

'And if it doesn't?'

'Well then. We decided, did we not? You will lay on a back-up to deal with any residual problems. I take it you have?'

'Put in a back-up? Yes. Two of the Ossis. And I shan't be far away.'

The phone warbled and he leant across to the bedside table.

'Speaking.' He covered the mouthpiece. 'Haussner.'

He listened for a moment, barked an affirmative, replaced the handset.

'They've told him where the container is. Back out at that car-racing track. Where it was before. On the way to Burghaven. It'll take him forty minutes to get there.'

Kurtz uttered a short dry laugh.

'We might have guessed. Never mind.' He took the phone from Roehl, dialled. 'Frisch? Kurtz here. Listen carefully. The container is on a trailer at a disused car-racing track just off the motorway south of Burghaven. Here's how you get to it . . .'

When he was finished he cut the call, pressed a single button.

'Room 318. Send up a porter. Have my bill ready, and a taxi. To the airport.'

He straightened, tall, thin, skeletal, looked down at the tub of lard beneath him.

'That's it then. I hope it works out for you. None of this would have happened if we'd used Prolebentek in the first place . . .'

'Prolebentek? You said the firm was called EuReCycle, Zürich.'

'Prolebentek's a subsidiary.'

'Sheen Associates wasn't my idea. Nerone suggested them, and since they were a quarter of the cost of EuReCycle the clients insisted. Can't blame them.'

The fact was they had all agreed that Kurtz was on a backhander from EuReCycle, and that was why the Swiss firm was so expensive. Since they were already paying Kurtz a top executive's annual salary for a fortnight's work . . .

A knock on the door—the porter. They both stood. They did not shake hands. They did not even share a spoken farewell, or conventional if insincere wishes for good luck. The association had not been a happy one.

On the gravel outside Drenkmann's neo-gothic mansion (it had been built as a hunting lodge for the last Elector) Renata paused at the Toyota's driver's door. Meier straightened on the other side.

'I'm sorry,' she said. 'But I'm too wound up over what's going to happen in the next hour or so to drive.'

She pushed the keys across the bonnet, and walked round the back while he came round the front. He unlocked manually, forgetting there was infra-red central locking, leant across to open the passenger door. It was only as she got in beside him that she caught the whiff of peppermint on his breath overlaying the hotness of neat vodka. Neither had been there earlier.

'Shit,' she said.

He glanced at her, firmly slotted in the ignition key, started the engine.

'I'm OK,' he said.

Nevertheless he released the handbrake before putting the gear lever into first position, and the car lurched closer to the stone curbing that edged the lawn than was necessary as he put it into a tight curve. They followed Sheen's Mercedes down the drive to the main road, but presently let it get well ahead.

CHAPTER 36

It was almost dark when they saw the headlights coming down the concreted track beneath the tall firs.

'One car only,' El muttered. 'Like we stipulated.'

'That's a relief anyway. Right. Off we go.'

The Twins, the Terrible Twins—the phrase was unavoidable for El—melted away into the darkness on the other side of the stand, brief silhouettes against the sky holding their machine pistols in their left hands, away from their bodies and pointing upwards. Their rubber-soled boots whispered briefly on the stand's tiers, then they were gone.

On the other side the car, a middle of the range Audi, took a half turn, stopped.

'I suppose we'd better go down.' El, the anger that had burned in her for so long suddenly dowsed by a surge of fear, glanced at Sharon.

'I guess so. We don't want them up here.'

El pulled a master switch and the area where the Audi had come to a standstill filled with light—but a dull weak sort of light—from four inadequate floods. Enough though to pick up the short needles of hazy rain which had begun to fall. A minute or so later they climbed the steps out of the pit area and took a step or two towards the car. Two men got out. Haussner and the tallest of the Ossis. Where were the others? Sharon asked herself. In the Schiller-park, watching Kurtz's arse for him. Haussner in front—his Asterix moustache had already picked up silvery droplets.

They all stopped. Ten metres separated them.

'You are alone? Just you two?'

'Yes.'

Haussner glanced round, into the dampening darkness beyond the lights.

'I find that hard to believe.'

El shrugged.

'Who's your friend?'

El shrugged again.

'A friend,' she said.

Haussner threw a backward glance at the tall Ossi behind him.

'All right. Where is it?'

'Down there. Beyond that building on your right. You'll need the torch we asked you to bring. There are no lights down there.'

Haussner thought it through then quickly instructed the Ossi who pulled out a pistol and stayed put, confronting El and Sharon. Haussner moved off out of the circle of light. The implication was clear: if he was attacked while he examined the container, El and Sharon would be shot.

El watched, saw the glimmer of a torch and briefly the three-metre square of the facing side of the black cube container. Then it focused on black tape which Haussner ripped from the labelling and serial number. The torch played over them for a moment or two, then went out. The Ossi shifted from foot to foot and suddenly spat on to the concrete. Haussner came back towards them.

El cleared her throat.

'Happy?' she called. A sudden waft of fragrance played across her nostrils—sweet conifer, released by the warm humidity.

It was not a word he used much.

'It is . . . all correct.'

He re-entered the sphere of dull light. El choked back what she wanted to say: don't push him, she warned herself, let him find the way.

He walked back to the Audi, reached in, unclasped a mobile, dabbed in the numbers.

'Chief,' he said. 'It's here. It's the right one.'

Chief, the word flashed across Sharon's cortex. That's not Kurtz he's talking to, but Roehl. Did it make a difference? Not really. Her left hand searched out her ID from her back pocket, her right hand found the butt of the Walther P5 in the small of her back stuck inside the waistband of her jeans.

'Knut Haussner. I have here a warrant for your arrest. Duly signed by the State Public Prosecutor . . .'

They knew he'd go for his gun and anyway the Ossi was ready to shoot. She and El hurled themselves backwards and in opposing directions, hitting the concrete as the burp guns farted out slugs at lethally close range from the black shadows beneath the firs. Haussner and the ex-STASI Ossi were cut down in one and a half seconds.

El picked herself up as Jace and Ash came out into opposing but not opposite segments of the circle of light. As they came they pushed empty magazines into the deep pockets of their combat trousers, slotted in full ones.

The ex-STASI moaned in a pool of black blood and Ash fired off a single round into the side of his head. El stood over Haussner. He looked up at her with dull but frightened eyes.

'I could,' she said, 'piss on you. But you know I think you might quite like it if I did. So I won't.'

She turned her back on him and walked into the forest. She did do a wee. That's Asti for you. As she pulled up her jeans she heard another round slam through brains and into concrete. Shot while resisting arrest. Police issue Heckler and Kochs. No regrets.

CHAPTER 37

The mobile bleeped. Renata reached down, released it,
glanced though the window now streaked with light rain,
as the southern suburbs, for the most part the detached
villas of senior businessmen and civil servants, rolled by.

'KOK King here.'

'Sharon. Go ahead.'

'It went . . . according to plan. We're all OK.'

Renata bit her lower lip. That almost certainly meant
Haussner and whoever came with him were dead. She
suppressed a sudden shudder of angst.

'Who turned up?'

'Haussner and just one of the Ossis.'

So, Renata thought, Kurtz will have two behind him.
We should be able to handle that—Arslan, Meier and me.
But again she shuddered: she would have liked it better
if Haussner had had two Ossis with him. Three was
asking for too much, she knew, but two would have been
nice.

Sharon had not finished.

'There are two things worry me. First, Haussner did
not speak to Kurtz. He spoke to someone he called "chief".
I didn't do the redial since it might have alerted the
opposition but it could have been Roehl. Second. Just as
it was all over and I was about to report to you a trailer
truck turned up, on the track from the autobahn. It has
Swiss number plates, it belongs to a Swiss firm called
Prolebentek, and the driver and his mate are Swiss. The
driver's name is Frisch, his mate is Dürrenmatt. Or so

they say. They have a pump-action short-barrelled shot-gun in their cab and they refuse to say why they're here. They say they were heading for the docks but took a wrong turning . . . I think . . .'

'Sharon, you've done well. Hold those men. I'll get back to you.'

She looked at Meier.

'Can we speak to Arslan?'

'I don't think so. Not unless the English have a mobile and you know the number.'

'Then you have to catch them. Before they get to Schillerpark.'

'But you said we were to be at least two minutes behind . . .'

'Do it Meier.'

He put his foot down, shifted into fifth, the car surged forward. Renata's foot too pushed into the floor. She bit her lip, muttered beneath her breath—come on, come on. Meier glanced at her.

'It would have helped if I had a siren . . .'

'But you haven't. Do your best.'

It was clear to her. Arslan and the two Engländers were driving into a trap. Kurtz was no longer planning to use Sheen's boat to get the container out of Germany: he'd found some other route, one which at least began with this Swiss trailer-truck. He didn't need Sheen any more, and Sheen knew too much . . .

Clustered in landscaped lawns with ornamental trees the first high rises, pillars of light this early in the evening, rose around them. With a stab of recognition, which came as a surprise because she had never approached it from this side before, she realised they were close to Aldo's apartment. Then it happened.

The flashing light of a protected crossing, and a U-bahn train stop in the middle of the road. A woman and child,

the woman head-down against the rain, possibly misjudg-
ing the Toyota's speed since all she'd seen were approaching headlights, stepped off the pavement. Meier's reaction
was slow, slower than it should have been, slow and
wrong. He both braked hard and pulled out, away from
the curb, and the road surface was greasy with the
rain . . . The rear of the car swung towards the woman
and child, gathered momentum. Too late and too fiercely
he spun the wheel, tried to correct the skid by steering
into it. The car slewed the other way and the rear end,
just behind Renata's seat, smashed into the heavy sign
post that marked the train stop. The force of the blow
hurled her into Meier and the side of Meier's head into
the side window.

For the briefest of moments she sat there and wanted
to cry like a child. Then for a moment she thought Meier
was dead, but no, he moaned, seemed to try to shake his
head. She became conscious of her own pain, mainly in
her mouth which was filling with blood. She must have
bitten her tongue. Nothing worse. Almost mechanically
she opened her shoulder purse, searched for a tissue, and
found two keys on a keyring. The tab was a black
enamelled horse prancing on a yellow field . . .

The Schillerpark. It occupied ten hectares or so of grass
with occasional patches of low density woodland. A brook
ran through it, there was a beer-garden, and on the one
low eminence a monopteron: a small round classical
temple—very simple, just eight Corinthian pillars sup-
porting a shallow cupola with an empty platform beneath,
a singular place from which one could see most of the
park and much of the city. Because of the beer-garden,
occasional concerts and festivals, the Schillerpark did
not, between the spring and autumn equinoxes, close at
sunset, but was somewhat laxly patrolled by a private

security firm—two retired policemen with a retired German Shepherd dog. Bicycles were allowed but not cars, although there was access for service vehicles and staff parking on the east side.

Arslan told Herbert to park the Mercedes on a parking meter in front of the Regional Parliament, then he shepherded them across the road, past the Museum of Twentieth-Century Art, and through a turnstile set next to the big ornamental gates, cast-iron with gilded points. The narrow asphalted paths that threaded the park were lit dully by occasional lamp-standards—originally gas, now electric. Arslan, Sheen and Herbert walked, strolled almost, from one pool of light to the next, towards the hill and the floodlit monopteron. From not all that far away they could hear music, an accordion, a cornet. In spite of the light rain it was warm and the beer-garden which was mainly covered with canvas awnings and rimmed with fairy lights was doing reasonable business.

'"Hear the little German band, taa-ta-ta-ta-taa taah",' Herbert warbled to himself.

'"Where the brass band plays tiddly-om-pom-pom,"' Harry added.

They laughed, but a touch nervously.

Then, when they had covered little more than a hundred metres, Firat stopped.

'You go on on your own now. I'll circle around, never far off, until I sight Kurtz. KHK Fechter and KHK Meier will be in the vicinity too by then. We'll be watching you closely, but hopefully not so close as to frighten him off. As soon as the deal has been concluded and he's paid you the money, we'll move in for the arrest. You keep well clear at that point since he may try to resist. If we don't meet up straight after the arrest then go back to your car and wait for me there. OK? Good luck!'

And he melted into the shadows.

Harry and Herbert looked at each other, grimaced, grinned uneasily, and walked on towards the hill and the monopteron—a little island of light suspended in darkness, still a good half kilometre away.

Our brains are constantly bombarded with sensory data: intoxicating and repulsive smells, voluptuous caresses on our skins and abrasive roughnesses too, sounds magical, intense, bewitching, terrifying and seductive, and above all for we are the most visually complex of animals, we are besieged with colour, fogged with light and damned by darkness. It is not yet too well understood how, in earliest infancy, we learn to control, edit, ignore, reinterpret and corrupt this avalanche of sensation. Clearly nurture as well as biology is involved. Nurture working on the biological imperative to survive creates the particularised prison house the culture into which we have been born accepts as acceptable.

There are drugs that will sweep away these self-inflicted barriers; psychological distress too can wipe them out. We have read of, and some of us have experienced, the ecstacies of untrammelled perception: there is the reverse side too, the terrible paranoia that can descend on the soul of someone from whom the protective prison walls have been withdrawn. As vulnerable as hermit-crabs we'll scurry anywhere—or freeze, retreating into schizoid catalepsy.

Add in morphine addiction, as was the case with Roth, and someone under the influence of powerful designer hallucinogens is yours or anyone's.

He crouched beneath a weeping willow whose long streamers of leaves fully out ahead of all the other trees made a curtain of emerald light that promised heaven on the side that faced the floodlit monopteron. Behind him similar leaves became sub-aqueous tentacles of seaweed between him and the dark slopes below: they hid but could not keep out the possibility of putrescent monsters or the walking drowned, streaked with phosphorescent decay. Taken together the whole made a cathedral-like dome supported by a gnarled and twisted trunk, ribbed and writhing, the leg perhaps of a dinosaur which he knew could rise and stamp on him, crush the life out of him. A symphony of wild noise filled his ears: the hiss of rain, the rustle of leaves promised the Eros of tender caresses in front, the Thanatos of snakes and scorpions behind, while the distant music was a derisory, mocking melody suggesting the Bacchanalia of naked women who tear the living flesh of seers from their bones.

But he was all right.

Hunkered as he was with the butt of the VZ 58 V Czech-made assault rifle on the grass between his feet, with the breechblock pressed in his crotch and his hands gripping the wooden rifle-casing beneath the barrel, whose muzzle, directly in front of his eyes, glowed with ruby light, he was more than a mere man: he was a machine, soft and hard, vulnerable but deadly; the gun was not a weapon but an extension of his deepest soul, a projection created by desire and will. He could see how the blood that flowed through the veins in the backs of his hands branched into the spidery capillaries that fed his fingers and from them flowed into the glowing steel.

He was also rewarded with a purpose. Without a purpose, an aim to hold on to, this flood of sensory data whose interpretation he could no longer control or order, but which welled up from depths far below the reach of custom or reason, would have been insupportable, would have overthrown his already tottering mind. But he had a mission. In front of him and above the white temple shone with a celestial radiance, a perfection of form and meaning: it was the very centre of the universe, from which all structure and logic emanated, the centre which must hold or all goes down into darkness, chaos, the Pit from which Creation came—and he was its Guardian. He knew it was under threat. Two demiurges from deep space, one with a face like a skull, the other marked by a hideous scar, were on their way to destroy it ... he had been told these things, he had been shown photographs, he was not sure when, he could not remember where, but he knew what to do when they came, he knew how.

Meanwhile there was the ecstasy: the carpet of emerald grass every blade of which stood out clean and separate, stiletto-sharp, beaded with pearls and diamonds of rain in front of the Temple, and the pall beyond, not black but the deepest darkest purest blue, the colour of Heaven itself . . .

CHAPTER 38

One key opened the mechanical lock on the street door, a short sequence of remembered numbers produced the buzz and the click which released the electronic one. A ceramic bowl filled with a fern viridescent in the harsh light of the hall stood in front of the lift, beyond it a steel fire-door opened on concrete steps to the two-storey parking area below. The door clanged behind her but the stairs were permanently if dully lit; two angles brought her on to the top floor—her trainers squeaked like mice on the crimson gloss that covered it as she ran towards the numbered bay.

It was there all right.

Sleek, the bodywork a steely bluish grey, the gleaming chrome, the charcoal black hood, she had forgotten how close to the ground it was, how like an animal. The feeling became stronger as she sank for the first time in her life into the low flat bucket of the driving seat, more a soup plate than a bucket: the soft hide, bull-blood red, welcomed her with an embrace— left closed for days its breath reeked of dried meat. For a moment she was swamped with a nostalgia and longing that almost overpowered her, it needed will to fight it back, will and a moment or two to get it under control.

She remembered how he had had a routine that never varied. It was, he said, a ritual to ensure a safe journey. First he put the key in the ignition but did not turn it. He checked that the gear-stick was in neutral, that the handbrake was engaged. Then he took black chamois gloves from the dash and pulled them on.

They were still there. Her fingers were long, the gloves were not too big. She put her feet on the pedals. He had been no more than a couple of centimetres taller than her, she did not need to adjust the seat. She reached behind, found the seat-belt and clunked it into place, remembering with a tiny smile how he always used to curse these aberrations, these additions to a car that had been flawless when it was made thirty-five years ago without them. Sometimes he said he only used his belt because she was a police person who would book him if he did not . . .

All this slowed her down, gave her time to remember that this was no ordinary car. She remembered there was a pump, a petrol pump that had to be allowed fifteen seconds or so of gentle ticking before she attempted to get the engine to fire. She gave the key a half-turn and waited, listened, counted, then the full turn. The engine coughed. She resisted the temptation to pump excess gas into the carburettor, tried again, it coughed and caught. Now she could press the accelerator and the deepening throaty purr swelled around her.

As she pushed the stubby gear lever into reverse, let out the clutch and very gently steered the car out of the bay, she sensed the hypersensitivity of the car's response to the controls, the power, speed, manoeuvrability waiting to be used. Through some primitive magic that had to do with the way her buttocks fitted on the seat, with how her sentient living hands inside the skin of an animal grasped the polished organic teak of the steering wheel with its three stainless-steel spokes radiating from the enamelled buttercup hub with the black prancing horse, she felt not that she was the soft machine inside a hard machine but that they were as much at one as a brain, a mind inside a skull, is at one with the torso and limbs it controls.

To get out she had to go down to the second floor, which meant two tight hairpins, and then up a long ramp to the street. At the top there was a grille but against his landlord's as well as her own advice Aldo had always left the infra-red signaller which would raise it in the glove compartment in front of the passenger seat. Again a moment of strangeness—always in the past it had been her job to fetch it out and hand it to him. Why was he not there now to do it for her? She leant awkwardly across to let down the veneered lid. Why was he not here to take it from her?

She put the car across the sidewalk. The large chrome fender with two over-riders shaped like the sabres of a sabre-toothed tiger, jutted into the brightly lit six-lane carriageway, with the tram-like U-bahn in the middle. The whole point of what she was doing flooded back. How long was it since Meier had crashed the Toyota? Five minutes, ten? Would Sheen's Mercedes have reached the Schillerpark already? Perhaps.

She swung out into traffic, not too busy now, the workers home, the night-life not yet under way, searched the dash for the wipers, found a black bakelite leaf which continued to move back and forth in rhythm with the wipers. She put herself in the fast lane, there was nothing in front for at least three hundred metres, eased her foot down. For a second she was frightened by the surge, the pressure in her back, then the exhilaration she had experienced when Aldo drove returned, but spiked with the thrill that it was she now not him who... She creamed past a U-train, the long chain of lit windows above her like the deck of a liner, and heard the blare of its horn and the clang of its bell as the front receded in her rear-view mirror beneath a shower of sparks from the cable overhead. On the other side the disgruntled driver of a BMW 535i Sport, already twenty kph above the speed limit, also blasted his horn, held it so Doppler-effect shifted it down a semi-tone as she sped away. Why were they all hooting at her?

Shit, lights. In the lit parking bay she had not thought to turn on the lights. She half-grimaced, half-laughed, reached for the switch, then pulled her hand back. No. She would fly like a dark arrow into the heart of the evil ahead, they would not see her coming, but they would know of it for already behind her rose the banshee wail of a traffic cop on a 2000cc BMW bike and behind him the guinea-pig yee-ip, yee-ip, yee-ip of a green and white Polizei car. Let them all come, she cried out, let me bring them all in storming behind me like a comet's tail.

A road sign on a gantry gleamed above, forked arrows: *Centrum* to the left, *Parlament Schillerpark* to the right. She swept into an underpass, blasted a dawdling Merc out of her way, there were now only two lanes, and bit her lip: what was she doing without a gun? What could she achieve unarmed? Then she blasted the horn again, a challenge now to those in front, she had a weapon all right, she and the car together, they, it, she was all the weapon she needed.

CHAPTER 39

Two elderly English gents out for an evening stroll. Both tall, the thin one in a dark slate-coloured raincoat with too many buttons and flaps, the solid bulky one, with a bit of a limp, in a weatherproof anorak and a peaked flat hat.

'I don't like this,' said Sheen. 'Not one bit.'

'It's getting a nasty taste, I grant you. Feels like a trap.'

'Maybe.' Sheen wheezed, chronic smoke-induced emphysema suddenly acute. 'Maybe. But that's not what I meant. Truth is I'm finding this hill a bit steep.'

Herbert glanced at him: Sheen's face was grey, almost as grey as the sockets round his eyes usually were. The sockets themselves were purple. The skin glistened with more than rain. He looked up through the silvery haze of light from the floods, one of which was over to his right, fifty metres away, at the glowing white perfection of the monopteron above them. They still had a good hundred metres to go and the final grassy slope looked steeper than any they had been on so far.

'"On a huge hill, cragged and steep, truth stands and he that will reach her about must and about must go . . ." In short we'll get there not head-on but by degrees.' Herbert took his boss's arm and steered him over to the left, across the slope. 'It's not doing my hip any good either.'

'That sounded like poetry. Though it don't rhyme.'

'It is. An' it does. "Hill" and "Will".'

'How come you know so much poetry Herb?'

'Wandsworth. Class of 75. Open University Arts Foundation Course. An' a coupla units after that.'

'Ah, I never had your advantages. I envy you.'

'Come on, Harry. You did time too.'

'Not enough Herb, not enough.'

Chuckling now at the jokey absurdity of all this, they passed ten metres below a large weeping willow whose newly open leaves brushed the bright green grass. The light silhouetted the trunk, which, to Herbert's educated eye, had an unsightly bulge on one side. The hazy rain gusted on a strengthening breeze and Sheen pulled his coat collar up.

'You know Herb what's going to be the worst out of all this?'

'No, Harry.'

'Sciatica.'

'Let's hope you're right.'

'You never had sciatica.'

'No, Harry. Not a sufferer myself. Bad enough having an arthritic hip.'

'Well, let's hope I'm wrong.'

Wheee-eeee, whee-eee, and yee-ip, yee-ip from the distant streets below.

'Some joy-rider had his number took.'

'Not our problem, Harry. Bear right a bit here I think, get in front of that large tree.'

'There's a bench beneath it.'

'Excelsior, Harry. Upwards and onwards.'

'Ah. That's one I do know. "There was a youth through snow and ice . . ." Hang on, I'll get it straight . . .'

Below them, trying to keep in visual touch without drawing attention to himself, weaving from tree to tree and yet striving to look like a casual out for a walk, Arslan was also hoping to catch sight of Dr Kurtz before the Engländers reached the monopteron. He too heard the sounds of a police-chase surging through the city, louder, nearer, wondered if somehow it was connected, if somehow it explained why still there was no sign of Fechter and Meier. He needed to be sure they were watching his back before he made his move. Like Herbert he felt a sudden surge of unease: he wanted to call to the Engländers, tell them to hang back for a bit, wait until their position was more secure. Then he saw how they abandoned the straight climb to the top, began the first leg of a zig-zag approach. Good. That would give them all a minute or two more.

He reached a mature maple, leant against it, looked down the hill. The slope levelled a bit, ran on to the brook and an ornamental bridge, humped in keeping with the chinoiserie of the small pagoda beyond the beer-garden. Loops of coloured light bulbs swung beneath the awnings like the chains of gold coins his aunts and female cousins back home still kept—not just as personal ornaments but as inflation-proof insurance against disaster.

People were beginning to leave now, perhaps driven away early by the shift in the weather. Between the bridge and one of the exits he saw a large fat man offering a brief farewell to a younger man in a black leather jacket before turning back into the garden. The younger man pulled out a mobile phone, jerked up the aerial. A frisson raised the hair on the back of Arslan's neck: but why? Surely he was just calling a taxi to the park entrance.

Arslan pulled a paper pack of Bafra from the zip-up breast pocket of his windcheater, got a disposable lighter to work behind his cupped palm, inhaled smoke from the dark aromatic tobacco. Sharon King came to mind—the black, *Die Schwarze, siyah.* How she tried to annoy him by smoking Virginian, which he hated. It had been stupid, that business in the lift, on the way to the Green HQ. He wondered how she was making out at the car-racetrack. That bastard Roth, letting them all down again. Suddenly, and the thought surprised as well as hurt, he hoped she'd be all right.

The sirens were much nearer, seemed almost to be in the park itself.

He looked round the tree. The Engländers were on the next tack, coming back across the hill, would shortly pass in front of a big weeping willow a hundred metres below the monopteron. At this rate they would not reach it for another three or four minutes. But there was something, someone else too. Below them, but above him and out to his left another man was edging closer to them, tree by tree, flitting across the spaces, but clearly always using the cover so the Engländers would not see him: to Firat though he was dead obvious. Black leather jacket like the guy he had seen with the mobile, talking to the fat man . . .

It was suddenly clear, and clearly wrong. Without verbalising his sudden understanding of the situation he simultaneously realised the fat man he had seen silhouetted against the lights of the beer-garden was his ex-boss KHK Hans Roehl. And the man stalking the Engländers was not there to protect Kurtz, who still hadn't shown although he was five minutes late.

With the loosely packed cigarette clamped between his teeth, he unbuttoned his jacket, shrugged the holster in his armpit so it sat right for a quick draw. As he stepped out from the cover of his tree he drew deeply on the cigarette, thinking to chuck it: the glow close to his eyes, greenish from the saltpetre, brought on a moment of night-blindness and dizziness too . . .

He did not hear the gunshot. The bullet hit the side of his head, just above his ear, smashing bone but failing to penetrate his brain, before the sound could get there. For anyone else nearby the wailing sirens almost drowned the noise.

Roth had had enough. His hands had begun to shake and he sensed the chemical power streaming through the capillaries that fed the cortex of his brain was beginning to fail. If the man with the skull face and the man with the scar would not, of their own volition, climb the hill to the altar that awaited them, then he would have to make them. He stood. The sudden movement produced a sensation as if warm tingling sparks of light were being shed from his skin the way water slips from your body if you suddenly stand up in a bath. He hoisted the rifle across his body, right hand round the polished wood of the pistol grip, finger curled on the trigger which seemed to throb and burn, left hand clenching the rifle-casing: that way he got the shaking under control. He pushed through the screen of spear-shaped willow leaves. They brushed his face and clothes, streaking them with what he instantly knew must be blood, the cold blood of a reptile. In the strange reflected light from the monopteron it was deep purple, almost black.

'Oh shit,' Herbert muttered, and his hand went for the Makarov Sheen had bought from a stall in the Novgorod street market. Roth fired once, from across his chest, not sighting the shot. The bullet smashed into Herbert's left thigh, spun him round, threw him into the sloping wet grass. Harry Sheen backed away, stumbling, broke into a shambling run that took him away and down. The rifle cracked again but this bullet smacked into the tree with the bench beneath it. With it came a shout, high, harsh, a command. Sheen froze, half turned. The man was nearer now. A livid heavy face, eyes wild, mad. He shouted again, gestured with the gun.

Herbert, sitting with his right hand pushing his cap into his upper leg, blood welling between his fingers, still managed a hoarse strangled call.

'Harry? He wants you to go up. Up to the temple thing. Do as he says . . . Oh, hell, hell hell but this hurts.'

Sheen faced the hill, began to climb. The slope was very steep near the top; the grass was longer, filled with early moon daisies which swayed and shook with the wind and the rain. He slipped, reached forward, began to haul himself up pulling on the grass and flowers, scrabbling with his feet, often on one knee then the other. Each gasp of breath was a load that had to be hauled into lungs scorched with pain, the blood roared in his ears.

The service entrance to the Schillerpark was a big double gate set in a high wall. It was guarded, but open: the staff were allowed to park inside and an hour or so before the beer-garden closed the guard opened the gate. Which was precisely what he was doing when Renata decelerated on screeching tyres and put the 250 GTS California into a ninety degree skid turn in front of him. With a couple of pensions to look forward to within the next six months the guard took no chances. He got out of the way.

Off the main roads the park was suddenly and frighteningly dark. Fumbling for a moment—with her memory of the car as well as her fingers—she found the right button, a protuberance like an organ stop, which, like an organ stop, she realised needed to be pulled not twisted, and pulled twice, through two settings, to get full beam. Light speared a funnelling tunnel of poplar, swung across a small car-park, raced down one of the tarmac paths. With wheels on the grass first on one side then on the other the car began to sway, rock and jolt like a suddenly frightened colt. Then, not directly in front of her, but over to her right she could see it, the monopteron, a *tondo* of light suspended like a medal in darkness. She braked, spun the wheel, and knuckles white, the jolting now thumping through her spine in spite of the Connolly upholstery, with the sump thudding and the wheels occasionally spinning, she surged towards it.

In spite of the pain, the horror of the mess that was his upper left leg, and the virtual certainty that he was dying, Herbert now had the Makarov in his right hand, was desperately trying to steady it with his left, drawing a bead on the rear left quadrant of Roth's head. At twenty yards, increasing, he knew he could hit him. The problem was if he were to be sure of saving Sheen, he had to kill him—outright. A head shot, not a body one. And taking one thing with another, that was not going to be easy. He heard something coming, but did not dare take his eyes off the back of Roth's head to see what it was.

Roth looked—turning even further away from Herbert to do so. He saw two enormous round eyes, swaying up the slopes towards him. They gave off an incandescent beam, silvered with rain, which bounced off the tree trunks they swung between, hurling long shadows up towards him. And as it came into the outer periphery of the light reflected from the monopteron he could see the black squashed oval of its mouth above the polished steel of its teeth. It roared and howled through the night.

Roth swung back to the monopteron. The man with a skull for a head was still below it, looking over his shoulder, but he had his hands on the temple's curved lip which was the outer edge of its base, was clawing at the slippery stone for the purchase he needed to get up on to it. Good enough thought Roth and this time swung the assault rifle up to his shoulder.

Herbert squeezed the trigger, saw how the bullet plucked Roth's shoulder, spinning him round and back a yard or so, but failing to drop him. Fucker shoots low, and his thumbs, one on top of the other, dragged on the cog-like teeth of the hammer, but before he could loose off a second round, or Roth could respond to what had happened to him, Aldo Nerone's Ferrari caught Roth behind his knees, hurled him up over the long gentle swoop of the bonnet, across the windscreen and down into grass below.

Headlights, sirens, swirling blue and red. The two leather-jacketed ex-STASI Ossis who had waited in the shadows decided that enough was enough. Time to go. They pulled up their collars and walked briskly off into the darkness. Soon they were jogging, and when they hit the tarmac path below, they ran.

CHAPTER 40

'The two ex-STASIs were picked up. I thought you'd like to know that. One of them still had the gun that probably hit Arslan. Forensic will check it out. Incidentally the earlier prognosis has improved. It's possible he'll survive.'

Which oddly enough will please Sharon, Renata thought. Sharon had wept on hearing how badly the Turk was hurt: 'He fancied me,' she had moaned, 'and I was getting used to the idea.'

Once again Renata was sitting in the low, sway-backed black leather and chrome chair and gazed sightlessly at *Cohesion 3*. Drenkmann rattled his pipe in the copper ashbowl on his desk, searched for and found a small silver penknife. For the next minute or so he gouged at the clinker in his pipe, producing a sour squeaky sound, before rattling the bowl again as he tipped what he'd loosened into it. Occasionally he glanced up at her over his half-lenses.

Meanwhile Renata was angry. With herself.

'I was stupid. A fool. I let them manipulate me.'

'The Engländers?'

'Yes, the Engländers. Those two men from Hamburg. They weren't there to protect the girl. They were there to kill Haussner . . .'

'He'd have killed the girl, and KOK King too, if they had not been there . . .'

'Yes. But there was no need to kill Haussner. They set it up so they could, so they had to. That's what they wanted. And the old ones. I don't think they went to that rendezvous with Kurtz so I could have him arrested. I was silly to think I could get people like that in court, testifying . . . No, Herbert Doe had his gun and he would have found an excuse to kill Kurtz if Kurtz had been there. That's what they wanted. But Haussner is the one who mattered. He was the link between the thugs on one side and Roehl and Kurtz on the other. Through him we could have got to Roehl, and through Roehl to Kurtz and the people who employed him. And now nothing. Nothing.'

Drenkmann blew through the pipe. Almost it whistled. He gave it another scrape and this time got a clear passage of air. With his thumb he lifted the lid from a tin of Whisky Flake.

'Roehl has resigned. I have the letter here.' He pointed the stem of his pipe at a small pile of papers at the end of his enormous desk. 'That's enough.'

'Enough?' she cried. Sought for words. 'He ought . . . he ought to be . . . Hanged.'

'I grant you it's not ideal. But it's enough. Two of his deputies are going with him.'

'And you're letting it go at that?'

'Oh yes. If the Supreme Public Prosecutor brought charges they'd be forced to fight. And that would mean an ongoing scandal for months, even years. There are at least three very senior politicians, one of whom is now in Bonn . . .'

'A scandal that would certainly lose Burg to the right and cost you your job.'

This was plain speaking. And therefore very bad manners. Drenkmann's view of plain speaking was that if there is a pile of shit everyone can see, there's not a lot of point in talking about it. Get out a shovel if you like, but don't talk about it. He let her sweat for a moment, let her think he might just terminate the interview, maybe her career too.

'This way,' he said at last, 'the new man in Serious Crime will be able to get a few more resignations, and generally clean up the whole department.' He stuffed tobacco into the pipe bowl, glanced up, over the gold wire of his half-lenses, down at her. 'It's a job you'd like, but you're not getting it. There are ways of going about this sort of thing, and I doubt if you'd appreciate their value or efficacy.'

She wondered, just as he wanted her to, what job if any was still on offer.

'But there's still the matter of the incident at the Burghaven Reactor, Radwasthaus and so on. A man died. There was a colossal cover-up. People have been exposed to potentially very harmful radiation . . .'

The Zippo rasped, ignited, and he sucked the flame into the bowl. Smoke billowed round the flame and the flashes.

'And that,' he rumbled on, 'is precisely where everything has worked out as it should. There have already been resignations. Prosecutions will follow.'

She waited.

'We don't yet know what went wrong at Burghaven. There is talk of corrosion fouling up the control systems, of human error, of cost-cutting, and so on. And of course there was an attempt, a wholly reprehensible attempt, at a cover-up. What you have done has brought all this to light. There will now of course be a long and very detailed enquiry, properly conducted by responsible people. At the end of it they will make recommendations, and public servants will advise the politicians on whether or not these recommendations should be followed through. Meanwhile the Burghaven Reactor is to be closed down and decommissioned.'

She remembered how he had said fear and greed were

not the best foundations on which to base the safety of a dangerous industry. Did this mean that because of what she and her team of misfits had achieved radical changes would be made? Perhaps even that a second generation of reactors might not after all be built? That the existing ones would also be closed down? She glanced up at him, or rather at the smoke that swirled around him. But already, pipe in one hand, pen in the other, he was initialling the sheets in front of him, and his dour secretary was at her elbow.

She stood, he glanced up at her.

'You did a good job with lousy staff. We'll see you have sound replacements. Any other recommendations you might like to make will not fall on deaf ears.'

Replacements? For Roth, Becker and possibly Arslan. But not for Aldo. She felt her eyes fill, but got out before the tear fell. Emotion still got the better of her every now and then. Reaction, she supposed. The reason too why her period was late . . .?

Harry Sheen, Sam Pratchard and El brought flowers, chocolates, and a bottle of Baileys to Herbert's bedside.

'I'm a happy man.' He beamed up at them. 'I got the new hip I been waiting three years for. For free and all. Solid aloominum.' He patted the leg. 'Pity they can't rebuild every part the same way. Eh, El? We'd 'av 'ad some fun if they could.'

He began to hum and diddle-diddle: something from Verdi's *Falstaff*? Maybe. He broke off.

'No offence meant, El?'

'None taken, Herbert. I couldn't half have fancied you twenty years ago. I mean—what must you have been like twenty years ago?'

'It's all right for you two,' Harry Sheen interjected. 'You do know we're broke, don't you? Down the toob.'

'Well,' said Sam Pratchard, 'there may be silver lin-
ings . . .' He dabbed away at his pocket calculator. 'Your
Jace had a tale to tell of Russian arms gone missing from
Brandenburg barracks where the Ruskies were based. He
has a line on 'em, and if the profit margins are what he
says they are . . .'